A GENT   ~ ER

EMMA ORCHARD

B
Boldwood

First published in Great Britain in 2025 by Boldwood Books Ltd.

Copyright © Emma Orchard, 2025

Cover Design by Rachel Lawston

Cover Illustration: Rachel Lawston

The moral right of Emma Orchard to be identified as the author of this work has been asserted in accordance with the Copyright, Designs and Patents Act 1988.

All rights reserved. No part of this book may be reproduced in any form or by any electronic or mechanical means, including information storage and retrieval systems, without written permission from the author, except for the use of brief quotations in a book review. This book is a work of fiction and, except in the case of historical fact, any resemblance to actual persons, living or dead, is purely coincidental.

Every effort has been made to obtain the necessary permissions with reference to copyright material, both illustrative and quoted. We apologise for any omissions in this respect and will be pleased to make the appropriate acknowledgements in any future edition.

A CIP catalogue record for this book is available from the British Library.

Paperback ISBN 978-1-83633-843-7

Large Print ISBN 978-1-83633-842-0

Hardback ISBN 978-1-83633-841-3

Ebook ISBN 978-1-83633-844-4

Kindle ISBN 978-1-83633-845-1

Audio CD ISBN 978-1-83633-836-9

MP3 CD ISBN 978-1-83633-837-6

Digital audio download ISBN 978-1-83633-838-3

This book is printed on certified sustainable paper. Boldwood Books is dedicated to putting sustainability at the heart of our business. For more information please visit https://www.boldwoodbooks.com/about-us/sustainability/

Boldwood Books Ltd, 23 Bowerdean Street, London, SW6 3TN

www.boldwoodbooks.com

To my husband, Luigi

PROLOGUE
JUNE 1817

It was very late, or very early. The sky was lightening in the east, and the blackbirds beginning to sing to welcome the end of the short summer night. Even here, in the heart of fashionable London, there were a few such wild creatures clinging on to life among the trees and bushes of the central private garden, which made a brave attempt to mimic a little rustic wilderness. The grand square with its tall, impressive mansions had been briefly busy earlier, as carriages brought weary party-goers home after another glittering ball, and wearier servants tended to them. But it was quiet now, its inhabitants slumbering in silk-hung bedrooms and crowded servants' attics, and the square was empty.

But not everyone, it seemed, was fast asleep. A lone figure, cloaked and hooded, slipped from the mews at the rear of one of the grand houses, and stood waiting in the shadows near one of the corners of the square. If there'd been anyone to observe, it would surely have been obvious that some sort of desperate flight was in progress. It must be an elopement. The fugitive – a woman – was struggling with a heavy portmanteau, and there was an indefinable furtiveness about her movements, an evident tension in her tall frame. She appeared to be young, well dressed and anxious. It seemed she was that most interesting of persons, a runaway debutante, a lady of quality. A fanciful observer would have been tempted to guess at the intriguing nature of her whirling thoughts: can I trust him? Will he come as he promised, and at the time he promised? Will we be pursued? And most of all: is it right, what I am daring to do for love, or is it reckless madness that will end badly, in my ruin and a lifetime of regret?

But whatever her private fears, she did not have long to wait. A dilapidated hackney carriage rattled slowly into the square, breaking the tranquillity. It was a brief interruption – the vehicle stopped, the door was released by some passenger already inside, who did not descend to make a romantic scene but leaned out and held the door wide in a practical manner with a dark-clad arm so that the woman could enter. It closed behind her, softly but decisively. A moment or two later, the carriage was moving again, heading east. Its ultimate destination might be guessed – Gretna Green? The Continent? – but could not be known.

Inside, where the invisible observer's curiosity would surely lead him to trespass if he could, there were embraces, passionate kisses, murmured endearments. It was a vital moment, certainly, in the lives of two young people, and there could be no turning back now.

'Will my plan work?' The hood had fallen back to reveal golden curls and a flushed, vivid face; the fugitive was beautiful.

'Of course it will, my love; you are so clever.' Her companion, still in shadow, was reassuring, and clasped her hand strongly.

'I suppose we shall know soon enough…'

The carriage rattled off, into an uncertain future, and the square was quiet again. When the young lady's flight was discovered, there would be panic, tears, anger, and perhaps pursuit, and even violence. There would inevitably be public scandal. But for now, the blackbirds were left to sing undisturbed.

1

FOUR DAYS LATER

It was a truth universally acknowledged, Dominic reflected, that two persons of high rank might become engaged to be married as effective strangers, without having spent any time at all alone together and without having the least idea of each other's true nature. Whether such behaviour should be described as sensible or advisable – that was another question entirely. But that was not, it must be admitted, a particularly helpful question for a man to ask himself as he dressed, with habitual care, for his own betrothal party.

Dominic had, of course, been alone, briefly and for the first time, with the Honourable Miss Nightingale when he had asked for her hand and she accepted. But those few moments could hardly have been said to further their acquaintance in any meaningful way.

He had been expected in Grosvenor Square, the day he proposed, and was punctual, after his brief formal conversation with her elderly father the day before. The butler's face reflected his knowledge of the circumstances; the tall young footmen standing impassively in the hall no doubt knew it too.

He was shown into her aunt Greystone's drab sitting room, where the young lady awaited him, composed, pale and silent.

An inner door had rather pointedly been left perceptibly ajar, making Dominic all too conscious that the older lady must surely be lurking behind it in the adjoining chamber, listening. Had he been overcome with lover-like ardour, impelled to overstep the bounds of propriety, no doubt she'd have bustled in and set matters right. Since he had felt no such compulsion to make urgent love to Miss Nightingale – the very idea was ridiculous – he'd never know what the eavesdropping duenna might have said or done. Perhaps any hint of a serious conversation, any attempt by him to ask his new fiancée if this bloodless and old-fashioned marital arrangement was really what she wanted in life, might have produced the same result, or even a far swifter interruption. Indeed, signs of overwhelming passion on his part, though improper, might have been excused much more easily by the lady's so-called protectors. Better an excess of enthusiasm than the merest hints of doubt or reluctance on either side, he mused cynically as he tied his snowy cravat now, frowning unconsciously into the cheval glass as he adjusted its folds.

But it was not to be that sort of marriage. Not a passionate one. Presumably it would have to be, one day, or rather night – or what would be the point? – but at present the strictest decorum was being observed. This, perhaps, was why none of it felt quite real to him, as though all of this were happening to someone else and he a mere detached observer. He had no means of knowing how *she* felt.

Sir Dominic De Lacy – Beau De Lacy, as the polite world knew him – was famous throughout the haut ton for his address, for the exquisite refinement of his manners and his dress, and the ironic detachment with which he viewed the world. No doubt the words in which he expressed his admiration and proffered his suit to the young lady had been superbly chosen, polished to perfection, and of course not inappropriately or unfashionably ardent. He couldn't recall what he'd said, now, just a few short weeks later, and it really didn't matter. The fact that it didn't matter struck him suddenly as terrible. Surely it was the kind of important thing a man should remember forever?

He pushed the unhelpful, uncharacteristically dramatic thought away, putting on his immaculately tailored black evening coat with his young valet's silent, reverent assistance. He'd always disliked melodrama, the display of excessive and uncontrolled emotion – perhaps because his widowed mother was so deeply devoted to it – and his whole persona had been constructed quite deliberately in opposition to the concept. He was unfailingly cool, languid, lazy, unenthusiastic – proverbially so. He knew that it was rumoured in Corinthian circles that he had just once in his life become visibly agitated, but it was also admitted that this had occurred late in the previous century, and he had been a schoolboy at the time. Certainly nobody had ever seen him in such a state in recent years, nor could they imagine it. Nor could he, for that matter. Especially not this evening. So, matters matrimonial were proceeding exactly as they should, without the intrusion of anything so inconvenient or even downright vulgar as feelings.

It must be noted, though, that the plan that was unrolling so smoothly was not of his making. It had been revealed to Dominic quite recently – by his fond mama, in fact – that his father had long ago entered into discussion with Lord Nightingale about the desirability of a match between the Baron's elder daughter and Sir Thomas's only son and heir. Since his father had been dead these nine years, Dominic was scarcely in a position to ask him if any of this was true, and to doubt his surviving parent's word would be quite shockingly unfilial. But he'd been unable to prevent himself from asking why such an interesting and important fact was only now being conveyed to him for the first time.

The fateful interview had taken place in his mother's sitting room, which was decorated in mourning shades of lavender that no doubt contributed to its oppressive atmosphere of perpetual gloom. Lady De Lacy, drawing on the support of her smelling salts and clasping the thin hand of the unfortunate female relative who lived with her and catered to her every whim, had informed him repressively that the young lady in question had only recently reached marriageable age. Plainly it would have been premature, even improper, to enter into discussion of such matters before that happy date. 'Your poor father,' she said, shedding tears, 'had no opportunity to talk all this over with you, young and heedless as you were when he was torn from us. Imagine your reaction, if he had told you when you were nineteen or twenty that he had a suitable girl in mind for you, a girl who was at that time a mere schoolroom miss. You would have laughed in his face! And alas, he did not live to see you reach maturity so that you could ever discuss your future in a sensible fashion.'

All this was true, and silenced Dominic quite effectively. He greatly regretted the fact that his father had died before they had developed a relationship of mutual confidence; he must blame himself, and the reflection that he had been no more or less of an idiot than any other youth of twenty summers was no consolation at all.

'And of course, dear boy,' she went on inexorably, 'if you had chosen another girl as your bride in the intervening years, as you so easily might have done, nothing need ever have been said on this most delicate subject. The agreement between our two families is very far from being a matter of common knowledge, and could never have been described as binding, merely your sainted father's dearest and final wish.' At this melancholy reflection, she shed more tears into her delicate lace handkerchief, and her little wisp of a cousin sighed in sympathy.

'I am happy to hear it is not to be considered binding, Mama,' he had replied drily, his sardonic manner effectively masking his emotions, as it so often did, 'since I am nine and twenty years old, and yet before today I knew nothing at all about all these plans that have been made for my future. I cannot recollect ever having laid eyes upon the young lady, or even having heard of her existence, and I might have expected you at least to have presented me to her at some convenient moment. But I dare say you may think that I am being unreasonable. I so often am.'

This was, in boxing cant, a low blow, since Dominic was perfectly well aware that his mother regarded even the slightest opposition to her wishes on his part, or anyone else's, as the height of unreasonableness. It was with a little wry amusement, then, that he watched her change tactics with admirable speed and say gushingly, 'My dear son! What is this foolishness? You know that it is my fondest hope to see you married at last, and happy! If you had chosen a bride yourself, ten years ago, you would not have heard the least objection from me, and you might now be the father of a hopeful family, with all the joy that brings. Then there would not have been the least reason to advert to Miss Nightingale, and your poor father's cherished plan.'

'Ten years ago? If I had been so imprudent as to wish to marry at nineteen, Mama, I am sure I would have heard the most vehement objections from you, and from my father too. In fact, I do seem to recall that when I was at Oxford and you discovered that I had become romantically involved with a young woman you did not hesitate to describe as entirely unsuitable—'

No one could ever call Lady De Lacy slow-witted. 'I am not speaking of *that* sort of disreputable entanglement, with a woman of low character,' she said reprovingly. 'I wonder you should mention, even indirectly, such an improper liaison! A mere folly of immaturity, such as young men are sadly prone to, as I am sure even you would now admit yourself.' He waved a graceful hand in agreement, and she continued, 'I refer, naturally, to a sincere and lasting attachment to a young lady of birth and breeding. I am only too well aware that you have formed no such desirable connection, despite a decade spent in the best society, which – one might imagine – has offered you many excellent opportunities to do so.'

'Alas, Mama, that is all too true.'

It was an undeniable fact. Dominic would have said, before this surprising conversation, that he had met every debutante of even moderate eligibility who had made her come-out in the past decade. If his mother had not brought them to his attention, their own mothers, sisters, aunts, cousins, grandmothers or godmothers had inevitably done so. He had danced with them, so many of them, at private balls and public assemblies. In his heedless youth, he'd gone occasionally to Almack's Assembly Rooms, and been positively besieged by them there – but he was wiser now, and avoided the dreary place like the plague. He had met the young ladies of the ton, and continued to meet them, while riding in the park, at Venetian breakfasts, ridottos, rout parties, at the theatre and the opera. At the races. In Brighton. On the hunting field. The only places he didn't meet them were Jackson's Saloon, Cribb's Parlour, the fives court, and other exclusively masculine places of entertainment – or, of course, other places, best not mentioned, where women might indeed be found, but ladies decidedly would not.

It was also true that, after ten years, all the blushing flowers of the polite world had, in Dominic's eyes, begun to blend together into one indistinguishable mass of curls, giggles and muslin. He wasn't such an arrogant cockscomb as to think that they were all the same in reality – they remained individuals, with their own characters and their own private hopes and dreams, presumably, and it couldn't possibly be true that they all wanted desperately to marry him, although it quite often seemed as though they did. But not one of them, in the highly artificial circumstances in which he and they inevitably encountered each other, had ever touched his heart, or even slightly piqued his interest. And here he was, almost thirty, with a duty to his ancient family name. That being so, perhaps it was high time he put aside childish dreams of love that seemed unlikely ever to be realised. Maybe his father had known from his own bitter experience that one might be lucky enough to find love, and one might undertake a suitable marriage, but rarely – never? – with the same person.

'What – apart from my father's hitherto secret wish, of course – makes this young lady above all others so outstandingly suitable?' he said.

It was a sign of wavering resolution on his part, and trust his mother to pounce on it. He endured a lengthy encomium to Miss Nightingale's beauty and virtue, her noble birth, the very respectable size of her portion, her mastery of every accomplishment, her prowess in the saddle, even – as a distinct afterthought – her intelligence. She sounded far too good to be true, and probably was. He knew nothing to her discredit, knew nothing about her at all save what he was being told, but her father was another matter. 'Lord Nightingale has the reputation of being rather eccentric,' he ventured after a while, when the flow had lessened a little. 'Has he not lived apart from his wife for several years?'

'What of it?' said his parent robustly. 'There has been no open breach, no mention of anything so shocking as divorce, not the least breath of scandal, and I am surprised, Dominic, that you should even hint at such a thing! Lady Nightingale merely prefers the countryside, and her husband Town. They are both notable scholars, you know, with a wide correspondence and a great deal to keep them busy, though I do not mean to say, of course, that Miss Nightingale herself is a bluestocking, or... or a writer, or anything of that disagreeable nature.'

He wondered why his mother should consider intellectual achievements in a woman so very undesirable, but did not feel equal to arguing the point just now. 'Naturally not. I feel sure you would not suggest her otherwise, ma'am. She sounds a very paragon of perfection.'

'She is! Dominic, I know you are being tiresomely satirical, as ever, but truly, it is past time that you should be thinking of marriage. The future of the family demands it, and if, as you pretend in your odiously affected way, you cannot distinguish one lovely and eligible young lady from another, the plain truth is that you may as well marry this one and be done, since it cannot possibly make the least difference to you!'

Cousin Sarah, whose unobtrusive presence it was possible to forget for long periods of time, clucked ineffectually at this stinging and most unmaternal remark, and Dominic smiled at her. 'There is no need to distress yourself, Cousin,' he said gently. 'I assure you that I am not in the least offended. Perhaps my mama is right, and perhaps my father was, though alas he cannot be here to tell us why he thought so. Perhaps it is indeed time.'

It was a great concession, and Lady De Lacy was duly sensible of it. She might have preferred that her son should hasten immediately to the Nightingale mansion in Grosvenor Square, to offer for the young lady before he should have a chance to change his mind. But when Dominic insisted with great firmness that he should as a bare minimum be able to identify his prospective bride by sight before he asked for her hand, his mama conceded with surprising grace.

The Season was in full swing, and perhaps it was no surprise that an opportunity to encounter Miss Nightingale and her chaperon and aunt should have presented itself most conveniently that very evening, at Lady Sefton's ball. Naturally, Dominic had been invited; naturally, his mother was confident that Miss Nightingale would also be there. A less cynical man might have described it as providential.

Dominic, if he attended such dull affairs at all, generally arrived shockingly late, but on this occasion he entered the glittering ballroom precisely at the time specified by Lady De Lacy. To do otherwise would be rude, he knew, and the whole situation was awkward enough without offering an egregious insult to the woman he must accustom himself – unless anything unforeseen should happen to prevent it, perhaps a meteor strike, a royal death or an invasion by the French – to think of as his prospective bride.

He bowed punctiliously over Miss Maria's hand, and that of her duenna Mrs Greystone, a harassed-looking woman in puce satin trimmed with Mechlin lace. He didn't care much for the puce, but he could find no fault with Miss Nightingale's dress and demeanour. He didn't recall ever having set eyes on her before, now that he saw her, or even having heard her name mentioned in conversation, though he was slightly acquainted with her half-brother Francis, who was a man of about his own age who he'd seen occasionally around the town, but at Cribb's Parlour and the like, he thought, not at balls and fashionable soirées. He banished a fugitive longing for the uncomplicated, undemanding masculine comfort of Cribb's Parlour from his mind now.

The young lady was tall and elegant in white silk. He'd have remembered her, he was almost sure, if he'd met her before. She was not willowy and fragile, but robustly built, along fashionably ample lines; she looked like the strong horsewoman his mother had claimed she was. Perhaps that much, at least, was true. And it would be perverse to deny that she was attractive. Her features were classical in their regularity, and in their marble immobility – objectively, she was beautiful, only that she lacked all animation. Her eyes were large and blue, her golden hair curlier than the current mode but arranged with propriety and taste, her smile quite mechanical. She reminded him rather of an automaton he had once seen displayed. See the simulacrum of a lady! Watch her speak, and marvel at how lifelike she is. But it was entirely wrong to blame her. He was sure he was not a whit better in her eyes. How could he be? In that sense, if in no other, they should make a fine pair, and could be set in a shop window as an advertisement.

Her voice, when they conversed, was low and pleasant. She said nothing of any note, but then nor did he. If he saw no particular sign of her much-vaunted intelligence on this occasion, he couldn't flatter himself that he made a more creditable showing. It was a horribly awkward situation for them both, and worse for her. She must be conscious that he was here to look her over; she might as well have been a horse at Tattersalls, or some other piece of expensive bloodstock, and what could she do but endure it, no matter her private feelings? She was, he thought, close to paralysed with acute discomfort, which was understandable, and concealing it with an effort that he found admirable. A less perceptive man would surely have noticed nothing amiss. He consoled himself with the thought that a woman who had enough sensibility and good taste greatly to dislike the circumstances in which she found herself might, just might, be someone he could one day communicate with in an honest fashion.

If he couldn't have love in marriage, or anywhere else – and, after ten years spent in the best society without a single hint of it, and without being too horribly self-pitying over the matter, it seemed he couldn't – he could at least have honesty and mutual respect. It didn't seem too much to ask for. If Miss Nightingale had been giggling, arch, triumphant, shooting him vulgar and flirtatious glances under her lashes, looking around to see who was watching them, the situation would have been unendurable. Be damned to his mother's plans and even his father's dying wishes, if she'd been that sort of creature. Perhaps he'd been hoping she would be… But she wasn't. She was a lovely young woman who was just as trapped as he was, and for the moment that would have to be enough. If he couldn't imagine kissing her, making love to her – and he couldn't, any more than to one of the marble statues in his hall – he must hope that that desire would come eventually, for both of them.

Dominic asked for the honour of a waltz with her, and they danced; she was coolly graceful and correct, and once more recalled the automaton he'd seen, which had moved in a similar fashion. They exchanged a few more commonplaces – the weather, the great crowd at the ball, the sad news of the King's continuing ill-health – and then a short while later they stepped out together a second time. On this occasion, they spoke, though he had no idea how the topic arose – perhaps she raised it – of their shared admiration for the distinguished author of *Evelina*, who, he was able to tell her, had been a regular correspondent of his late father. His mother would no doubt have been on the lookout for signs of excessive erudition, but he was merely glad to have something slightly more substantial to discuss. This innocuous subject allowing them to converse with rather less awkwardness, the dance passed more swiftly.

He was aware of a little hum of interest from their fellow guests, of sharp eyes upon them, of whispers of gossip. It was quite unexceptionable, for a lady and a gentleman to be partners twice in an evening, but it wasn't the sort of thing Beau De Lacy normally did. He wasn't the type of man to flirt with debutantes or raise expectations he had no intention of fulfilling. And so conclusions would inevitably be drawn. Correct conclusions, as it happened.

Later, Dominic would wish he'd taken a little more time and a little more care – had asked Miss Maria to go driving in the park with him, perhaps, setting down his groom so they could converse in something like privacy. But, aware of how much she seemed to dislike the public gaze, he'd decided not to wait, not to prolong pointlessly this unpleasantness and uncertainty. Miss Nightingale clearly knew of his intentions, and he thought – entirely and disastrously wrongly, as it turned out – that she would be more comfortable when matters were decided, and public interest had peaked and inevitably waned. People, even in the haut ton, got married every day, after all. The novelty could hardly persist, and other subjects for gossip would inevitably arise.

After a little while – too soon – he'd gone to see her father, had received his gracious permission to address her, and then had formally proffered his suit to her and been accepted. The announcement had been inserted in the fashionable newspapers, and he received the congratulations of almost every one of his acquaintance; many of these people might even be sincere in their good wishes for his future happiness. It was a highly suitable match, after all, in terms of age, birth, reputation and fortune. Marriage settlements were being drawn up: generous ones, on his part, to give his future wife as much financial independence as was possible. The date was set, just a few weeks away. Why wait? Though it was no concern of his, he presumed that bride clothes were being purchased, and a wedding gown, and all manner of feminine fripperies.

Now it was the evening of their engagement party – another step in the swift, inexorable progress towards their union. And still they'd had no private conversation.

2

It would be inaccurate, for a number of reasons, to describe the evening of the engagement party in Grosvenor Square as the night everything started going wrong. It was merely the night the prospective bridegroom found out, that was all. For one thing, Dominic was very soon to discover that the wheels had come off the carriage of his betrothal long before, and he had been entirely and humiliatingly unaware of it. For another, the celebration, from his pathetically ignorant point of view, started well, though later when he reflected it upon it he was forced to admit that he'd carelessly ignored several obvious warning signs, struck as he'd been by a sudden, unexpected and most welcome sense of attraction towards his intended bride.

It wasn't anything as grand as a ball. Lord Nightingale hadn't held a ball, with all the trouble and expense that such an occasion entailed, to celebrate his elder daughter's come-out, and he had no intention of holding one to mark her engagement. His Lordship had made this quite clear – that the disruption to his comfort and his studies was not to be thought of – when Dominic had called on him to ask permission to address his daughter, but since Dominic had attended more than enough balls already in his life and didn't care if he never went to another one, least of all one held in his honour, there'd been no unseemly dispute upon the matter, or on any other.

He'd found the old gentleman to be an odd mixture of scholarly vagueness and shrewd self-absorption. He was later to hear the Baron described, by someone who might be supposed to know, as 'the most infuriatingly selfish man who was ever born, and the most impossible to live with'. But it wasn't really to be expected that he would show sign of such intractability in the brief, formal interview they shared.

The fourth Baron Nightingale was a curious creature indeed, almost a caricature by Gilray of a classical scholar. When Dominic paid his momentous visit, his host was wearing a dreadful frockcoat, covered in nameless stains, and a horrible old grey wig that made the fastidious Beau feel itchy, and sat surrounded, as in a nest he'd made for himself, by a great disarray of ancient books and scattered manuscript papers. His library was stuffy and faced north, away from direct sunlight, and would have benefited from an open window or two, to let in some air. It was not a room his guest would have cared to spend long in, and he couldn't help reflecting that if it served as a reflection of its owner's mind and temperament, as it appeared to, Miss Nightingale might well be only too happy to leave her father's house behind her forever. He could give her a better life than this, at least.

The old fellow's satisfaction with the entire situation had been evident. The match was clearly most agreeable to him, but Dominic felt somehow that his future father-in-law's pleasure had little to do with Miss Maria herself, but was instead rooted, he must assume, in his own undeniable eligibility in terms of social standing and fortune. The older man didn't know him from Adam, and couldn't have the least idea whether or not he'd make a good husband. Since he'd never offered for anyone's hand before, Dominic didn't know if it might be traditional for the lady's father to interrogate the suitor as to his character and morals. He'd almost expected such an examination, had been prepared to face it – he was no rake, far from it, and there was nothing in his past of which he need be greatly ashamed – but it did not occur, and he was a little surprised.

If the Baron felt any deep attachment to Miss Nightingale, regret at losing her companionship or concern for her felicity, he showed no sign of it. A sentimentalist, or a loving father, might have spoken of his daughter's sterling qualities, might have said, 'I hope, sir, that you will be good to her, and make her happy.' But there was no sign of any such tender emotion. Perhaps the old fellow was merely reserved, Dominic thought doubtfully. But it felt like more than that. He could not help imagining a list among the piles of papers, and this one item – Arrange Maria's Marriage – ticked off from it, allowing the Baron's mind to move on to matters he considered more important. An interesting antiquarian discovery at Pompeii, perhaps, or a disputed line in Chapman's Homer. He found it hard to picture this dry, old scholar having anything to say to his own late father, although Lady De Lacy claimed they had known and liked each other well enough to plan their children's marriage. Sir Thomas had been a man of great energy and wide liberal sympathies, who had lived in the present day and concerned himself with living people, not the dusty past. But how well had he really known his father, or his father's friends, or what they discussed together? In truth, it hardly mattered, since he was committed now, as a matter of honour, and it was too late to withdraw.

The engagement celebration was to be a rout party to

signify the union of the two noble families. Lord Nightingale had waved a careless greyish hand and said that the women would take care of all the arrangements and were well aware of his wishes. From his manner, Dominic did not doubt it, and surmised that there'd be no music or dancing, very little or no food, and as little drink as the Baron could get away with. Though he was wealthy, nobody could accuse the man of being a hedonist, or addicted to luxury, or even personal comfort. His home, though it was clean and, apart from his library, tidy, had obviously last been decorated a considerable time ago, and it seemed clear that no extraordinary effort in that regard could be expected for the party. Everybody would stand about the slightly shabby rooms talking and drinking indifferent wine, would congratulate the happy couple, and then presently go away again, either to their beds – or someone's bed, at any rate – or to some more relaxed, enjoyable event where they'd at least be fed, watered and properly entertained.

Dominic would freely have admitted that he didn't have much – any – experience of arranging and hosting festivities of this nature. His mother, on such occasions, would complain that it was an enormous amount of work, though as far as he could see Cousin Sarah and the servants undertook most of the labour, and once the evening was over Lady De Lacy would take to her bed, claiming to be prostrate with exhaustion, for days afterwards.

With this in mind, he wasn't particularly surprised when he arrived in Grosvenor Square escorting his parent on the night of the celebration, to see Mrs Greystone, once again in her puce gown, in a highly agitated state and apparently on the verge of tears; the strain of organising the party, not to mention all the wedding preparations, must be affecting her, he thought, and was sorry for it.

She'd seemed quite distracted enough the last time he'd seen her, a couple of days before. They had encountered each other quite by chance in the curious location, for a lady of quality, of Lombard Street, in the City; he'd been there on financial matters relating to his marriage. The old lady had started nervously at the sight of him and murmured something unnecessarily elaborate about delivering an urgent letter to the post office in order to catch the evening's mail. This struck Dominic as an odd thing, because her brother was a peer and could surely have franked her correspondence for her and saved her the trouble, but it was most certainly none of his business. She'd then, her manner still flustered, gone on to volunteer the information that Miss Nightingale was a little indisposed at present. His natural concern at the worrying news had only appeared to cause her more distress, even though she'd assured him it was nothing at all – merely a slight summer cold, and dear Maria, the most tractable and sweet-natured of girls, didn't want the least fuss made.

Mrs Greystone was even more troubled now, answering remarks addressed to her almost at random and occasionally wringing her hands in what appeared to be, but surely could not be, despair, then catching herself up and clutching her ebony fan so tightly that the fragile thing looked likely to break under the pressure. He was glad to see that his mother assessed the situation in one swift glance and took the lady aside, compelling her to sit upon an uncomfortable-looking green brocade sofa and take a restorative glass of wine, which did appear to do her some immediate good.

But the matter of his hostess's strange behaviour vanished instantly from his mind when he laid eyes on Miss Nightingale. As they stood together to receive her father's guests and respond suitably to their congratulations – they were mostly a motley assortment of cousins, older members of the extended De Lacy and Nightingale families rather than friends of his or persons he'd any desire at all to spend time with – he was happy to see that she must be considered completely, even miraculously, recovered from her brief illness. She was in high bloom in pearls and a charming gown of cerulean blue silk with a gauzy white overdress, looking better, in fact, than she had on any other occasion on which he'd seen her. There was colour in her previously pale cheeks, and she must have caught the sun during some outing in recent days, despite her cold, for her straight nose was scattered with a few freckles, which were surely new. In general, she now resembled a living woman rather than a statue from antiquity, and in Dominic's eyes, at least, it was a decided improvement.

She'd also cut her hair, which perhaps contributed to her more modern and approachable air. Was it quite usual for a young lady so ruthlessly to chop off her long, lustrous and much-admired golden locks in favour of a short crop a couple of weeks before her marriage? Dominic couldn't say. Did he mind, or think he should have been consulted? He didn't. He detected in himself distinct signs of liking it. The change revealed the graceful arc of her long neck, unburdened by heavy curls, the fine shape of the back of her head with its feathery wisps of short hair, which somehow made him want to run a finger lightly down that swooping curve, to where her bare, creamy skin met the edge of her gown, and then around... For the first time he was conscious of a fugitive spark of sexual interest. More than that – desire. He had no reason to assume that it was reciprocated, but in the circumstances, with their wedding so close, he welcomed it as something that could perhaps be built upon, slowly and with infinite care and patience. It was surely better if at least one of them felt something more than complete indifference towards the other.

Unsure if it was wise, once the stream of arrivals to be greeted had slowed to a trickle and then stopped he could not refrain from complimenting his betrothed upon her novel and flattering way of arranging her hair. She regarded him in a measuring sort of way, and this too was new, as was her manner, which was somehow brisker than he'd known previously. She seemed about to speak – perhaps actually to offer something beyond platitudes for the first time in their acquaintance – but she was interrupted before she could do so. This was, after all, supposed to be a formal, public celebration of their impending nuptials, and must be marked as such. Lady De Lacy took swift charge of matters, since Mrs Greystone appeared to be incapable of it and Lord Nightingale disinclined to exert himself in the task, and at her instigation glasses were raised to toast the happy couple, brief speeches made, not least by Dominic himself, and renewed congratulations offered by the assembled guests. The bride to be blushed becomingly, and murmured her thanks, and everything passed off entirely satisfactorily, the company now resolving itself into various conversational groups.

'Thank goodness that's over!' said Miss Nightingale unexpectedly in his ear, her breath brushing his flesh and making it tingle. 'Now you and I must talk in private, sir. Urgently!'

He had no time to object, even had he wished to; her hand was on his arm, urging him away, and in a moment or so he found himself truly alone with his betrothed, back in the sitting room where he'd proposed to her. On this occasion both doors were firmly closed, and Miss Nightingale leaned back against the one they'd entered by, treating him to that oddly assessing glance once more. Her cheeks were still flushed, and he now realised that she had only been superficially composed before. But she was revealing her underlying agitation plainly now. Whatever the reason she had drawn him here in such a determined manner, he didn't think, unfortunately, that it was to further their acquaintance in any of the enticing ways that had so recently occurred to him. She didn't look in the least like a woman with an amorous purpose in mind; in fact, she appeared more likely to dress him down than kiss him.

Still he felt no sense of impending doom, no hint that his life was about to be up-ended, shaken vigorously, like a feather mattress by a chambermaid, and put down in a way entirely new to him. 'Ma'am,' he said, 'Miss Nightingale—'

She shook her head emphatically, her bright curls bouncing. She seemed – though surely she could not be – irritated, even angry.

'I'm not Miss Nightingale,' she said with emphasis. 'That's Maria, my older sister. I'm Miss Margaret Nightingale – Meg. We've never met before, Sir Dominic. And I must tell you that my sister has disappeared.'

3

Sir Dominic De Lacy stared at Meg with an expression of incomprehension that would have seemed foolish on a face less handsome. He was, it pained her to admit, excessively, even ridiculously, good looking. Maria had inexplicably not thought to tell her so in any of her letters, though it wasn't the sort of thing that Meg herself would have neglected to mention when discussing her own future husband. His features were strong, masculine and regular – his nose straight, his cheekbones sharply cut, his chin strong and his eyes a pleasing shade of grey. His mouth was particularly finely sculpted, and his artfully dishevelled hair a warm honey brown. He was tall, too – Meg was accustomed to towering over men, but this gentleman was well over six foot and had several inches' advantage over her. His immaculate black evening suit fitted him to perfection, and if the breadth of his shoulders owed anything to padding, she could see no sign of it. She knew, as did anyone who paid attention to such matters, or had done her research, that he was a notable whip, a consummate horseman and a superb amateur boxer. A leader of fashion, too, and one of the wealthiest and most eligible men in the haut ton. And her sister, his betrothed, the woman he had chosen above all others to be his bride, instead of being gratified to be so singled out, had run away from him, vanishing utterly into the teeming streets of London.

'What did you do to her?' she said fiercely, determined to catch him off guard while he was still dealing with the severe shock she'd given him. He might be the epitome of male elegance, the image of every hero of every novel she'd ever read, Mr Darcy or Lord Orville made flesh, but that didn't mean he couldn't be a secret monster of depravity too. She would not be so foolish as to judge him by appearances. Had he forced his attentions on poor Maria, or otherwise offended her tender sensibilities by unforgivably boorish behaviour? She, Meg, needed to stop gazing at him like a mooncalf and find out.

He shook his head, as if to clear it. 'I?'

'Yes, you! Who else?'

'I have not the least notion what you're talking about,' he said firmly.

She scoffed in disbelief. 'My sister has run away – at least I must assume she has – because she is horrified by the prospect of marrying you. Why else would she go so suddenly, and without telling anyone? All I know is, she's gone. And I demand you tell me why!'

It seemed to Meg that anger was kindling deep in those grey eyes, anger to match her own. 'If what you say is true, I'd quite like to know myself. I assure you, I have done nothing to her. Though we are betrothed, I scarcely know her. I must admit that I was aware she was experiencing some discomfort since our engagement became a subject for public speculation, but she never spoke to me of it, and I had thought her merely embarrassed by the scrutiny we have inevitably been undergoing. I see now that I was quite disastrously wrong. I suppose you're twins?'

'Of course we are, as must be perfectly obvious to anyone of the meanest intelligence! Is that all you can think to say?'

'Madam, I think I'm reacting rather well, considering I've just been deceived into publicly celebrating my engagement in front of half the stuffiest old dragons of the ton with a woman at my side I've never met before in my life. Did your father not think to make some excuse – a sudden indisposition would have served perfectly and occasioned little comment – and call the damn thing off, rather than prevail upon you, as I must assume he did, to engage in such a ridiculous and dangerous imposture?'

'Oh, he doesn't know,' said Meg a little more calmly. Perhaps she had been wrong in thinking that Sir Dominic must be to blame. It seemed there was some mystery here.

He appeared to be speechless for a moment. 'Lord Nightingale doesn't...?' he managed at last. 'How in the name of heaven is that possible?'

'Maria ran away four nights ago, we believe. As soon as she realised my sister was missing, my aunt Greystone sent an urgent letter by the overnight mail, asking if Maria had come to us – to my mama's house – and summoning me to take her place if she had not. But we knew nothing at all of the matter, and had not laid eyes on her or heard from her, and so I was obliged to do as Aunt begged me. I arrived last night on the stagecoach. You must have seen how distraught the poor creature is, which I am sure is quite understandable. But my father knows nothing at all of the matter.'

'He hasn't noticed? Not your aunt's distress, and not this... this outrageous substitution?'

'Well, he pays no attention to my aunt, or to females generally. Or people, really. All he cares for is his studies. And as for me, we haven't set eyes on each other for five years or so. My mother would tell you that he's forgotten he ever had another daughter. Although she is prejudiced against him because of the dreadful way he has treated her, I do think on this occasion she may be right.'

'Your hair…' He gestured at it somewhat helplessly with one elegant hand.

'If he's noticed it – which he very likely hasn't – he probably thinks I simply had it cut. You thought so, did you not?'

'I did. But I'm not your father, and I don't share a home with you. I assure you, I am barely acquainted with your sister, and we have never been alone together for more than the very brief interview in which I proffered my suit and she accepted it. But I find it almost beyond belief that one daughter – even if you are identical – could be substituted for another and a parent not notice it.'

Meg said, hysterical laughter suddenly welling up in a great bubble inside her and making her voice unsteady, 'My mother has always said… he isn't very observant!'

Sir Dominic let out a crack of sudden mirth that transformed his features and made him appealing rather than merely conventionally handsome. 'I would say that is something of an understatement!'

The shared moment of humour seemed to lessen the tension somehow. 'Are we truly still identical?' Meg asked him with unconscious wistfulness. 'My aunt said we are, but she was so desperate for me to take Maria's place tonight that I wasn't sure if she was being honest, or just hoped that it might be so.'

'My dear girl, don't you know?'

'How could I? I haven't seen my sister since we were thirteen.'

'I think you must explain. I feel as though I've entered a madhouse.'

'There's no time for all that! You need to help me find Maria,' she said urgently. 'I've thought a great deal about it, and now that I must accept that you're not directly responsible for her flight, or at least if you are you don't know that you are, I don't see who else I can ask.'

'It may be so. Of course I'm not refusing categorically to help you. But we can hardly leave the house together – we'll have to go back to the guests soon, in any case, or there will be a great bustle about our absence. It really would be madness to start combing the streets of London at this hour. Apart from the scandal it would surely cause, where on earth would we begin such a task? I need more facts. You must see that this is true.' He spoke gently, and Meg became aware of an odd lump in her throat. But she could perceive the sense in what he said, and sank into a sofa, unconsciously pleating and twisting the folds of Maria's fine blue and white engagement gown as she did so, anxiety and a sense of utter helplessness overwhelming her once more.

He sat down beside her, reaching out and gently disengaging her fingers from their convulsive grip on the delicate fabric. His hand was warm where hers was cold, and he held her chilly digits in a reassuring grasp. 'Tell me,' he said. 'Make me understand your situation. You must realise we only have a few moments.'

She said dully, 'Very well. My parents should never have married, you understand. It was an arranged match, his second – he is much older – and they turned out to be entirely ill suited, despite their separate intellectual achievements, or perhaps even because of them. Lord Nightingale has no time for clever women. For living women at all, in fact, or for normal human feelings. My mother said she first realised their incompatibility fully when he insisted, upon our birth, on naming us Maria Major and Maria Minor – as the Ancient Romans did, you know. He thought...' Her voice cracked again, though this time with incipient tears rather than laughter. 'He thought it would be easier. Since we were twins, and identical. He couldn't understand how she could possibly have any rational objection.'

He was regarding her with a sort of fascinated horror. 'I had heard he was eccentric, but good God... Please tell me that isn't your name, you unfortunate girl. That sort of thing should surely be illegal.'

'No, she did manage to persuade him, but not that he was wrong – he can't ever be wrong, you must understand – merely that he should also commemorate his sister. Maria was his mother, you see, and Margaret his younger sister, and they both died prematurely. My mother said she thought it highly sensible of them, and that his older sister, my aunt Greystone, had often appeared to regret not following the same path. But possibly she exaggerates. She is a writer, you know, as I aspire to be, and is not always to be trusted to tell the literal truth, but rather favours what may make a good story.'

He seemed relieved, and not noticeably shocked by this revelation of authorial unreliability. 'So you are Margaret, and she is Maria? That's much more normal.'

'Oh, no. She is Maria Margaret, and I am Margaret Maria. That way – he told Mama as she lay recovering in childbed, and this I am afraid I do believe – if one of us should soon die, or otherwise turn out to be unsatisfactory, he should still have commemorated both his mother and his sister. He was pleased, she said, because it is so efficient.'

'Efficient.'

'Yes. Do you begin to see what he is like?'

Sir Dominic sighed, perhaps in the realisation that he had entangled himself with a most peculiar family, with consequences for his own peace of mind that could not yet be guessed at. 'I do, but I think,' he said, 'that we must go back now before we are missed. Can you not tell me everything else, quickly?'

'She's gone, and nobody has the least idea where. The rest is just details, don't you think? We're wasting time when we could be looking for her, sir!'

He was still holding her hand – she feared she might have been clinging to him – and he squeezed it comfortingly and went on, less reassuringly, 'I know you're worried about your sister, and concerned that she may be in some dire peril, and I share your concern. But you do understand that you cannot find her tonight. We know so little; it is not sensible to contemplate wandering about the streets calling her name. No, we must meet again tomorrow, and you will tell me all the rest, everything you can think of, without hurry. Would it be possible for you to ride with me early in the morning, do you think? Is there a groom you can trust to accompany you?'

'There is,' she replied, disappointed by his refusal to hare off immediately into the night with her, but reluctantly admitting that there was a great deal of cold good sense in what he said. But she'd also noticed that he hadn't actually said that he would help her. Not explicitly. A true gentleman would never break a promise, it was claimed, which was no doubt why he hadn't made her one. Yet. 'The servants all know who I am – the older ones, at least – and Robert will be happy to accompany me and let me talk privately with you. They're all most worried about Maria too.'

They left the room together and headed back into the

salons, which had been made into one large space by the opening of a set of double doors. The party was still continuing, though some of the guests had already left and the room was decidedly thinner of company. Meg couldn't deceive herself that their entry went unnoticed – she was hotly aware of curious looks shot in their direction, and a few knowing smirks. Lady De Lacy, who undoubtedly had observed her son's absence along with that of his supposed fiancée, looked quite delighted. It was all too easy to divine what she, and the rest of those present, believed they had been about. A betrothed couple might be allowed just a little indulgence in such matters, she supposed, but in these most unusual circumstances the prurient attention could only be unwelcome.

On another occasion she might have recoiled with mortification at the commonplace minds of her father's guests, but she had no time for that now. Her only concern must be to discover what had happened to her sister, and make sure she was safe and happy. Sir Dominic didn't appear to be the monster of her wildest imaginings – if she was any judge at all, he'd been truthful when he'd told her that he'd had very little contact with Maria and no private speech with her – and so perhaps sharing her secret with him had been a wise decision. He seemed kind, at least. But she couldn't yet say whether he was prepared to shoulder the burden of responsibility and help her. She was in desperate need of help, and so she must persuade him, and she would. It was too important a matter to let considerations of propriety or ladylike behaviour stand in her way. Not that they generally did, she was obliged to admit. If necessary, she would even cry, a feat she rarely attempted.

Meg Nightingale wasn't of a nature easily discouraged or cast down, but the idea of scouring the crowded streets of London – a place she did not know her way about, home to well over a million people – for Maria, who could be absolutely anywhere and might not even be in the city any more, was undeniably daunting. It was to be hoped that Sir Dominic would be able to think of something, where she in her current panic could not. He was a man of the world and of some resource, plainly, even if he understandably didn't know her sister at all well. Perhaps they'd devise some scheme together. She would know better tomorrow, and must be quite ruthless in making use of him, for her sister's sake.

4

Meg met Sir Dominic, as they had arranged, a little way inside the gates of Hyde Park, by a stand of mature trees. She hadn't been here, or anywhere else in London, for five years, of course, and her childhood memories of the place had inevitably faded, but his instructions had been clear and Robert had known exactly where he meant. It was still early – a cool, clear morning with the promise of heat to come, and though there were other riders about, mostly men, alone or in pairs, nobody seemed inclined to approach them, and so they had a certain measure of privacy. Robert kept a discreet distance, his face impassive, after he'd saluted Sir Dominic politely.

Their horses were restive on this fine day, and so they decided to ride a little before dismounting to talk. Sir Dominic was mounted on a glossy black stallion, and Meg on the well-mannered bay gelding that her sister generally rode. She'd brought few clothes to London in her haste and anxiety, and so was wearing Maria's riding habit, which fitted her snugly enough; it was a dashing confection in her sister's favourite blue, with a great deal of military lacing and a daring cap to match. She thought, from the warm expression in Sir Dominic's eyes, that the ensemble must become her – but that was of no significance, of course. No doubt he had liked Maria as much, if he'd seen her in it.

He said, after they'd trotted together in silence for a while, 'You must know that I have a great many questions.'

She shook her head in frustration. She had the perilous sense of time speeding by while she did nothing, as in a fever dream of running with desperate haste and getting nowhere. 'I daresay you do. But are they relevant? I know my family is most odd, and I don't mind telling you about it if you care to know, but can any of that really matter now?'

'Perhaps not; it is too soon to say. You've been corresponding regularly with your sister, I take it, since you have been living apart?' She nodded assent. 'But you don't have the least idea where she might be, or even why she's gone, apart from the understakable assumption that she's fled because the idea of marrying me is repugnant to her?'

Even in her preoccupation, she felt rather sorry for him. If he really had done nothing wrong, as seemed to be the case, this must all be a great shock. 'She didn't tell me so, you understand – or anybody else, as far as I know. She only said you'd offered for her, with our father's approval, and that she'd accepted. She said you seemed very agreeable.' Meg looked across at him, and found that his mouth was twisted into a wry smile; she could hardly wonder at it, so very faint was the praise. She'd written back, saying as much, asking if her sister was sure she wanted to do this serious and irrevocable thing: to commit herself for life to a man she found merely agreeable. Maria hadn't answered her letter but had instead – run away. Which was an unequivocal answer in itself, she supposed.

'Agreeable,' he repeated, as though the word tasted ill in his mouth. 'Well, obviously not all that agreeable, since the undeniable fact is that she's gone. I suppose I should be grateful she didn't wait a little longer and leave me at the altar – but I wish she'd talked to me, instead of this. I must blame myself, for not conveying to her the fact that she might repose her trust in me and tell me of her qualms. Her natural qualms at such a serious change in life. How could I expect her to know she might depend on me, otherwise?'

'Might she?' Might I? Meg wondered. He still remained uncommitted, as far as she could see, for all his fine words and his air of sympathetic understanding. 'Why did you offer for her?' she asked abruptly, looking across at him where he rode by her side. He didn't look like a fortune hunter, he looked more like someone who'd be hunted – but what did she know? She must admit that most of her knowledge of the world came from books, and she could not help but recall how easily Miss Elizabeth Bennet, for example, like the heiress Miss Darcy before her, had been deceived by Captain Wickham's plausible charm. Might this gentleman be another such? 'Was it her portion that attracted you? Our grandmother left all her fortune to my father's eldest daughter in her will, and I believe it to be very large. You might as well tell me, you know, if that's the reason. I expect,' she said kindly, 'that you're very expensive, so I can quite see why you might wish, or even need, to marry an heiress like Maria.'

He laughed, not offended, as Meg realised rather belatedly he might easily have been, but apparently genuinely amused. 'I am indeed extremely expensive – do you imagine that looking as well as this comes cheaply? – but I assure you, I am perfectly able to sustain my outgoings, and to support a wife, for that matter. I am a wealthy man, Miss Margaret, and I promise you that I have not the least interest in your sister's fortune. I don't –

didn't – intend to touch a penny of it, in fact. It was to be put in trust for her, and for our future children. I could show you the written marriage settlements, if you don't believe me.'

'Oh,' she said, rather at a loss. And then, 'Your children, of course – I expect you need an heir. You are quite old, I suppose.' And then she let go of the reins for a moment and clamped one gloved hand over her mouth. 'I don't know why I said that.' If Meg had been writing such a scene, she would never have had her heroine blurt out such a shockingly gauche thing to any gentleman.

He was still laughing rather ruefully. 'Because it's true? I'm nine and twenty, if that seems old to you, chit of a girl that you are, and yes, my mother has made it quite plain to me that it is time I should think about setting up my nursery. She told me, in fact, that this match was made years ago between your father and mine. No more eligible young lady than your sister could possibly exist, she informs me.'

That didn't seem like much of a reason. 'So you asked Maria to marry you because your mother told you to.'

His mouth quirked again, as if in self-disgust. 'And it was my father's dying wish, don't forget. Perhaps it really was, though he never told me so. My mother kindly reminded me that I was nothing more than a callow young fool when he died, not fit to be trusted with serious topics. Filial obedience is a virtue, we are told. I'm certainly told as much, with tedious frequency.'

'Do you always do what your mama tells you? I find that very hard to believe.' They were straying far from the topic at hand, Meg was aware, and she was hardly being persuasive, pushing him like this, but she couldn't seem to help herself. She found him oddly fascinating, probably because she might put him in a story. That must be it.

'Practically never, when it comes to unimportant things. But she is so far right in that I must marry somebody, you know. Why not your sister?'

She turned her head as she rode and stared at him. What an extraordinary way to make what must surely be one of the most important decisions in one's life. 'I think you're very strange.'

He was smiling wryly now. 'I dare say you do, but I could return the compliment. For my part, I don't think anyone whose father – whose whole family – is so deeply peculiar has any right at all to cast aspersions on anybody else. You appear reasonably normal to me now, compared with the rest of them, but then we have only just met. The true depth of your oddness is yet to be revealed to me, no doubt. But I hope at least we've established to your satisfaction that for my part I don't know a single thing that can help. At the moment, it seems as though I can't be any sort of help at all. Therefore I must ask you again to tell me what *you* know. There may be some detail that is important. For instance, why did you not make your come-out with your sister this year, as one might have expected?'

She rolled her eyes impatiently. 'It's completely irrelevant and we're wasting time, but very well – quite simply, my father wouldn't countenance it. He certainly wouldn't pay for it. I didn't mind, because I didn't want to attend the London Season particularly, or go to lots of silly parties, except that I would have been able to spend time with Maria. I would have liked that. I miss her.' She was aware that her voice betrayed her wistfulness; there didn't seem to be any way to prevent it, but at least he didn't comment.

'You're completely estranged from Lord Nightingale?'

'I suppose so. Yes. When my mother finally told him that she was leaving him, he told her she could go alone or take me – he really didn't care – but he wouldn't allow her to take Maria, his beloved mother's heiress. Because of what he said, Mama was faced with a terrible choice. And already at thirteen I'd begun arguing with him, and causing the most frightful scenes, while Maria appears to be much meeker and never does. So in the end Mama thought it would be better for me to live apart from him, with her, lest he crush me with his disapproval, as he had tried so hard to crush her. She hated separating me from my sister, and she hated leaving Maria too – she has apologised to us for it a hundred times – but she felt it would be bad for me, and also for my relationship with Maria, for that matter: to stay and be so disregarded, and always at odds with him, and have her goodness and my wickedness thrown in my face constantly.'

'Does he care for her so very greatly, then? I didn't get that impression when I spoke with him, I must admit.'

'I don't believe so. I'm not sure he cares for anyone living – not my aunt, and not even my half-brother Francis, his son and heir. Nor does Maria care for him, to judge by her letters. But she never disagrees with him or defies him, just smiles and says, "Of course, Papa. Just as you say, sir." No wonder he likes it and says it reminds him of his dear gentle little sister, who was supposedly a perfect pattern-card of virtue. My mother certainly never behaved in such a fashion, any more than I did. They used to fight terribly.'

'You said that she "appears to be" meek. Is she, genuinely? I'm sure you can see why I ask.'

'I don't think she is. She's a daydreamer, she lives in her own head most of the time, but I've always believed, and Mama has too, that underneath it all she's strong and determined. It's just that she rarely shows it to the world.'

'So running away from a marriage that was distasteful to her – rather than speaking up and making her objections plain and facing all the disagreeable consequences – would be quite in keeping with her character?'

'Yes, I believe it would. I don't think for a moment that she'd ever have allowed herself to be forced into marrying you, you know, if she truly doesn't want to.'

'What a comfort that must be to us all, and particularly me,' he said drily.

They'd slowed to a walk, the horses having trotted off their fidgets, and by common consent they dismounted, Meg sliding from the saddle with an agility that denied the least need for Sir Dominic's assistance. They were back under the trees again now, and Meg sat down on the grass – which was probably something a correct young lady wouldn't do, for fear of dirtying her habit, but she had more important things to worry about just now – and looked up at him, frowning. She needed to involve him, to make him care, for she could see that at the moment he really didn't; he was just somewhat interested, which might be more enthusiasm than he usually showed for anything much, lazy, cool and exquisite as he was, but still wasn't enough. This was her sister's life at stake, not the cut of a waistcoat or a lapel. 'She took clothes with her,' she told him with some association of thought. 'Not all of them, of course, but more than a gown or two. Her maid has shown me the gaps in her wardrobe. She packed her hairbrushes, too, and all manner of small personal things. It was well-planned in advance, obviously. There was no disorder or confusion among her possessions, nor any sign of haste or panic. And – I suppose it must be some consolation, and I cling to it – she definitely can't have been taken against her will. I'm not expecting you to rescue her from some gang of kidnappers, or anything of that nature.'

He didn't engage with that. 'The servants knew nothing of her departure?'

'Not a thing. Her maid, Hannah, is our old nurse. My mama made sure she stayed with Maria to support her and keep her safe. She, any of them, for that matter, would surely have tried to stop her, to ask her why, if she'd had the least notion anything was wrong. They've all told me as much. They suspected nothing, and she must have slipped away with the greatest secrecy.'

'Does she have friends whose aid she might seek, or are there any servants who have left your father's employ that she might conceivably go to for aid and shelter? I can't imagine from all you've said that Lord Nightingale is the easiest of masters. There must be people who have quit his household in recent years and who might be willing to help her.'

Meg smiled up at him approvingly. These were good, solid questions, she thought – it was plain that Sir Dominic, despite his fashionably languid appearance, was far from stupid and could be most useful, if she could draw him in. 'Yes, to both questions. She went to school for the last five years, a very correct seminary that prepares ladies for their come-out. Accomplishments, you know the sort of thing. The back board, and watercolours, and singing sickly songs in Italian while looking sweetly pretty. My mother had been teaching us herself before she and I left, and continued to teach me, but not that sort of nonsense. You see, my father doesn't approve of extensive and serious education for women.' She was pleased to see him shake his head in disapprobation of her parent's old-fashioned views; he could hardly care what she thought of him, so he must be sincere. 'He believes that my mama's bluestocking ways were what made her so very unsatisfactory as a wife, and therefore the breakdown of their marriage, and my quarrelsome nature too, had to be her fault. Nothing to do with the fact that he's utterly selfish and quite impossible to live with.'

'Why am I not surprised to hear any of this?'

She smiled briefly in acknowledgement. 'So yes, Maria went to school, and I recall from her letters that she made a number of friends there, many of whom made their debut this year with her. I know their names, and so do Hannah and my aunt. But I can't very well go around asking them questions about her, or about where she is now, can I? That's partly why I need your help so desperately.'

'Why can't you?'

'Because I'm supposed to *be* her!'

5

Dominic was forced to conclude that his companion had a point. 'I can spend time in their company,' she went on reasonably, 'and try to see if they are behaving oddly, though it'll be difficult to tell for certain as I don't know them at all, apart from what she's told me in her letters. I have asked my aunt to give me details of anyone Maria is particularly close to, and she has done so, but she's so very distressed over what's happened that she can't be much help beyond that. She's taken to her bed with a spasm today, Hannah tells me. Or several spasms. And palpitations, whatever they are.'

'My mother suffers from them too. I've always supposed them to be imaginary, but perhaps I'm being unfair. They do sound most disagreeable. But let us not be distracted by such incidental matters. It is plain that you must continue in your deception. Very well. And the servants who have changed their situations? It sounds as though that aspect of the problem might be easier to deal with. If any of them are living and working in London, or near London, I assume their fellow servants will know, and perhaps they'll even have their directions?' She nodded. 'Well then, my valet or my groom, both of whom are utterly trustworthy, I promise, can be admitted into the secret so that they can help us interview them in a discreet manner. Does all this sound like a plan?'

Miss Nightingale had seemed more cheerful for the last few moments – clearly the idea of positive action appealed to her lively nature – but now she said doubtfully, 'We can do all these things, and we must.' Dominic could not help but notice that his companion was very keen to involve him much more deeply in the matter than he had so far promised to go, with her clever use of the innocuous little word 'we'. 'Don't think I'm not grateful for your help, sir, because I am, but I'm very conscious that the clock is ticking all the while. When is your wedding to be? I collect it is quite soon, but Maria didn't say.'

'Can you wonder she didn't, since she apparently had no intention of actually participating? In three weeks' time,' he responded rather hollowly. 'At St George's, Hanover Square. As one might expect.'

'And what happens if we can't find her before then, sir?'

'The wedding will have to be called off,' he said resolutely, frowning down at her. 'Really, it must be. There's no other option. If I were more sensible, I'd put an end to this farce directly myself rather than tacitly support you in it. It's quite plain your sister doesn't want anything to do with me, and really, you know, I'm an easy-going sort of a man as a general rule, but I don't experience a great desire to spend the rest of my life with a woman who'd rather run away from her home and family in the middle of the night than become my bride. I hope I'm not excessively conceited, but you can't expect me to like it nonetheless. I should speak to your father without delay.'

'I quite understand your feelings, but you must see that you can't do that,' she said persuasively, her large blue eyes liquid and earnest. 'For heaven's sake, Sir Dominic, your engagement party was just last night! There'd be a fearful scandal, and your reputation, and your family's, would suffer for it, as well as Maria's. *You* can't call an end to the engagement – men can't, can they? – so if you intend to put it about that my sister has cried off, you'd have to tell my father the whole truth to make him cooperate with the lie. And that would be most unkind to my poor aunt, and to Maria herself, if she means in fact to come back, which for all we know she might. You can surely imagine how Lord Nightingale would react to such a blow to his conceit. He'd cast her off in the most dramatic of fashions, making a huge public fuss like a great spoiled baby and doing everything he possibly could to be excessively disagreeable. I assure you from my own knowledge, he can be most unpleasant when he is thwarted. It's only fair that we at least *try* to find out where Maria is and why she left. We mustn't despair yet.'

That 'we' again. Such a small word, and so dangerous. He felt himself weakening in the face of her determination, and looked down at her with a lurking smile in his grey eyes. 'You are a young lady of great energy and resolution,' he said. 'To set off in such haste, too, to come to the aid of a sister and an aunt you haven't seen for years – your loyalty is admirable.'

'Nonsense,' she said, flushing a little. 'They needed my help. They still do. And Mama would have come too, though obviously she could not be expected to stay under my father's roof, which would be extremely awkward, only she is very exercised with finishing her latest novel, which does not progress as it should and is due to be delivered to her publisher next month.'

'Ah,' he said. 'I see.'

He was determined to keep his inevitable reflections to himself, but Miss Margaret appeared to have divined them by some mysterious means, for she said, 'I don't suppose you do, you know. I can see you think that she is being selfish, not coming to help, but you're wrong. We have not very much money, and for the most part Mama is obliged to support us with her writing. I have been able to make almost no contribution as yet, though of course I hope I shall in time. This means she has commitments she must fulfil. A legal contract! I expect you think that successful writers like my mother earn a great deal of money for their labour, and live in great luxury on it, but I must tell you that it is not so.'

'I'd never considered the matter particularly before,' he replied, 'not being of a literary turn myself, but I might have imagined that your father supported you both, or at least supported you, as you are his acknowledged child and his responsibility, at least till you are of age.'

'He is supposed to, but he does so very grudgingly, and the payments are always late, or mysteriously go astray, and certainly are not to be depended on always to keep a roof above our heads, the servants' wages paid and food on the table. Paper, too, is quite shockingly expensive, you know, and postage, and books, which are a necessity for existence, naturally.'

'Naturally they are. The more I hear about your father,' Dominic said rather grimly, 'the more I am inclined to dislike him enormously, and, for that matter, the more I wonder that *my* father should have entered into any sort of agreement with him, least of all one of such an important nature. My own father was quite another type of man, I assure you. But friendship – especially if it is of many years' duration – is a mysterious thing, I suppose.

'We may be refining too much upon the matter, of course. I will never know my father's motives now, though my mother's seem clear enough. One is, after all, obliged in the end to marry someone in particular. And your sister is highly eligible by anyone's standards. But we are wandering from the point. Will you draw up a list of former servants and their directions, so that you can share it with me? I assume you are to attend Princess Esterhazy's ball tonight?'

'I am – Maria is – although I am by no means sure that my aunt will be well enough to accompany me. She is still quite overset. Would your mother consent to act as my chaperon, do you suppose?'

'Need you ask? Nothing could delight her more,' he said drily. 'And she'll be a most inattentive duenna, I promise you. I dare say we could disappear together for hours and she would turn a resolutely blind eye to it. She will be in alt when I tell her that I have seen you already today and you have requested that we collect you this evening.'

Miss Nightingale grimaced, wrinkling up her freckled nose in a manner that made her look quite astonishingly unlike her sister. 'Oh dear, I expect she will be. She will be devastated if you are obliged to tell her that the match must be called off, will she not, when she has done so much to promote it, whatever her reasons?'

'She will, and I suppose I must be sorry for it. But I challenge you to present me with an alternative. Can you, in all seriousness, envisage any possible combination of circumstances that leads to your sister walking up the aisle and joining me, of her own free will, in three weeks' time? Because I must be honest and say that at this moment I cannot. And I warn you that I will not accept an unwilling bride. I may be expensive, elderly, and altogether quite a frippery fellow, in your eyes, but I am not a complete fool.'

'I never said you were... some of those things,' she responded with dignity. 'You can't imagine, now that I know what has happened – because my aunt's letter was extremely incoherent, so that I had no real idea what I might find when I got to London – that I mean to try to force Maria to marry you? I would not do such a thing even if it lay within my power. It does seem quite clear that she doesn't want you, which is her right, and I must respect that, even if I fear my father won't. My first concern is to see her safe. That's all I care about, really. If she doesn't want to come home for some other reason, and I would be the last person to blame her for it, we can deal with that together. If I end up having to reveal to my father that she's gone and I took her place, and that she has no intention of returning, I will do that for her. *I'm* not scared of him. She's the one who's been forced to live with him these past five years, after all, while I was much happier with Mama even if we do lack for money. I'm sure no number of pianoforte lessons and silk dresses could make up for that.'

'You must be right. I'm sure you would tell me that you often are,' he said, smiling. 'But you told me you came up to Town by stage?' What entertaining, unexpected company she was – he had not the least idea what she was going to say next, and he was conscious of an unaccountable desire to prolong the interview beyond its natural duration. Dammit, he knew he was going to help her. Of course he was. 'Without even a maid to accompany you?'

'Are you shocked, sir?' she replied tranquilly. 'I suppose it is highly irregular. But my mama has brought me up not to regard social conventions overmuch, and the last thing I needed was to bring someone with me who might go chattering indiscreetly about my sister's disappearance while there might still be a chance of keeping it secret. It was a great adventure, I assure you, and most interesting to have the opportunity to talk to people I did not know, though it was not, of course, terribly comfortable, and very slow. We don't keep a carriage, and I couldn't possibly have afforded to travel post, in any case. It didn't occur to my aunt to send me any money for the journey, and no wonder, so distressed as she is, poor thing.'

'I am sure the journey offered you many opportunities of observation that you will quickly turn to good use as a writer. But I haven't thought to ask you if Mrs Greystone knows anything that might point to your sister's whereabouts. I assume she does not?'

'Not the least thing in the world, I assure you. She is my father's sister, you know, and quite in awe of him; Maria would never confide in her, for fear she'd fall into a fit of the vapours and tell him everything.'

'Perhaps tonight we may discover if any of your sister's friends are in her confidence, instead?' He couldn't help realising that he was saying 'we' now too; it must be infectious.

'I hope so,' she said doubtfully. 'We can only hope that none of them realises I'm not her – but then, why should they, since I have never appeared in society and don't live in London, and they probably barely know I exist? I have a list of them already, though there's no point sharing it with you – it's not as though you, of all people, can go round interrogating debutantes, or even talking to any one of them on your own for very long; everyone would think you'd run mad, especially now you are betrothed. But I'll make up another list, of servants who have left, which is a very good notion of yours and where you can perhaps be useful.'

He bowed. 'Thank you; to be of use to you is my sole aim in life, naturally, ma'am.' He hoped it wasn't true even as he said it, but feared it might swiftly become so. 'If you can contrive to have it sent over to my house quite soon, I can make a start on it. Otherwise the afternoon will be quite wasted in my usual idle and inconsequential pursuits. Perhaps you can send your sister's maid, Hannah? I'd like to talk to her, in any case.'

If she was aware he was teasing her, she showed no sign of it. 'I don't think she knows anything, or she'd have told me, but of course I will, if you wish it.'

They parted cordially, Dominic throwing Miss Nightingale up easily into the saddle and watching her trot sedately away with Robert a discreet length or so behind her. Her back was very straight and her seat excellent; she made a brave figure in her bright blue habit, and despite his earlier lively amusement he was frowning as his eyes tracked her out of the gates and into the busy street.

He was aware of a strong and growing sense of foreboding, though he hoped he had revealed nothing of his fears to his companion. He greatly admired her fierce determination to help her sister, and he supposed it might be possible that one of Maria Nightingale's bosom bows might be keeping secrets for her, or that she'd taken shelter with a trusted servant who'd known her since childhood. But if neither of these avenues of investigation led anywhere, they would swiftly find themselves at point non plus. They'd have to tell Lord Nightingale and insist that he call out the Runners, hoping desperately that they had resources denied to private persons, and be damned to all hope of concealment. There would be a dreadful scandal – but that was the least of his worries.

It seemed certain that Miss Nightingale had fled of her own free will, but that was not to say that she was safe now. She could have found herself in all manner of peril a few minutes after she'd left her father's house. She could be held against her will in some house of ill repute; she could be injured, or dead. She could, in fact, be floating in the river at this minute, a lifeless, nameless corpse, just one among many. London was a dangerous city, full of hazards for a young woman on her own, and it was all too possible for a vulnerable and friendless girl to fall prey to one of them and disappear forever without leaving any trace. What then? All Meg's high courage and desire to be active would help her little if the days passed, and then the weeks and months, with no news. Her father's anger and the scandal of a broken engagement could soon be as nothing to what she might have to endure in dread and constant anxiety. And her life, it seemed to him, had been hard enough already, though she made light of it. It struck him as cursedly unfair.

6

Dominic rode home, frowning, and gave precise instructions to his servants. They were far too well trained to betray any surprise at the peculiar tidings he gave them regarding a middle-aged female domestic of respectable appearance named Hannah, surname unknown, who would shortly be calling upon him in St James's Square and who was to be shown directly into his presence.

Meg had not delayed, it seemed, and so her old nurse arrived early in the forenoon, ushered in and announced by a carefully expressionless butler, and Dominic was soon urging her to take a seat in his snug, well-furnished library so they could converse. She took a comfortable chair without tiresome preliminaries, though she refused his offer of refreshment, and regarded him shrewdly with a pair of bright brown eyes, not the least disconcerted by being alone with a strange young gentleman in his private residence. Hannah Treadwell was a stout woman in her forties, dressed in the muted colours and practical fabrics suitable for a woman of her station, but with an air of quiet self-confidence and self-possession that made her a person of some substance, if one had the wit to see it.

'Mrs Treadwell,' Dominic said. 'Thank you for coming. I believe you have a message for me?'

'Yes, sir,' she said with great composure, handing over a document she produced from her capacious reticule. 'Miss Meg and I have put our heads together and set down the names and – so far as we have them, or could get them – the directions of the new employers of everyone who has left Lord Nightingale's service in the last couple of years. We didn't include outdoor servants who had little to do with Miss Maria, or anyone who stayed in their posts but a few weeks, as some did. It's still not the shortest list you ever saw, sir, I'm afraid.'

He took it from her with a word of thanks. 'Where do you think Miss Nightingale has gone?' he asked her abruptly. 'And are you as worried about her as her sister is, ma'am?'

'She never has confided in me, sir. I wish I knew something that could help you to find her, but I'm afraid I don't. And yes, I am worried. She has her head in the clouds, that one. For all that, she's stronger and more determined than she looks, but she has no more idea of the ways of the world than a babe of seven summers. How could she?'

'I'm sorry to hear that.' She was regarding him steadily, her thoughts unreadable, and Dominic felt compelled to add, 'I'm not seeking her out so she can be forced to marry me, you know, Mrs Treadwell. I've no interest at all in a reluctant bride. But if she has gone because of me, which I must assume she has, given the timing, I bear some responsibility for her safety. I should have spoken to her in private and made sure that she was willing to accept my offer, and not being constrained by her father. I knew all was not well with her, but I misunderstood the reason.'

'I doubt she would have told you even if you had pressed her, sir. She's very reserved in some ways. I brought her up from a baby, and she didn't tell *me* anything. I asked her, too, if your offer was to her liking, and she said it was. She wasn't tripping around her chamber strewing rose petals and singing for joy, but she's always been quiet and she said you seemed a most estimable gentleman, and that she was surprised, in fact, that Lord Nightingale had chosen so well, him being what he is. I sensed nothing at all amiss, so why should you?'

'I have wondered – and I didn't want to ask Miss Margaret, for several excellent reasons – if there was any chance Miss Nightingale might have another suitor, one whose advances she knew her father would never approve. Might she be in love with someone she knew must be considered highly unsuitable, do you think, ma'am, and have run off to Gretna with him?'

She didn't answer him directly, looking at him shrewdly and saying instead, 'You take it very cool, sir, I must say, if that's what you think.'

He said, a little impatiently, 'It would be foolish to pretend to be deeply in love with someone I scarcely know. And as for the blow to my self-esteem, I believe I will survive it. Better to know now exactly how things stand, don't you think, when matters can still be mended, rather than after the wedding when it's far too late, and both of us bound to come home by weeping cross?'

Hannah sighed in apparent agreement. 'Well, if that's the way of things, I must be honest and admit it's crossed my mind. But I can't say who it might be. There's no young men visit her father's house, I promise you, or none of the kind that'd be likely to appeal to her, or any woman with eyes in her head. Scholars, that's all, and antiquarians; poor, dusty creatures, every one of them. And she was spending most of her days at that fancy school up till a month or two ago, where she barely met a man from one month to the next. Trust the mistresses there to make sure of that, or what are they being paid such a pretty penny for? She's not the type to be falling in love with her old dancing master or the boy who cleans the boots, or any of that foolishness. It would surely have to be someone she'd met since her come-out. Some dashing young blade who'd turned her head. But sir, I have to think I'd have noticed the change in her, being on the lookout for it, as you might say, with her so pretty and innocent and such a good catch. So I'd be obliged to say no.'

'I don't know whether to be glad or sorry,' he said. 'It would be a great scandal, of course, but it would also be an explanation of sorts, rather than all this devilish uncertainty. I'll look at your list of servants, ma'am, and think how best to make enquiries among them, but I'm not overly sanguine. If she's told you nothing, nor her sister, are we to think she would so easily confide in another she cannot know half so well, and seek their aid instead of yours? And that's a point I had not previously thought of. Why would she not go straight to her mother, above all people? Surely she could be depended upon to support and shelter Miss Nightingale, if her husband was indeed forcing her daughter into just the sort of arranged marriage that has caused *her* so much unhappiness.'

'I don't know, sir. I honestly don't. I wish I did. And if you're thinking to ask next if she might have gone to her half-brother, Master Francis, I can promise you she hasn't – she's barely met him half a dozen times in her life, if so many. I doubt she even knows where he keeps his lodging.'

There seemed nothing more to be said, and Mrs Treadwell made her departure, leaving Dominic frowning over the paper she had left him. After considering it for a while, he rang the bell and asked that his head groom and his valet be sent to him. Another unusual request – why both together? – but once again the butler showed not the least sign that anything was amiss, and in a short while Messrs Fishwick and Pargeter joined him, and both took their seats at his invitation, looking at him questioningly.

'I am in the devil of a fix,' he told them bluntly. 'I presume you have heard that I am – or I was – to be married.' Dominic realised suddenly that he should already have told his staff the news himself; should have set matters in train to receive his bride into his house, which would become hers – and yet he hadn't. Had said nothing, had done nothing. Somehow he'd known instinctively that the damn thing wasn't real and wasn't going to happen. But that didn't signify now. 'I say "was", because Miss Nightingale has disappeared. Run away, I must assume, because she didn't wish to marry me.' He really was getting excessively tired of saying that to people.

'Disappeared since last night, sir?' his valet Stephen Pargeter ventured incredulously. He was a young, bright-eyed, endless enthusiastic fellow who was also an excellent valet, and once Dominic had trained him out of expressing that puppyish enthusiasm in the forenoon, for example by overly cheery morning greetings or loud, emphatic opening of the curtains, they'd developed a fine working relationship. If Dominic cherished a suspicion that Pargeter regarded him as a work of art, rather than a human being, and himself as the artist, he prudently kept the idea to himself.

'No, several days ago, apparently. Ah – I take your point, Pargeter. The engagement party was indeed only yesterday, though in my mind it seems to have taken place months ago. The world remains in ignorance of Miss Nightingale's departure because her identical twin sister has, for reasons I won't burden you with, taken her place. But she's also asked for my help in finding her. And I think I must give it.'

'How are you going to do that, sir, if she isn't supposed to be missing? Can't exactly call in the Runners,' volunteered Jack Fishwick. Jack was a much older, more grizzled man than the young valet, and had known Dominic from the cradle – had taught him to ride his first pony, in fact, and was prone to remind him of it if it seemed he was likely to forget.

'It's cursed awkward, Jack,' Dominic admitted. 'But I now have a list of servants who've left Lord Nightingale's employ in the last couple of years, and with whom she might conceivably have sought refuge. I need your help, both of you, in making enquiries to see if she's with one of them. I pray she is. I'm told by a reliable source that she almost certainly hasn't made for Gretna with some fortune-hunting cub, but I think that's still worth a little investigation, too – the inns where you'd make your first change of horses seem like the best idea. Barnet, to start with, for the Great North Road, if I give you the date and a description of the young lady. I know I can leave that to you, Jack.'

He grunted. 'The Mitre, and the Red Lion, and a few others, I dare say. I'll take it in hand. And what shall I do if I find she did pass through with some young swell on her way to Scotland, sir – send word to you and follow them?'

'Certainly not. It was days ago, man – they'll be wed across the anvil by now, or certainly would be by the time you caught up with them.' Seeing his concerned expression, Dominic said, 'I've no desire to stop her, or drag her back and force her to the altar. What the devil do you take me for? I've merely promised her sister I will do all I can to discover her whereabouts and see if she's safe. I can't engage myself to do any more. If indeed she has eloped, her father must be told – and there'll be a hell of an uproar, I dare say, and all of us embroiled in it. Her sister and her aunt are understandably keen to avoid that. But there's nothing any of us will be able to do to avert it, in the event of a flight to Scotland with all the scandal that implies. I want you to set off as soon as you can have a horse saddled. Five nights ago, late in the evening or in the early morning, and the young lady is tall, blonde and attractive, and very fashionably dressed, I'd imagine. The sort of woman people would remember if they saw her, we must hope. They'd surely suspect an elopement the moment they set eyes on her – anyone would.'

Pargeter, who seemed to be having some difficulty staying still in his seat, said, 'What shall I do, sir? I am most anxious to help in any way I may.'

His puppyish eagerness almost made Dominic smile as he passed over the list. 'See if you have friends in any of these households, man. If you do, take it from there.'

The young man's bright eyes scanned the document. 'I do, sir, as it happens, in three of the cases. I am acquainted with the valets in two of these houses, and the butler in another.'

'Good. Then lay out my clothes for tonight, and go. Seek out your friends. Ply them with drink – I'll cover your expenses, naturally. Keep a clear head yourself, and make enquiries – discreet enquiries, I need hardly add. This is a great deal more important,' he said as Pargeter hesitated, plainly torn over his conflicting duties, 'than handing me into my coat for some damn tedious ball. Be off with you both!'

They rose hastily and departed, though Jack shot him a glance from under his bushy eyebrows that promised a more honest and extensive conversation between them when Pargeter, the young upstart, should not be present. But he went, and would perform his task with speed and efficiency, Dominic knew. To make enquiries on the Great North Road was almost certainly a waste of time – but it had to be done. It would be foolish to neglect this most commonplace of explanations for Miss Nightingale's flight. He hoped she had run off with some plausible young fellow, and that Jack found solid evidence of it – but Mrs Treadwell had been so positive that she had not.

He'd sent a note to his mother at her home in Clarges Street, informing her of Mrs Greystone's indisposition and of the interesting fact that he'd engaged to take Miss Nightingale to the ball tonight and offered her services as a chaperon. With tongue firmly in cheek, he'd written apologising for speaking on her behalf; he hoped this scheme was agreeable to her nonetheless. His messenger had come rapidly back with an enthusiastic assent, and words of approbation for his conduct over the last couple of days that made him wince. Apparently, he had turned over a new leaf, to his mother's delight, and appeared to her as a man transformed, and one ready for the responsibilities his marriage would soon bring.

Sooner or later, his fond parent would discover that she was sadly mistaken to think that matters were proceeding excessively well. They were, in fact, viewed purely in the light of his own speedy entry into matrimony, proceeding excessively badly. Though he thought that only a part of the blame could justly be assigned to him, he wouldn't be at all surprised to discover that his mama, once she knew all, disagreed emphatically with this. If he had made more of a push to engage Miss Nightingale's affections from the outset, he could almost hear her saying... And perhaps she'd be right to think so.

Dominic cursed the restrictions of his position. He too had recognised a few of the names on Mrs Treadwell's list – he was, unsurprisingly, acquainted with some of the new employers of Lord Nightingale's former servants. But he could hardly go up to them at White's or Jackson's or anywhere else and ask them if, perchance, anyone associated with their household might be sheltering a young lady who bore a striking resemblance to his own fiancée. If he'd actually wanted to create an unholy scandal, that would be the quickest way of stirring it up. He was, until this evening, helpless to do more – and he didn't place any great dependence on being able to achieve anything then, either, though Miss Margaret plainly had a touching faith in him. It seemed to him that if Miss Nightingale was determined to remain hidden, or if the worst outcome had come to pass and she by now was either dead or in the power of those not kindly disposed towards her, there was very little chance of finding any trace of her, however hard they tried. In comparison, a flight to Gretna Green, even in the company of a fortune hunter, even with all the scandal that would inevitably flow from it, seemed a much more desirable discovery.

7

Meg was fortunate to have maintained such a regular correspondence with Maria, even though – in an act of quite characteristic pettiness – Lord Nightingale had refused to frank his older daughter's letters, and so the sending back and forth of missives had come at a considerable and equal cost to the two sisters. But they had both been determined to keep up their relationship despite their long, involuntary separation, and Lady Nightingale, for her part, had always encouraged them to do so. It had been an important aspect of Meg's life for the past five years, and now she was all the gladder of it, because it had made her familiar with the minutest detail of the household in Grosvenor Square.

When it had become clear that she would have to take Maria's place, at least temporarily, she'd had the reassurance of knowing that her sister saw little of their father from day to day. He had not even noticed Maria's four-day absence before Meg's own arrival, accepting without question or any show of concern Mrs Greystone's claim that Miss Nightingale was suffering a slight indisposition (such a vague and useful phrase) and keeping to her bed.

In fact, though her heart had begun to beat uncomfortably fast at the prospect of seeing him for the first time after five years, she had barely set eyes on her parent in the days she'd been here, though she was always aware of his lurking presence in his library. She'd shared the breakfast table with him, to her concealed dismay, but, remembering with unpleasant vividness his dislike of matutinal company and how bitingly he had expressed his disinclination for being obliged to endure trivial feminine conversation at such an hour, she had merely poured him his coffee in submissive silence. Poor Meg, she'd thought – five years of this silent tyranny, five years of living as it were in a tinderbox, endeavouring to avoid provoking by some innocent remark an outbreak of extreme paternal ill temper. No wonder she'd so enjoyed her time at school. It must have been a paradise compared with this.

She detected in herself a growing tendency to open doors cautiously and make sure Lord Nightingale wasn't passing like a disagreeable ghost through the hall or up the stairs before she ventured out; despite this, she had a strange little encounter with him the day after the engagement party, when on catching sight of her on the landing he said abruptly, as though already in mid-conversation, 'That's settled! Good, good! Excellent!' He was exhibiting the closest to ordinary good humour she'd ever observed in him, and, presuming him to be referring to Maria's marriage, she murmured some wordless form of assent that appeared to satisfy him, all the more because it relieved him of the necessity of replying. And then they parted, she shaking her head once he could no longer see her. The more she saw of him, the odder she knew him to be – but then, he had always been so.

His Lordship rarely dined with the ladies of his household, to precisely nobody's regret, but generally ate alone in his study or with fellow scholars at his club. As Mrs Greystone was still confined to her own room by nervous prostration, Meg took her evening meal in Maria's chamber upon a tray, with Hannah, on the evening of the Esterhazy ball. She was reassured to hear that Sir Dominic had promised to begin enquiries into the servants upon the list.

'He seemed like a sensible man,' Mrs Treadwell told her, 'and asked me all manner of reasonable questions, including what he didn't quite like to ask you, Miss Meg – whether your sister might have eloped with someone.'

'To Gretna Green?' responded Meg, eating her summer pudding with a thoughtful air. 'I suppose it must naturally occur to him as a possibility. But I do think it most unlikely. Surely you'd have noticed if anything of that kind were afoot, Hannah, even assuming that she didn't for some reason want to tell you, or me, or anyone.'

'That's what I said to Sir Dominic. And who would she be running away with? I asked him. Some young gentleman she's barely acquainted with? I do doubt it.'

'She hasn't mentioned any man at all in her letters, apart from Sir Dominic, and him very briefly. If she'd met someone else and he'd begun wooing her, surely she'd have said something about him in her letters at first, in all innocence, before the affair took on a clandestine nature? And if she were truly in love with someone else and being forced to marry by my father, I can't imagine any reason why she wouldn't share it with me. She's hardly likely to think that I – or Mama, for that matter – would take my father's part and not support her.'

'Sir Dominic said the same himself, and I agree. There's something else beyond a simple love affair going on here, Miss

Meg, you mark my words. I felt proper sorry for the gentleman, I have to say. He's taking the whole thing a great deal better than you might expect. It can't be very pleasant for him to find himself in this situation, can it?'

'No, it can't. And if the whole thing blows up into a frightful scandal-broth, he'll be as deep in it as the rest of us, when as far as I can see it really isn't his fault. You don't think he did anything to drive Maria away, do you, Hannah? I confess I did at first, but I don't now.'

'Beyond asking for her hand? That I surely don't. I liked him. He was nothing but polite and pleasant to me, asking my opinion and listening to what I had to say as though I'd been your aunt or any other lady. And there's no denying he's very handsome and well set up, for what that's worth. A great catch, that's what he is. And considering how much she dislikes living with your father, and no blame to her, your sister must have a powerful reason not to want to have him and make her escape that way.'

'Yes,' said Meg, pushing aside her bowl and setting down her spoon with a decisive clink. 'Yes, she must. If we only had the least idea what it could be!'

* * *

There was an undeniable awkwardness in the evening ahead – not least in the short carriage ride from her father's house to the ball close by. Meg was cloaked, ready and loitering about in the hallway, pretending to be absorbed in studying the large brown capriccio paintings of classical scenes that hung there, when Sir Dominic called for her. His mother remained in the waiting vehicle, but there was no time for private speech, not with the butler and the footmen standing by, able to overhear every word that passed between them. He bowed low over her gloved hand, and she took his arm and accompanied him down the steps. 'Nothing,' he said as they crossed the pavement, in response to a question she clearly did not need to ask. 'One of my men has returned from the first stage on the road north with no news to report, and set off out again, and the other is still absent. They are both now attempting to make contact, in a subtle manner, with members of the households in question. At present, I have no information for you, and I assume you are in the same case. And here is my mother, waiting eagerly to see you.'

He handed her up the steps and took his place opposite her, while she made herself as comfortable as she might be at Lady De Lacy's side and greeted her politely.

Meg was glad the journey was such a short one. There was no denying that she was of a venturesome disposition, unlike her more serious sister, and she'd already admitted to herself that in other, less anxious circumstances she might have enjoyed the imposture she'd been forced into. She led a very quiet life at home, with a restricted circle of acquaintance, and this could be a rare adventure, if she might only know that Maria was safe and well. But nobody, she thought, could really relish this aspect of it – deceiving a lady who was so nearly concerned in the matter of her sister's engagement, and so likely to be distressed and embarrassed, not to mention angry, if any part of the truth ever came out. And at this moment it was hard to imagine how it could fail to do so, unless they found Maria very soon and discovered that, no matter the reason for her flight, she was willing now to continue with her engagement and her impending marriage. Which seemed, on the face of it, increasingly unlikely as the days passed.

Lady De Lacy was a handsome, gaunt woman in her fifties.

She was tall, like her son, but darker, and her hair was a rich brown streaked with silver, abundant and beautifully arranged. She was very fashionably dressed in damson silk with a fine black lace overdress, and she took Meg's hand now and pressed it warmly. 'My dear Miss Nightingale,' she said affectionately, adding further to Meg's discomfort, 'I am so happy you asked us to accompany you this evening. It hardly needs to be said that we were delighted to do so, were we not, Dominic?'

'Of course we were, Mama.' Sir Dominic's face was in shadow, but Meg thought she could detect a mixture of rueful amusement and discomfort in his deep voice; she was, she realised, beginning to know him, and to perceive the emotions that his languid demeanour generally cloaked. He couldn't be liking any of this any more than she was, and he'd not had quite as long to get used to the idea.

'I'm most grateful for your kindness, ma'am, and so is my aunt. She keeps to her room, but she asked me to thank you, and to apologise for her absence. She is not strong, and the strain of organising last night's party overset her already fragile constitution. I hope that she will be better presently, but just now she cannot think of going into society and tiring herself further.'

'Please tell her tomorrow that I quite understand,' Lady De Lacy replied graciously. 'I am quite happy to chaperone you whenever you may need my aid, and I do feel deeply for your poor aunt, for there is no denying that, despite my deceptively robust appearance, my own health is not all it should be...'

Meg murmured in sympathy, and was able afterwards to sit back and make the most mechanical of responses to the older lady's flood of words until the carriage drew up at its destination, and Sir Dominic descended with languid grace to assist the ladies in exiting the vehicle. With one on each arm, he led them up the steps and into the grand mansion, to merge into a huge crush of people.

This was, in fact, Meg's first ever ball, though she had no intention of revealing this embarrassing fact to anyone. It was the sort of life experience a writer should have, she considered, and must be helpful to her, especially since she could expect to see little of such exalted society again. She could not help but look about her with interest, observing the lights, the flowers, and the magnificently dressed guests. She must thank heaven for Hannah, who had known exactly what she should wear: a beautiful gown of gold silk with an overdress of gauze in the exact same shade, scattered with brilliants that would catch the candlelight. At her throat she wore a simple string of pearls, which must once have belonged, she supposed, to one of the women, now deceased, for whom she and her sister were named.

Meg's mama had disliked London society for all the years that she was obliged to be a part of it, and now that she had quit it she steadfastly proclaimed herself profoundly indifferent to such things as fashion, and the vain display of wealth and status through jewels and fine fabrics. Lady Nightingale, it need scarcely be said, held views of an advanced nature, both politically and on the position of women. She didn't give a fig what she wore as long as she was warm and dry, and had never encouraged Meg to concern herself with the details of dress, or such trivial matters as whether one gown or another became her more. Many of Meg's shapeless day-to-day garments had been knitted or sewn by her mother or herself, as anyone looking at them could have guessed instantly, and they were both undeniably much better writers than knitters or needle-women. Meg had absorbed Lady Nightingale's philosophy, naturally, and agreed with it to a large extent, but that didn't mean, she now discovered, that she was completely indifferent to such a grand occasion, or to the notion that she was looking rather well in all her finery. To be aware of such a sensation and to find it agreeable was shallow, she knew, and all the more reprehensible because anxiety over her sister's plight should entirely suppress such trivial feelings, but apparently it didn't. Her emotions were in turmoil; at one moment she felt cheerful and optimistic about their chances of discovering that Maria was perfectly safe and well, and at the next she was overcome with panic and fear.

She shed her gauzy evening cloak in the chamber designated for that purpose, and set her hand rather firmly on the arm of Sir Dominic's dark coat again, unused to being among so many people – more, she realised, than on any other occasion in her life. Lady De Lacy was still nearby, but drawing further away with each step, as she paused to greet friends and acquaintances, of which she appeared to have very many. Meg was conscious of eyes upon her, but more aware of her companion's intent regard. 'Do you go out into company a great deal at home – and where is home?' he asked her now in low tones. 'I don't recall that you have ever said.'

She realised that he was aware of her disordered nerves, and moreover that he was questioning her to distract her from them. 'Mama and I are fixed near Bath, in a snug village house she inherited from her parents. Luckily our home was placed in trust for her as part of her marriage settlement and falls outside my father's control,' she told him. 'And no, we don't. We go into the town sometimes for the bookshops and so on, and even the occasional concert, but we don't mix in polite society outside our village, or attend the public assemblies, or anything of that nature. Mama does not care for such things, and I have too little experience of them yet to know whether I do or not.'

'And so, since you have not, as we previously discussed, made your come-out in London either, am I to assume that this is your first ball?'

So much for keeping that somehow shameful fact to herself. 'Yes,' she admitted rather defensively.

He was smiling ruefully. 'Forgive me, but I should then ask you – can you dance?'

8

Dominic was touched, he found, by the emotions Meg was trying and failing to conceal. No doubt she was concerned for her sister, focused on their mission, but despite herself she was also excited, as was only natural. Her eyes were bright and her cheeks slightly flushed, and she was looking about her with great interest. He should remind her that enthusiasm was not at all à la mode, and that her sister had surely learned not to display it, and so she should not either, for the sake of her impersonation, but he found himself oddly reluctant to crush her obvious pleasure. It seemed to him that her life held little enough novelty.

Of course it must be her first ball; he wondered, not for the first time, if Lady Nightingale was not, in some respects, as selfish a parent as her peculiar husband, keeping her younger daughter close at her side and away from all society. What did she mean Meg's life to be – was she to have no chance to travel, to see more of the world, perhaps to marry? Or was she already destined for a match with the local curate, or some ink-stained literary scrub her mother knew? It was an oddly uncomfortable thought.

She said now, 'Can I dance? Why, yes, of course I can – in theory, at least.'

He could not help but smile. 'In theory? You mean you've read about it in a book? If that's so, this is going to be a very strange evening, stranger even than I had anticipated.'

'Not entirely from a book,' she said with dignity. 'My mama is very fond of music, and made sure I learned it, and to dance too. She considers it healthful exercise.'

'I dare say she does. "Healthful exercise"! Have you, Meg Nightingale, ever danced with another human being – a male human being, at that – in a public place? Be honest with me, now!'

'Yes!' she replied, flushing. 'Though we do not attend fashionable assemblies, our village is quite sociable, and I have often danced with our squire, Sir Nicholas, or his son Robin, or our curate, Mr Relish. We are very gay, especially at Christmastime.'

'I knew the curate would come into it somewhere,' he said resignedly. 'I should have thought to ask you this crucial question long before this. Well, we shall manage with a few of the more usual dances, I expect – and after all, we are here to converse with your sister's friends, are we not, rather than to wear out the soles of our evening shoes in idle pleasure? But I shan't ask you to partner me in the waltz, and if anybody else should ask you, I strongly recommend you refuse. I'm sure your sister has waltzed a score of times at Almack's and elsewhere, but I don't suppose Mr Relish is a great waltzer, is he?'

'I couldn't say. It's not danced in our village. I'm sure everyone would consider it most improper. You must think us a parcel of sad rustics.' She looked quite crestfallen, and he cursed his own clumsiness. Why should she know how to waltz, and what did such nonsense matter? He had tarnished her enjoyment, and it was the last thing he wished to do. But to apologise would only make it worse. Whatever had happened to his famous address and careless ease of manner?

He grimaced. 'There's no sensible way to answer that remark – to say yes would be unpardonably rude, but if I said no you probably wouldn't believe me. And I'm sure for your part you believe me a frippery, shallow fellow – we already know you think I'm old – who cares for nothing but the arrangement of his cravats and the shine on his boots. You don't have to reply to that, either. Perhaps we're both right, or perhaps neither of us is. I can teach you to waltz, Miss Nightingale, if you wish it. It would be my great pleasure to do so. But tonight we have more pressing concerns.' His last comment was a reminder of why they were here, and was as much for his own benefit as hers; he thought he might quite enjoy taking her in his arms – in an impersonal and friendly sort of a way, of course – and teaching her the steps to the shockingly intimate dance that had taken the ton by storm in the last couple of years. But really, was this the time to be thinking of such things?

They'd made their way through the crush of people to the ballroom now, and his mother, who had surely been behind them when last he'd thought of her, was now mysteriously ahead of them, wreathed in smiles and urging them to take their places in the set that was forming. He couldn't say, 'Miss Nightingale doesn't care to dance' – his mama had presumably seen her, in the shape of her sister, do so many times before. To refuse such a commonplace request would be to draw attention to themselves, which was the last thing they needed.

It seemed it was, thank God, not a waltz or a quadrille, but one of the simpler country dances. 'I imagine even you will believe that I can manage *this*,' she muttered rather ungraciously as they took their place at the foot of the set and the music struck up.

'It could have been a cotillion,' he said when the steps brought them together.

'Well, it isn't,' she responded. 'And I am obliged to tell you that, despite your obvious fears, I can do that, as well.' He laughed, and might have sworn that she was on the verge of sticking her tongue out at him, but luckily she did nothing so unladylike, but twirled away from him with a poorly suppressed grin of triumph.

She was a graceful, lively dancer, he was obliged to admit, though to a close observer – he was, it seemed, a close observer – it was plain that she wasn't quite as accustomed to the activity as a young lady who'd supposedly made her come-out some months back and danced for hours almost every evening since really should be. She was obliged at times to concentrate on her steps, he could tell, rather than performing them by instinct, which dimmed her usual bright animation somewhat. The more sober set of her features as she danced, and, he thought, counted silently to herself, made her resemble her sister more completely than she generally did. But that was an odd notion, was it not? Because they were identical, or very nearly so. Or it was to be devoutly hoped they were, if this evening was not to turn to disaster and exposure.

The set ended, as even the most protracted ones eventually must, and she curtseyed, smiling up at him, her colour a little heightened. 'That round must be conceded to the rustics,' he teased, bowing in his turn. 'But does Mr Relish – poor man, what a name to be saddled with – make you obeisance in so distinguished a fashion? I may be conceited, but I find it hard to be believe he does. And the squire's son? What of him?'

'You are fishing for compliments,' she said, her fine blue eyes twinkling, 'and it is very sad to see something so pathetic in a man of your *age* and station in life. Mr Relish is a very worthy gentleman, I must inform you, though shy and undeniably not... not excessively graceful, and as for his name, his parents were so unaware of or so unabashed by anything unusual about it that they christened him Richard.'

'A name from a restoration comedy!' Dominic laughed. 'I expect the rude schoolboys shout things at him in the street. I might have been tempted to do so myself, when young. But you do not mention the squire's son, despite my question, and I am instantly on the alert for signs of rural romance.'

'The squire's son is a great clumsy boy of fifteen,' she responded, smiling, 'and I am quite often obliged to partner him because he's the only gentleman in the village who is taller than me. My feet have been purple with bruises before this, from him treading on me, and the more self-conscious he becomes, the worse he dances. It's mortifying for both of us. But shouldn't we be looking about us for Maria's friends?'

He admitted that they should, and they stepped aside from the dance floor and looked about them. 'How are we going to do this?' he said very low. 'I know you have their descriptions and their names, but I can hardly think that enough, now that we are here and I consider the matter more particularly. Should you not be approaching them, and presenting me to them if I don't already know them, so that we may have speech with them? But how are you to do that when *you* don't know them either? It's vital they don't have the least reason to suspect you, or we shall be in the suds.'

'Luckily – well, not luckily, poor girl, but providentially for our purposes – Maria is very shortsighted, like our father, and wears spectacles when she is at home, but not, of course, on such an occasion as this. Anyone who knows her well wouldn't expect her to pick them out from a crowd, or at any distance at all. So we may expect them to come to us. I am quite confident none of them will notice anything amiss. You worry too much, especially for someone who affects to care for nothing and nobody.'

'Hmm,' he said sceptically. 'Well, minx, I hope you're right, and even more than that I hope Mrs Treadwell and Mrs Greystone between them have prepared you well. If matters become too awkward and you are at a loss for words, I suggest you faint. Don't worry, I will be primed to catch you before you hit the floor. Probably.'

'Faint? I've never done such a ridiculously missish thing in my life!'

He could well believe it. 'There's a first time for everything,' he said, 'and it may be missish, but it's better – surely – than being publicly exposed as an impostor. And what would that make me? Why did I ever allow myself to be persuaded into participating in such a hare-brained scheme?'

Even as he spoke, they both became aware of a tall, handsome young lady making her way through the crowd, clearly most determined to converse with them. She had a square chin and great quantity of bright red locks, and these convenient facts enabled him to play some useful part in the farce that was about to unfold. 'This,' Dominic whispered urgently, 'is one of the Duke of Fernsby's many daughters. I could not possibly mistake the hair. As to her Christian name, I hope you know it, for I am quite sure that I do not. I seem to recall they're all rather sickeningly named for flowers.'

Miss Nightingale, getting into the spirit of her sisterly masquerade, peered myopically at the approaching figure and said with enthusiasm, 'Lady Primrose! How good it is to see you! Such a sad crush, I am astonished that you found us in it.'

'I know you only recognise me because of my hair,' said the young lady cheerfully. 'I expect I appear to you like a lighthouse beacon in a thick fog. How are you, dear Maria? You are in high bloom this evening.'

'I am very well, thank you,' Meg replied with equal cordiality. 'And you look well, too.' That rather disposed of that. 'May I present Sir Dominic De Lacy to you? I'm not sure you know each other. Sir Dominic, my dear schoolfriend Lady Primrose Beacham, daughter of the Duke of Fernsby.'

'We have danced together several times,' Lady Primrose informed him with great composure, 'on various different occasions, but I never gained the impression that you had the least idea who I was, beyond knowing me for a Fernsby by the hair. You're a friend of my brother Hugh's, aren't you, sir?'

Sir Dominic, somewhat taken aback by the lady's frankness, admitted that he did count Lord Thorp among his intimates. 'I'm sorry if I was ever discourteous, Lady Primrose,' he felt obliged to say. Could he expect yet more unvarnished comments on his character and behaviour this evening? he wondered.

'No, no,' she replied unconvincingly, her bright green eyes twinkling wickedly. 'I am sure you have danced with hundreds of debutantes over the last few years, and there's no reason why you should pay any particular attention to one of them above another – in fact, it would have been perilous for you to do so. And it's not as though you're one of those odious flirts our chaperons warn us against. You've always made it perfectly plain that you weren't in the least bit interested in any one of the young ladies that society throws in your way.' Dominic became aware that he was perspiring slightly into his fresh linen shirt. What would she say next?

'And now, of course,' she went on enthusiastically, 'all that is behind you, and you are to be married! And to dear Maria! I am sure I wish you both very happy. Just think, you need never dance with another debutante again. I am sure you will be much more comfortable in future, once you are no longer being pursued in such a preposterous fashion!'

What could he say to *that*? Yes? No? To Dominic's relief, the next set was forming up, and Lady Primrose's hand was claimed by a pugnacious young man with very tall shirt points who had apparently been looking for her everywhere and appeared quite cross that he had had to seek her out. She didn't seem in the least discomposed – it was hard to imagine what might discompose her, short of the roof falling in on them – and departed on his arm.

'Well,' said Meg rather dejectedly, 'that's that, and I don't think she knows anything that might help us, do you, sir? And she did *not* have the least suspicion that I was not my sister, as I am sure you will be the first to acknowledge. So your fears were quite groundless.'

He shook his head. 'She's one of your sister's closest friends, is she?'

'So I'm told.'

'I wonder if the rest of them are the same?'

'In what respect? I quite liked her, and I can see why Maria does.'

'So bruisingly frank and satirical.'

'I shouldn't wonder at it. *Are* you so hugely sought after? Or is that another of those questions that one can't answer without being rude or disingenuous?'

'It's definitely one of those. But if I'd been inclined to

congratulate myself upon the matter – supposing it were true, which we're not discussing – I'm sure the current situation has cut me right back down to size. One hundred per cent of the debutantes I have so far offered for have fled from me in horror, after all. It hardly encourages a man to think well of himself. Now, do you want to peer shortsightedly about again, to see if anyone else is approaching? Please do so, before I forget our situation and start imagining I'm here to relax and enjoy myself in your company.'

It was a long evening. They encountered several more of Maria's most intimate friends, and Miss Nightingale navigated the situation with surprising skill, not being obliged to swoon or otherwise cause a distraction. They danced together once again – Dominic insisted upon it, as a pleasant break from awkward conversations – but by three in the morning all they had to show for several hours' worry was the headache. They'd learned precisely nothing, and encountered no one whose behaviour was in the least suspicious.

Lady De Lacy had passed most of her evening in the card room with her cronies, but she had spent long enough in the ballroom among the beady-eyed chaperons to be aware that her son and his betrothed had danced twice with each other – and with no one else. In other circumstances, such markedly exclusive behaviour might have drawn a reproof from her, but it might be excused in a newly engaged couple, as showing a great and understandable partiality for each other's company, and she was clearly in the mood so to excuse it. She bade Miss Nightingale an affectionate farewell when they stopped in Grosvenor Square to set her down, and waited patiently while Dominic escorted her to her front door and saw her safely inside. The knowledge that his mother was watching them with entirely misplaced misty-eyed sentimentality cast a constraint over him, and he said only, 'I'll see you tomorrow, Miss Nightingale; I'll send a message. Perhaps my servants have been more fortunate in their efforts, and may have some news for me.'

When he rejoined her in the carriage, Lady De Lacy surprised him by making no comment – any comment she thought to make would surely have stung – but merely pressing his hand with what he was sure was a significant look, could he but see it in the gloom. He was grateful for her forbearance, but the mutual awareness of words unspoken hung so heavy in the space between them that she might as well not have restrained herself. See how right I was! he could feel her thinking. See how perfectly I – or, if we are being sentimental, your dear papa – have chosen for you. Do you not like your bride excessively? Do you not look forward eagerly to your wedding now, despite all your earlier foolish objections?

Yes, Mama, dear. And no.

No.

You were so nearly right, and so utterly, fatally wrong. And he had not the least idea what was to be done about it.

9
———

Dominic was not so inconsiderate a master as to expect his servants to report to him on the outcome of their investigations when he returned from the ball in the early hours. A cool grey dawn was breaking across London as he let himself wearily into his house. Pargeter was very much the sort of eager person who might stay alert to give such a report, unasked, were it not for the fact that his master had made it very clear that nobody was ever to wait up for him on pain of his grave displeasure, since he was perfectly able to put himself to bed.

He slept badly, a prey to all manner of confused and confusing thoughts, and woke unrefreshed at ten. Once he'd bathed, dressed and breakfasted, he summoned Pargeter and Fishwick, and sat down with them, without a great deal of hope, to hear what they might have to tell him. He already knew that the excursion to Barnet and its environs to check on fashionable blonde travellers on the road to Scotland had borne no fruit.

'I had a fair amount of success in tracking down my acquaintances, sir,' the young man told him, his open face and bright dark eyes more sombre than usual, 'but nothing beyond that. Two of the persons on your list are still employed as you describe, but none of them has taken any sudden absence from work or otherwise behaved in a manner that has raised any suspicion in their fellow servants. There's been no hinting at mysterious matters or signs of worry in the last few days, or anything of that nature. Any one of them *could* have been approached discreetly and secreted a young lady away somewhere without the least noise or fuss, though certainly not in their master's house. I can't completely rule out their involvement – but I don't believe it. You know how servants' halls are, sir, for gossip and for sharp noticing. A housekeeper or a butler, if they know their business, they're better than the Runners at ferreting hidden things out any day. And as for the third person, he's taken a new situation and it's in Scotland – left a couple of months ago. So that's a dead end, as far as I can see.'

Sir Dominic handed him the list. 'Thank you for trying, Pargeter,' he said resignedly. 'We always knew it wasn't going to be easy. Will you be so good as to cross off the names you've eliminated?'

As he took up a pen, dipped it in ink and carefully did so, Fishwick said easily, 'Well, sir, I knew some people in one or two of the same houses, but there was no point me and young Mr Pargeter doubling up our efforts, so to speak, so I took a couple of other names and set to work on them.'

'Any luck?' asked Dominic a shade impatiently. Fishwick, he knew, would take his time.

'Maybe.' He raised his hand pacifically. 'Now, I'm not saying for definite, sir. But maybe.' His auditors both sat forward eagerly as he went on, prolonging the moment, 'I had the same result as Mr Pargeter did with the first cove I tried. I'm tolerably well acquainted with the very man on the list, as it happened.

Footman, didn't know nothing about anything, wouldn't have had the wit to conceal it if he did.'

'Jack...' said his employer warningly.

Mr Fishwick grinned unrepentantly. 'But in the second place I tried, the staff were all agog. Lord Purslake's residence. Didn't have to press them to talk, would have been hard to stop them. It was all concerning a lady's maid – a respectable-seeming, quiet young female who'd come to them not long since from Lord Nightingale's house, bettering herself by moving from working for some elderly widow mort to Lady Purslake, who's no spring chicken herself but very fashionable. The girl had only been with them a couple of months or so, and now she's vanished. No notice given, no attempt to collect her back wages – just gone one morning with what she could carry.'

'Mrs Greystone's former maid?' said Dominic slowly. Fishwick nodded. 'What's her name – Jenny Wood, was it? And when did she go?'

'Matter of five or six days ago, so around the time Miss Nightingale went too, seemingly. Which does make it seem like it might be more than a coincidence, to my mind.'

'Good God, Jack, and to mine! Well done, man. I never thought this wild-goose chase would turn up anything, and yet it has, and on the first night of trying, too. But – don't think I'm undervaluing your efforts, both of you – we now have two missing women instead of one. The mystery has become greater, not less, and I'm not sure we can call that progress. Even if they are together, apart from offering some reassurance to Miss Margaret that her sister might be safe and in another's company, I don't see how it gets us any further.'

'Ah, now,' said Fishwick with evident satisfaction, 'that's because I haven't told you all!'

'There's a time and a place for being infuriatingly slow, Jack, and this is neither of them. Spit it out!'

'The reason they were all so fired up about the business, *sir*, was that one of the footmen claims he saw the young abigail a night or so ago, very late, in a place where a decent female had no business to be. In the Garden, in fact, near the piazza, dressed up to the nines and going into a house that's far from being honest – well, I expect you catch my drift.'

Dominic was frowning as he absorbed the impact of this news. This investigation was taking them to some strange and unexpected places – unwelcome ones, too. It was not beyond the bounds of possibility that a respectable working girl might tire of a life of domestic drudgery and decide to exchange it for the dubious advantages of selling herself, which was what a stay in Covent Garden and all the rest of it seemed to imply. No doubt such a thing had happened before. But even if this were so, did it not make it unlikely that Miss Nightingale could in fact be with her? For what possible reason? 'I do understand you, not being a complete greenhorn. I suppose it would be idle to enquire if the young man is sure of what he saw?'

'I think he is, sir, and I'll tell you for why. It seems this fellow had taken a powerful liking to young Jenny, her being a spruce wench and well set up. He'd been laying siege to her virtue with a great deal of persistence, she not wanting anything to do with him and making it very clear, and him not letting up in spite of it. It caused a bit of a ruckus below stairs, because the women of the household thought that was why she'd left so good a place with no notice – to avoid his constant pestering. And they, and all the decent servants there, which is most of them, have been blaming him for it and making his life a misery with their reproaches. The lad's a worthless one, a regular thatch-gallows, as you can imagine, but he don't care for being put in the wrong. So he came back to them all indignant about what he'd seen. Seemingly he was happy to have them think the worse of him for being out on the town and ripe for a spree, if it meant he could damage Jenny's reputation and paint her as a strumpet. To his mind, if she's one who prays with her knees upwards, as the saying goes, why wouldn't she lay herself out for *him* instead of pretending to be so virtuous? You know the sort of man, I expect – he has such a powerful sense of his own worth, he can't by any means stomach being set down by a lass.'

Pargeter was looking rigidly disapproving, as well he might, but Dominic said thoughtfully, 'I'm sure such creatures exist in every walk of life. He sounds a complete scoundrel. But if he's obsessed with the poor girl, I suppose he would know her when he saw her, assuming he was relatively sober at the time.'

'I'll go bail he was. He does seem certain it was her, and by his own account he tried to follow her into the house, too, which to my mind makes it more likely he was telling the truth rather than spinning a Banbury tale afterwards about some half-glimpsed face in a crowd.'

'So he remembers the precise building she entered, or he thought she entered?'

'He does, and I could say I managed to get it out of him, but I'd be telling an untruth, for he was eager to tell me, and everyone who'd listen, that it was a big place on the corner of Henrietta Street, hard by the market. A flash bawdy house, for certain, in that location, and he grumbled because he said there was a bully-back keeping the door, some old bruiser who would by no means let him in, him plainly being a servant and not a fine buck of the first head such as the place caters to. I've been to run my peepers over the place in daylight, early this morning, but there was not a sign of life, and no wonder. You know such kens – they're asleep when respectable folk are about their business, and only come to life when darkness falls.'

'I admit nothing,' Dominic said with a brief grin, 'other than the fact that you have done well, and it must bear further investigation. Even though it seems unlikely, on the face of it, that Miss Nightingale should choose to hide herself away in such a place and with such a person – a lady's maid who, to all appearances, has fallen into prostitution. I fear it must be a bizarre coincidence, and nothing more.'

'You won't tell her sister of it, sir, surely? It must cause her the most severe anxiety of mind!' burst out the young valet. He seemed quite as overset by the news and its implications as he expected Miss Margaret Nightingale to be.

'I think I must, Pargeter. My part in this whole sorry business is only to help – I can't be concealing things from her just because they have an unseemly aspect. Clearly, though, if anyone is to go there and seek further news, it must be me, not her. *That* would be quite wrong, not to mention improper, and I cannot by any means permit it.'

10

Without delay, Dominic sent a note to Miss Nightingale; it was discreet in its wording, but made it quite clear that he had news to share, and proposed that he call on her and take her driving later in the day. His messenger, one of his footmen, waited for a reply, which was a prompt acceptance.

It was another fine, bright afternoon, with a breeze that sent fluffy white clouds scudding fast across the blue sky, and in other circumstances Dominic might have agreed with Dr Johnson that there could be no greater enjoyment in life than to go for a drive in the sunshine with an attractive female companion at his side. But this was not to be an expedition of pleasure.

His high-perch phaeton had barely slowed outside Meg's father's house when she came hurrying down the steps to meet him, rather than dawdling gracefully out like an affected young lady of fashion. She was wearing a dark green pelisse laced with gold, and a velvet Circassian cap in the same shade sat on her bright curls; unlike a more traditional poke bonnet, it did not obscure her face in the slightest, and offered him an excellent view of her expression, which showed mingled eagerness and anxious curiosity. Once again he was struck by how the same lineaments could be so much more expressive in one woman than in another, supposedly identical.

Fishwick jumped down from the seat and handed her up into it, taking his place in the precarious tiger's perch at the rear. Dominic set his bays in motion, and was occupied for a moment in negotiating a snarl in the traffic caused by an overloaded furniture wagon, clumsily driven, that was partially blocking the exit from the square. He was a notable whip and a member of the Four Horse Club, but he was not so puffed up in his skill that he would disregard the need to concentrate at tricky moments. He had no desire to overset his precious cargo, or experience an upset himself; life was complicated enough already.

'Miss Margaret,' he said at last, the obstacle behind them and the way momentarily clear, 'I have brought my groom Jack Fishwick with me rather than my tiger today because any success we've had in our enquiries – and I must warn you that it is by no means clear yet that it *is* success – is entirely due to his diligence on your behalf.'

Miss Nightingale turned in her seat to thank Jack warmly, and he responded gruffly – clearly highly gratified – that there was no need for that at all, miss, for he was happy to help. Dominic went on, 'Jack and my valet, Pargeter, have been looking into that list of servants Mrs Treadwell gave me, and he has discovered something – perhaps merely a strange coincidence of timing, perhaps something more than that.' He went on to tell her the tale of the vanishing lady's maid and her unwelcome suitor; he did not mince his words when he came to describe the nature of the house in which the young woman appeared to have taken refuge. 'And so you see,' he finished, 'although it may be a clue, and there's no denying it's the only one we have at present, we have no reason at all to believe that your sister is sheltering in that place too, nor even that the former abigail knows anything of her whereabouts.'

'Jenny Wood,' said Meg musingly. 'Of course I have never met her, but I remember Maria writing of her in her letters. Life in my father's house, you know, was so very tedious before Maria made her come-out that she described everything and everyone to me, as a way of passing the time and making us feel closer in our day-to-day existence though we could not be together; I did the same when I wrote to her. And all I know of Jenny is that she was a most respectable young woman – intelligent, and skilled at performing her duties, and quiet. I think Maria was quite fond of her. She would not be at all likely, from what my sister said, to run off in such a manner, and to such a place. Her experience with the horrible footman sounds most disagreeable, but I would have hoped she had other alternatives, rather than…'

Dominic said, 'One would think so. She could have complained to her mistress, or, if she did not want to do that, perhaps because she feared this young man's anger and revenge, she might have sought another position. I agree that it is iniquitous that she should have to so uproot herself, when she had done nothing wrong, but the choice that she appears to have made still seems odd to me. I wonder if she has a home and family she could turn to for help, or if she is alone in the world?'

'I have no idea; I will ask Hannah. We do not know all the circumstances, of course,' Meg responded. 'It's possible poor Jenny tried to find another place, and for some reason could not do so, or not quickly enough for her liking. Has it occurred to you that this unpleasant young man may not be telling the whole truth – that he might have assaulted her, or otherwise made her life in that house unendurable, so that she felt obliged to leave immediately and simply had nowhere else to go?'

'You're right.' They were in the park now, and Dominic paused to set Jack Fishwick down, telling him they'd be back to pick him up in the same place in a half-hour or so. His mouth was a grim line as he set the horses moving once more. 'We don't know, and still we have no reason to believe that she has been in communication with your sister. But clearly we – I – need to investigate further, by visiting the place.'

'Of course we do,' Meg said, entirely ignoring the careful distinction he had drawn. 'And as soon as possible. Shall we go tonight? I think we should.'

* * *

Dominic hadn't been surprised when it became clear that Miss Nightingale wished to accompany him to Covent Garden. He'd expected her concern for her sister and her active, lively personality to demand immediate action, and also to demand that she should be a part of that action, as the one most nearly concerned in the matter. But the idea was clearly utterly ineligible, even preposterous, and he had anticipated no difficulty in persuading her of that fact.

He thought she had come to trust him after her early suspicion, and he'd imagined that every instinct instilled into a gently bred young lady over the years of her upbringing would, in the end, compel her to agree that he was right. She must eventually approve his intention of going alone to such a shocking place and telling her about the matter afterwards, however awkward that conversation might prove to be. He was known throughout the haut ton as a man of great address, and one equal to dealing with equanimity with any situation life might throw in his way. Such a person could surely quite easily convince a sheltered country girl of eighteen that no, she could not join her sister's fiancé on a night-time visit to a known brothel in Covent Garden – not that the time of day mattered one jot, nor the location of the house of ill repute – to enquire after one of its disreputable inhabitants.

He had been wrong. Painfully wrong. He had plainly over-estimated his own powers of persuasion, or entirely misunderstood the nature of Miss Nightingale's education under the direction of her bluestocking mother, or perhaps both. She was entirely immoveable. 'Of course I'm coming with you,' she said serenely.

Dominic was lost for words for a moment. When his wits returned to him, he waxed eloquent, and embarked on what he felt, even as he was giving it, to be an elegantly expressed and perfectly reasoned little speech – not that it should be in the least necessary – explaining, forcefully, but without any improper dwelling on sordid details, why it was quite impossible that Miss Nightingale should go with him to Henrietta Street, that evening or any other evening. Considering he was still controlling his high-couraged team of bays and steering his fashionably precarious high-perch phaeton through the throng of similar vehicles as he spoke, he must consider it to be an impressive effort. He didn't know what more he could have said, nor how better he could have said it. But it was all utterly futile.

'I won't take you,' he said baldly in the end, glancing at her resolute face for a second. It was all too clear to him that she did not appear to be in the least cast down or chastened by his refusal. He began to experience a sense of alarm.

'Then I'll go by myself. You've told me where it is, luckily.'

Dominic swore involuntarily, and his companion let out an unladylike little snort of laughter. 'Precisely so, sir,' she said. 'If you hadn't been so shortsighted as to give me the direction of the place, it would have been much harder, of course, but since you have, there can be nothing to prevent me from going there myself and making enquiries.'

'Every decent feeling revolts against the idea,' he muttered though gritted teeth.

'Does it?' she responded calmly. 'Perhaps I am devoid of decent feeling, then. My father always used to say so, when I was young and we were always arguing so dreadfully because I would not show him the respect he felt he deserved. He said many times that I was a hoyden, without manners or breeding. And now I am glad if he was right, if manners and breeding would make me so foolish as to refuse to do everything – everything, sir! – that lies in my power to help my sister when she may, for all I know, be in the most terrible trouble! She could be a prisoner in that house, along with poor Jenny – they could have been tricked there by some foul deceit. Have you thought of that?'

He had. Since he had understood with dawning horror how determined and unshakeable she was, many visions, all vivid, all utterly dreadful, had been presenting themselves to him, in a sort of depraved magic lantern show that flickered behind his eyelids. 'Jenny, for one, isn't a captive,' he said shortly. 'The fellow saw her returning from some nocturnal expedition, so she's clearly under no constraint. But yes, you are so far correct in that she could have tricked your sister there with some false promises of assistance. Dammit, woman, she could be in league with the people who keep the place, she could have *sold* your sister to them by prearranged plan, for all we know! And if you go there by yourself, she could do the same to you!' His mind was in such turmoil at his failure to impress upon her the seriousness of the situation that he couldn't prevent himself from adding crudely, 'I expect a certain unconscionable sort of villain would pay a substantial premium for a pair of lovely, gently bred twins! It is plain to me, Miss Margaret Nightingale, that you know nothing at all of the world and its iniquity!'

'Nonsense! And if Maria is indeed in such terrible trouble, there is all the more reason I should not delay, but go to rescue her as soon as possible. But I'm sure you are exaggerating. You really shouldn't let yourself fall prey to such Gothic imaginings, sir; it isn't all helpful.'

'Helpful?' he said in extreme exasperation. If he'd had a free hand, he'd have been clutching his hair, with no thought for its modish Windswept style or for anyone who might see him in a state of such unaccustomed agitation. 'Helpful? Have you *no* concern for your reputation, madam? Or for your sister's, if you have no care for your own? Imagine if you – which is to say, she – should be seen entering such a place, or even observed by someone who knows you, out at night, alone, with me! With any man! You would be utterly ruined! And it wouldn't do me enormous amounts of good, either, though naturally I can't expect you to give a fig for that, I'm quite aware.'

'Why should anyone who knows me see me?' she asked. He couldn't tell if she was being disingenuous or not. A vision of putting her over his knee and spanking her popped into his head, but he pushed it away as *unhelpful*.

'It's a bloody brothel,' he said between gritted teeth. 'A place where women sell themselves. Young men of good family – I'm sorry to break it to you – and older men, for that matter, go to brothels. Half the members of White's and Brooks's, half the people you've danced with at Almack's, for all I know, could be trooping in and out of the place on a regular basis. Forming queues in the street. My credit will certainly survive being seen there, if not scandalously accompanied by you; yours, I assure you, would not, whether with me or alone!'

'I've never danced at Almack's,' she replied, infuriatingly.

'No,' he ground out. 'I am well aware of that. But your *identical twin sister* has.'

'You're right, of course.' Her composure was unshaken; for him, it was otherwise. 'It is just as well to think coolly of these matters, and you do well to reprove me. I am most concerned for Maria's safety, naturally, but it would be idle to pretend that I have no care at all for her reputation. Of course I do! Otherwise I might as well have let you tell my father the truth some days ago, and allow the whole sorry story to become public. Naturally she – and therefore I – must not be seen in such a shocking place.'

He felt almost weak with relief. 'Thank God you have come to your senses,' he said faintly.

'I was never out of my senses, sir, I assure you. But I have thought of a better plan, and one that you cannot possibly object to, for it deals with all these heart-burnings in the most ingenious manner possible. Indeed, I do not know why I did not think of it directly, but I am excessively glad I have now.'

Dominic felt he was learning fast, and so his heart did not leap with joy at the intelligence his companion shared with him so confidingly. He hated to think what her better plan might be. He was tempted to take his eyes off the horses, the carriageway and the scene ahead of him, and look at her maddening little face again, but he did not. He also resisted the instinct to grip the ribbons more tightly, convulsively, with results in the behaviour of the horses that he could all too easily imagine. 'Tell me...' he said, his voice a trifle hollow. 'Tell me what deranged and probably dangerous scheme you have now devised to bring down my grey hairs with sorrow to the grave.'

'You haven't got any grey hairs that I can see, surprisingly, and if as I suspect that's the Bible, I wonder you should think this the time to be indulging in religious quotations.'

'It's something truly terrible, isn't it? I know it is. I insist that you tell me immediately.'

'It's not terrible at all. It's genius. I shall disguise myself as a boy.'

11

It must be considered miraculous that the phaeton didn't overturn. Sir Dominic said nothing in immediate response, though if his companion had been looking at his face his stormy expression would have spoken volumes, and for a moment he concentrated his attention on his horses, and on making his way back to where he had set down his groom. Had half an hour passed – an hour – a week? He was in no state to tell. But in any case, Fishwick was there, waiting patiently, and Dominic indicated with a few clipped, well-chosen words that the groom should climb up and take the reins and drive home, while he would walk a little with Miss Nightingale, and then escort her safely back to Grosvenor Square. Assuming, he thought but didn't say, he didn't instead murder her and throw her body in the lake.

'Is it quite proper, sir, that we should be seen alone together at this hour?' she said. He couldn't tell if she was serious, or if she had instead just commenced on a determined campaign to drive him entirely out of his senses and into Bedlam. 'There are a great many people about now, and I have observed many ladies and gentlemen nodding to you and otherwise trying to attract your attention, though you have snubbed them all.'

'Proper?' he said. 'Good God, you have the effrontery to speak to me of what is proper, and of your reputation? And if I have really ignored anyone, and you aren't merely trying to infuriate me further, I am sure that my friends and acquaintances will forgive me, and assume that I am completely and rather charmingly enthralled with my future bride, Christ help me. They don't know that the woman at my side is not, as she appears to be, a beautiful debutante, but a dangerous escaped lunatic.'

'You make a great deal of bustle over nothing,' she said, though a slight flush had crept up into her cheeks, he could not help but observe; he didn't know, and shouldn't care, whether it was because he'd called her beautiful or described her as a lunatic. Clearly, both things could be true at once.

They had found their way under a tree once more – Dominic was in no state to be able to recognise whether it was the same one they'd talked under yesterday, or another – and the fresh green leaves provided them with at least a little privacy. There was no doubt that, as she had said, it was not ideal to be seen entirely alone together, even in a public place and surrounded by so many people, but in this moment he was beyond concerning himself over the proprieties. *She* clearly had no true interest in proper behaviour, however much she might pretend she did.

'You cannot disguise yourself as a boy,' he said forcefully, turning to her. They were very close, and he might have thought that his height, his looming presence, would have intimidated her, obliged her to give ground and back away from him, but quite clearly it didn't. She tilted up her golden head and met his gaze boldly. There were sparkling gold flecks in her blue eyes, he saw – they hadn't been so close before for more than a second or two, and so he'd had no chance to observe them.

'That's a patently ridiculous statement,' she said. 'Obviously I can, and I will. It is quite providential that my hair is short, not long like Maria's. I am sure that nothing could be easier or more convenient. I have done so frequently at home – not disguised myself, precisely, for I intended no deception, but put on breeches and ridden, or climbed trees, when I was younger, with… with a friend of mine. I am sure there are a great number of my half-brother's clothes put away somewhere in the attics, and I shouldn't wonder if they fit me well enough for a brief outing in the dark; if there isn't anything suitable, I'll borrow something from one of the servants. I am sure once you reflect a little you can have no rational objection to my plan.'

He couldn't make her see that what she was proposing was insanely dangerous, and yet he must. He reached out, scarcely knowing what he was doing, and took her firmly by the shoulders, his gloved hands grasping the green velvet of her pelisse.

Still she did not pull away from him. He'd been intending to try again, now that he was holding her and making her attend to him, to find new and better words to persuade her of the folly of what she was contemplating. But whatever he had been about to say died on his lips.

He'd never kissed her sister, nor touched her in this disturbingly intimate fashion. He'd kissed her cold hand, he supposed – he must have done that in common politeness, when he took his leave of her after she'd accepted his proposal of marriage. But he hadn't kissed her cheek – hadn't at all wanted to – and certainly not her lips.

Meg's lips, though, were slightly parted, and looked soft, warm and infinitely inviting. They were tantalisingly close. It would be no effort at all to bend his head a little and taste them. He'd been so angry with her, but he wasn't any more. Anger had been overwhelmed by quite another, much more powerful emotion. He'd just now admitted something to his conscious mind that his body must have known for days. Since they'd first met. A shocking thing.

Her pupils were dilated, her eyes dark pools, and she was breathing a little faster now, her velvet-covered breasts rising and falling, just a few inches away from where his leather-clad hands still held her. He could feel the tension vibrating through her frame, just as it was through his, and though he should let go of her, by every rule and tenet of society and morality and decency, he simply couldn't. He was paralysed with a bolt of sudden, overwhelming desire, so strong it was almost painful; if he made any sort of movement, he feared it wouldn't be to let her go, but to pull her close. He wanted very badly to move his hands down her body. The tree trunk was at her back, and he wanted, needed, to push her against it as his mouth claimed hers. He wanted to lose himself in her, to forget everything but his desire to touch and be touched, to know and be known. He thought – though of course he could not be sure of it – that she wanted it too. He wanted the length of his body pressed hard against hers from shoulder to ankle, his hands exploring her, his tongue in her mouth and hers in his, their breath mingling, her hands on him too, under his coat, under his waistcoat, under his shirt. Damn the park and everybody in it. Damn the people and the horses and the whole polite world of London. He didn't care if they suspected, or even if they saw. The thought of being skin to skin with her…

He didn't do it. He stepped away, releasing her, and with an effort of will as powerful as any he'd ever exerted in his life before, he didn't let his hands slide down her body for one precious, forbidden caress before he moved away. One caress could never be enough, and must lead to more. To disaster.

He said, 'This is madness.' Even as he spoke, he didn't know what he was referring to – her crazy scheme to masquerade as a boy, a momentary impulse to kiss her that he hadn't, after all, indulged, or so much more.

12

Meg took off her pelisse and flung it haphazardly on her bed – on Maria's bed, in Maria's chamber, which she was occupying in this strange interlude to her life. She had encountered her father in the hall once more as she entered – it was not always possible to avoid him – but he had merely looked at her vaguely, as if uncertain who she was and what she was doing in his house. It would be sensible, she thought now, to ask herself the same question. What, precisely, was she about? Collapsing onto the stool that sat in front of her sister's dressing table, she gazed at her flushed, muslin-clad reflection in the old, spotted mirror.

She had known that Sir Dominic was about to kiss her. He'd been so angry with her – quite unreasonably, she thought – and he'd taken hold of her, intending to use the shockingly unconventional physical contact to stop her in her tracks, to catch and hold her attention so that he might impress upon her the seriousness of what he was saying. He'd had no other intention, she believed, than a frustrated need to make her *see*. But as soon as he'd laid hands on her, everything had changed.

There'd already been a highly charged atmosphere between them as they'd quarrelled – or as he'd quarrelled with her, for she'd never lost her temper though her heart had been racing. But he'd let his barriers down for once and shown her the genuine feeling that he hid beneath that perpetually cool, languid exterior – even if the feeling, in this particular instance, had been intense irritation. He'd been highly agitated, which she guessed was not a common state for him. And though she had been, and still was, convinced that she was in the right, she could not be unmoved by so much unbridled emotion in one normally so cool and restrained, and she the focus of it. His anger, after all, had been unselfish, provoked by nothing more than concern for her safety and her reputation. He might be mistaken, but he cared what happened to her, and not in a general way, but in a very personal manner. He was – protective, that was the word. Though she didn't need protection, she also couldn't deny that his concern gave her an unaccustomed warm feeling.

Then, too, she must admit to herself – her mother was a highly unconventional parent, but she asked above all that Meg be honest in her dealings with others and with herself – that being driven by Sir Dominic in his high-perch phaeton had been an unsettling experience for her. Not unsettling, that was to understate it: exciting. Arousing. They'd been pressed knee to knee, thigh to thigh, swaying perilously high in the air in the ridiculously fragile little body of his carriage, and only his skill, she knew, had kept them from danger. From death, even. He'd been obliged to moderate their speed, in the crowded London streets and then the park, with so many other vehicles around them, but if he'd had a clear road, he could have let the bays fly in thrilling motion. How wonderful that must be, how freeing. She could understand why he plainly loved it so, and it was all too easy to imagine sharing that pleasure and exhilaration with him. Not to mention other, less public forms of pleasure.

There was no way, looking at it objectively, that one man, however strong, could physically control two high-spirited horses if they chose to break free. It was a sort of magic, something that shouldn't work but did – a mixture of training, on the horses' part, and confident mastery, on his. Such competence must always be highly attractive, and he was so much more than competent. She'd been watching him secretly from under her lashes: his strong hands in their tan leather gloves, loose and seemingly casual on the ribbons; his grey eyes, measuring and assessing risk instinctively at every moment, his broad, powerful shoulders in his many-caped driving coat. Some part of her mind – or perhaps not her mind at all – had been wondering if he'd consent to teach her this mystery, and if doing so would involve his wrapping his arms about her, pressing his hard thigh even closer to hers, putting his arms about her and hands on hers, guiding them. That was an intoxicating thought...

It was, all in all, a heady brew. Perhaps that was partly why something electric and intense had sprung so rapidly to life between them, when, surely without realising what he might be unleashing, he'd overstepped the mark so shockingly and touched her.

The fault was his, then – since he could not know her private thoughts – but she must share some part of the blame, because she had not pulled away instantly as she should have done. He'd have apologised profusely, if she had; would have confessed his frustration with her stubbornness and his desperate desire to convince her that he was right and she was wrong. But she'd stood there in his grasp and looked up at him, and when his eyes had dropped to her mouth, dark with sudden desire, she'd known what he wanted. And she'd wanted it too. It must have been written clearly on her face for him to read.

His big hands on her... Possibly he'd been unconscious of it, but they'd not been still. They'd moved on her body, an almost imperceptible caress, his palms pressing her shoulders with just the right amount of firmness, his fingers and his thumbs making little circles on the velvet of her pelisse. Leather and velvet, linen and lawn, and warm skin beneath it, blood beating hard in both their veins. Little circles of fire, as his touch ignited heat in her, and delicious tingling sensations that spread down her arms, down her body. Her nipples had been hard under her chemise, gown and pelisse, craving his touch. The space of empty air between them had felt both impossibly large and tormentingly small, and it had taken all her willpower to prevent herself from breaching it in nature's oldest way, by melting into his arms, moulding her soft curves to his hard body in what he surely would have recognised as an invitation, whether conscious or unconscious, on her part. Would he have been shocked? She had no idea. She was a little shocked herself, at the strength of the impulse. He was a virtual stranger, this man, and he was engaged to be married to her sister. Her missing sister.

Meg was not naïve. She had not led Maria's sheltered life of a town-bred lady of quality, a proper schoolroom miss, walking to church two by two in a file of obedient femininity and never seeing a man apart from the finicky dancing master or the stout old teacher of singing. Meg had grown up in the countryside for the past five years, under her mother's loving but undeniably casual, distracted supervision. She'd climbed trees and stolen apples, had swum naked in the river, and lost her heart, or a great part of it, to her constant companion in adventures. To Will.

It had always been clear to her that she wasn't going to live the life of a debutante and then a prim and proper society wife, and so the idea of preserving her reputation had seemed ridiculous to her. Preserving it for what? She didn't know what her future held. She hadn't Maria's fortune – which freed her from some pressures but brought other ones – and if she cherished a dream of writing stories that others would want to read, as her mother did, she knew how precarious living by one's pen could be.

Marriage had always seemed like something that happened to other people. To Maria, perhaps, in all her meek, dreamy, ladylike perfection, but not to her. Her parents' union had been no sort of example to follow, and besides, she and Will, her childhood friend and later sweetheart, had never even discussed it. He was destined for a life as a substantial farmer, following in his father's footsteps, and that was all he wanted. He'd never tried to hide it, or to share her enthusiasm when she'd spoken of travelling and seeing all the world had to offer. What Meg's destiny might be remained unclear, but it wasn't to be mistress of Appletree Farm, supervising her maidservants and putting meals on the table for her husband and his men when they came home hungry from the fields, fretting if the weather was too hot and the butter wouldn't churn. There was nothing wrong with such a life, but it wasn't for her, and not because she was a lady and too good for it. That was nonsense. Lady or not, she'd be bad at it, that was the plain truth, and would make herself miserable, and Will too. If she'd loved him, or loved him enough to set herself and her own dreams aside, she might have learned, but she'd still never have achieved the casual competence of someone born to do it. And there were things she wanted – experiences, a taste of freedom – that Will and Appletree Farm could never give her. In his turn, he deserved better than someone who'd always be subtly discontented with her life, and him, and must make him unhappy too because of it. They'd both known all this, without having to speak of it.

So over the last few months they had drifted apart by slow degrees. She'd stopped climbing out of her window at night to meet him in the barn or in the orchard, and this spring, when she'd gone swimming by moonlight, cold water silky and enticing on her naked skin, she'd gone alone. She still saw him, in the village or the lanes, but they greeted each other as old friends now, and she thought he was a fair way to forgetting they'd ever been anything more. She missed his lazy smile and the feeling of his strong arms about her, she missed the way his long-lashed brown eyes closed and his breath caught when she pleasured him, and God, she missed his fingers or his mouth bringing her to a place where she lost herself in pure sensation. They'd learned all this together, and perhaps now some wild and foolish part of her was sorry that they'd always been cautious – had given way to passion up to a point, but always held back from the final and most dangerous intimacy. That would never happen now, not with Will. But no, she had nothing to regret – that truly would have been folly.

One warm spring evening a few weeks ago, when they had both been sitting quietly writing, words coming easily for Meg and the smell of apple blossom and green growing things sneaking in through the open casements, her mother had set down her own pen and said as much. 'It's for the best, my dear. I know it's hard, but it would never have worked. You don't want the same things in life.' She'd looked up, startled, about to utter an instinctive denial, but Lady Nightingale had said, 'Just because I haven't spoken of it doesn't mean I haven't known. Given me credit for my fair share of intelligence. I have always had a great deal of respect for your good sense, Meg – you chose well, for your first experiences of life, and you've chosen to end it at the right time. For both of you.'

She was speechless for a moment. 'You astonish me, Mama. I can't believe you've known about Will all along and said nothing. What would you have done if I'd come to you one day in tears and told you I was with child?'

'Scolded you for being so careless, and then held you and reassured you that it wasn't the end of the world. Dealt with it. Found a way. What have women always done, in such circumstances?'

'I'm not,' she hastened to add. 'I couldn't be, I never could have been.'

'As I said,' her mother responded tranquilly, 'I have always had a great deal of respect for your good sense. I don't say you would never throw your cap over the windmill. I'm sure you're quite capable of it, as are most women, but not for Will Powell.'

'You are an extraordinary creature, Mama,' she said.

'Of course I am, my dear, and so are you. Never forget that.'

Perhaps, Meg thought now, she was missing Will, missing his touch, and that was all. This past harsh winter had allowed what they'd shared for the last three years or so to wither and die; they'd never been able to meet all that often when the nights were long and cold, and this winter they'd stopped altogether, so that it was a long time since she'd kissed or been kissed, or felt a man's hands on her body and known herself desired.

But it was summer now. She'd put away her sensible, ugly stuff gowns and her thick flannel petticoats, and she was acutely conscious of her physical self, restless, unsatisfied, in

Maria's flimsy silk or muslin finery. The gowns she wore now were lower cut and more clinging than anything she'd ever worn before, and under them she wore short stays, which she rarely bothered with at home, which offered up her breasts in a way designed, she thought, deliberately to tantalise. Looking like this, for the first time, it tantalised her too, and made her excessively aware of her animal being and its needs. It had been a while since she'd realised that she was a sensualist in her deepest nature, acutely conscious of the feel of fabrics – rough or smooth – on her skin, the silky touch of water, even the breath of air across her exposed neck. She shivered, sitting at her sister's neat dressing table, her body taut with unfulfilled desire and the memories of Sir Dominic's hands on her, his eyes dark with longing, his muscular body so temptingly close...

She was always conscious now of *him* in particular, and if men didn't want you to look at them, they shouldn't wear snowy white shirts, coats that fitted them like gloves, and buckskin riding breeches. They shouldn't have muscular thighs in those tight breeches, and beautifully glossy, well-washed hair that almost begged to be touched. They shouldn't smell wonderful and wear shiny leather boots. (What was it about the boots?) There had been periods in history – she was well-educated, she knew such things – when men had dressed in a ridiculous manner, with long curly wigs, patches on their painted faces and all manner of ribbons and bows about their persons. When, despite all their satins and embroidery, they had scarcely washed. And still women had wanted them, presumably, though she had no idea why, other than the undeniable fact that nature was the most powerful of forces. But she'd had the fortune – she couldn't say whether it was good or bad – to be born now, in the age of clean linen and broad, blatantly muscular shoulders, and those damn boots.

If she'd been able to go to Will and demand with the confidence of all that lay between them that he pleased her, gave her release just one last time, perhaps she'd not have felt this unexpected yearning for Sir Dominic. Perhaps.

But after all, nothing had really happened today in the park. They had not kissed. He had barely touched her, and she had not laid hands on him at all, let alone pulled him close and… Though she regretted this, though her imagination insisted upon picturing variations upon it, she should not.

Nothing had really happened, she told herself again. Her sister's fiancé had given way to her calm insistence, in the end, and admitted that she of all people must be party to what happened tonight. She couldn't go as a young lady, as Maria – he was so far right. She really couldn't risk being seen and recognised as Miss Nightingale. She'd be ruined – more importantly, her sister would be. So it made sense that she disguised herself as a boy. She wasn't sure if he'd seen the reason in what she'd said, or if what had flared up between them and so nearly overwhelmed them both had shaken him so much that he'd not had the power to refuse her any longer. Perhaps he'd been worried that if they'd continued to argue he really would have ended by pushing her up against the tree and kissing her till the world reeled about them. She didn't care why he'd changed his mind. Honestly she didn't. Shouldn't. He was a powerful distraction and a constant temptation, but she must concentrate on the reason she was here, which was to rescue her sister, if she needed rescuing.

She rang the bell for Hannah and told her what she wanted: access to her half-brother's wardrobe. Hannah grumbled at first, but she didn't seem anywhere near as scandalised as Sir Dominic had been, not once Meg told her all that had been discovered. Hannah had known Jenny Wood, as

Meg had not, and was shocked by what she heard of her experiences at Lord Purslake's house, and her present location. As for her sudden disappearance, such flighty behaviour was entirely out of character, Hannah swore. 'If she found herself in such a pickle, she could have come to me, Miss Meg, and I'm sure she should know I'd have helped her, or any other servant in this house would have done the same, for that matter. For she's a poor orphan girl with nobody in the world to watch out for her apart from her friends. It's a crying shame, that's what it is! I'm proper upset by what you've told me, Miss Meg, and that's a fact!' She was as concerned now for Jenny's safety as she was for Maria's, and if Meg had to dress in masculine attire to gain access to the house in Henrietta Street and find out what was going on there, Hannah was quite prepared to do all she could to help her. There would be no need to go up to the attic to look for clothes, she said.

They made their way instead to the Honourable Mr Francis Nightingale's former chamber and shut themselves in. The bed-hangings had been taken down and the feather mattress removed, and all the rest of the furniture was shrouded in Holland covers. There was no danger of encountering him here, or of any other sort of interruption, because Meg's half-brother no longer lived in Grosvenor Square and rarely visited. She hardly recalled ever having seen him in her childhood, and was aware that, despite her years in London, Maria knew him scarcely better. He'd been a schoolboy when his father had married for a second time, and although he'd apparently had a cordial enough relationship with his stepmother before her departure, Meg had been told that his ties to his father had never been strong, and their paths rarely crossed. He was a grown man of thirty or so now, the clothes he'd left behind had been abandoned here for years, presumably, and surely nobody would know or care if some of them went astray.

Hannah went through to the small dressing room that adjoined the main chamber and opened the wardrobe, surveying its contents with her hands upon her hips. The heady scent of lavender was almost overpowering. 'Most of these things must be from when Master Francis was just a boy,' she said. 'He did come home from school sometimes, though he spent his summers with his late mother's family, as I recall. Your mother tried her best to be good to him, in place of his poor mama, but things were never as they should have been between her and your father, and that made it difficult. If the boy showed any sign of responding to her kind overtures, let alone growing fond of her and taking her part, his father made him suffer for it. You know how he is. Well, talking pays no toll. At least Master Francis is tall, that's one blessing. Try these...'

They picked up armfuls of clothing and took them back to Meg's chamber, where she would be able to try them at her leisure. 'There's different sizes here, you can see, from when he was still growing,' Hannah told her. 'I'm sure we'll be able to find something that'll do well enough for a few hours.'

Meg had put on pantalettes for her driving expedition with Sir Dominic, as any sensible woman did when a passenger in a high-perch carriage that was exceedingly difficult to clamber up into with grace and modesty. And so it was an easy matter to step out of her muslin gown and layers of petticoats and try Francis's breeches and coats on for size. Some of the garments were too large and some too small, some of them looked so ridiculous that Hannah was forced to mop her eyes and stifle laughter, but at length they settled on something that served the purpose. It wasn't a suit of clothes – the unmentionables that fitted Meg's long legs had jackets in the same fabric that were far too wide in the shoulder for her, while the jackets that fitted her well enough had matching breeches that were tight to the point of indecency, especially about the posterior. But she ended up, after a half-hour or so of trying, with a sober black coat and a pair of grey knee-breeches. A waistcoat was easier, as it could be adjusted in the back, and shouldn't be too close-fitting to the chest in any case, for reasons sufficiently obvious. It would be idle to deny that Meg's own figure was hardly boyish. But nobody would be looking at her at all closely, she hoped.

'I suppose,' said Hannah, surveying her critically, 'you're not meant to be a young man of fashion, after all. Because there's no denying you don't look anything like one.'

'No,' responded Meg, dropping into a chair and sprawling in it, enjoying the familiar freedom and striking what she flattered herself to be a convincing masculine attitude with a touch of careless swagger. 'But what am I, then? What's my story? I'm serious, Hannah. How old do I look and what sort of person am I? I need to know, if I am to be a proper young man!' The storyteller in her could not help but start to weave an identity for the person she was pretending to be.

'I suppose you must be a sort of overgrown schoolboy in hand-me-downs.'

Meg sat up straight. 'Oh dear. I must be a schoolboy, I suppose, or a very young man. And that rather begs the question of why I'm going to... to such a place, doesn't it?'

'Well, no, my dear. That it doesn't, I'm sorry to say, boys being what they are. But it might beg the question of why you're going there with Sir Dominic!'

Meg giggled, pleasantly shocked. 'Hannah Treadwell, you horrify me! Are you implying that they'll think...? I don't know quite *what* you're implying!'

'I'm not sure I do either, if it comes to it,' Hannah said, her cheeks rosy. She bustled to clear away the discarded clothing and would no longer meet Meg's eye. 'I can't tell if people will know straight away that you're a girl – I know you, so I can't properly judge how convincing you look. But you be careful, that's all I'll say. It's all very well to do this for your sister's sake, but make sure you don't lose your head and enjoy it too much! There's a reckless streak in you that could lead you into all sorts of danger. I hope to heaven that your mother never gets to hear of this, never mind anyone else. What she'd say to me if she heard I'd helped you, I don't like to think!'

'She'd thank you, and say we need to do everything we can to rescue Maria,' replied Meg stoutly. She was confident that this was true.

'Maybe,' Hannah replied, unabashed. 'And maybe she'd say that if you're not careful you'll need rescuing too, and then where will we be?'

13

It was close on eleven on a moonless night, and Sir Dominic De Lacy, accompanied by his silently amused groom Jack Fishwick, was waiting restlessly in the shadows at the end of the mews behind Lord Nightingale's house in Grosvenor Square. There was, at present, nobody else about, for which he was devoutly thankful, since he knew himself to be lurking in a highly suspicious manner. Should the patrolling Watch happen to pass on their nightly rounds, he would no doubt be questioned, and possibly apprehended as a dangerous criminal and threat to the King's peace. A housebreaker, or worse. Or, perhaps, the escaped lunatic he'd earlier accused Miss Margaret Nightingale of resembling. The boot was on the other foot now, and such an eventuality seemed all too likely. He ought to have some plausible story prepared to account for their presence in case of being questioned by officers of the law, but his mind was blank and his mouth unaccountably dry. He didn't imagine that the arrival of Miss Nightingale, in masculine attire, would help matters much. Most likely, it would make things worse. And that was before they went anywhere at all, least of all attempted to gain entry to the dubious establishment in Henrietta Street that was the objective of their crazy journey.

A few weeks since, before he'd been so familiar with the name of Nightingale, his life had been peaceful and ordered. Rational, predictable. Safe. He had his friends, his sporting life – riding, driving, boxing, raising and training thoroughbred horses. If there was any excitement in his existence, he found it there, in the exhilaration of speed and physical exertion. More sedately, he looked after his extensive estates and the people who depended on him for a living, conscious that it was a heavy responsibility that merited being taken seriously. He read a great deal, enjoyed the opera and collected pictures in a modest way. Drinking to excess and gambling, the pastimes of his wilder youth, had begun to bore him long ago, and he'd never been promiscuous by the (admittedly lax) standards of the day. His physical, sexual needs were a small part of his life now, attended to – such a cold phrase, but undeniably accurate – by a woman he'd known for years who lived discreetly near Russell Square and welcomed a select few gentlemen as visitors. Sukie. To call her his mistress seemed inaccurate: yes, he gave her generous financial gifts, but they didn't flaunt their relationship nor make demands of exclusivity on each other; it was none of his affair what she was doing when he wasn't with her, as long as she was careful of her health, which he knew she always was. He thought of her as a friend as much as anything else, someone he could be at ease with, but the prospect of parting ways with her upon his marriage, as he'd intended, had caused him little distress. He'd have given her a suitable final present; she'd have smiled and understood and wished him well... It was a while since he'd visited her, he realised. He couldn't imagine doing so now; he had not the least desire to see her. His relationship with Sukie, if one could call it that, seemed a long time ago; like something that had happened to a different person.

As for his needs beyond the physical... it wasn't at all the thing to think about them, or even to admit having any. He'd certainly never discussed such a thing with any of his friends, or with anyone else at all. One did not speak of such matters. He wasn't sure, after the turmoil of the last few days, if he'd ever expected or hoped that such needs might be fulfilled in marriage, or, at any rate, in the kind of marriage he'd come to accept he would make. If challenged, as Meg had challenged him the other morning when they rode together in the park, he'd have struggled to explain in a convincing manner why he'd agreed to his mother's suggestion of Miss Nightingale as his bride. To say, Why *not* her? and shrug, was surely unsatisfactory. Meg had clearly thought it so, had told him he was strange. Perhaps he was. It was certainly strange, to put it no more strongly, to have been so quick to fulfil his father's wish – which might after all have been some casually expressed fancy rather than a deeply felt desire – when his father could never know of it, or give his approval. Or perhaps he'd just been tired of looking for something he'd come to believe didn't exist, or didn't exist for him. He needed to sit down and think seriously about all this, but now was hardly the moment. His life a few weeks ago had consisted of nothing but days that had had to be filled; now, there never seemed to be any damned time.

And it was hard to say, returning to the immediate hour and its most pressing concerns, why he had agreed to this preposterous scheme. Perhaps he hadn't. He couldn't remember now; that is to say, he recalled perfectly well all his strong and reasoned arguments against doing this mad thing, and Meg's ridiculous responses, and he recalled nearly giving in to temptation and kissing her, but after that everything was rather a blur, and here he was, nonetheless.

And here she was, coming along the mews towards him, swaggering with what she no doubt considered to be a masculine gait. It was quite dark here, and he couldn't see her very well. He wasn't sure he wanted to. He groaned softly, and his companion suppressed some sound that might have been a cough, but was more likely a snort of ribald amusement. 'Are you laughing at me, Jack, or just at the universe in general and the fickleness of destiny? Because I know there can't be anything in the least amusing about this fine young fellow who's coming to join us, or the prospect of the evening ahead. Nothing at all fucking funny about any of that, as far as I can see.'

'Just clearing my throat, sir,' Fishwick replied impassively. 'Phlegm, I dare say. This night air isn't good for a man. Dangerous, it is.'

'Isn't that the truth?'

She was upon them now, and all other deeper concerns were banished. Her borrowed clothes fit her far better than they should, clinging to and revealing her long legs in a way that did little for his peace of mind. But as if to balance that, she had a horrible, shapeless excuse for a hat set at a jaunty angle on her crisp curls. What little ambient light there was allowed Dominic to see that her eyes were bright with anticipation. 'Shall we go?' she said eagerly.

Dominic was relieved to move away from his lurking post, although he dreaded passing into better-lit areas. There would be a greater chance of them being seen, and also, he'd be able to see her properly. But he wouldn't be distracted from their mission. He wouldn't. He needed instead to distract himself, urgently, from looking at her, from lingering on the lines and curves that were normally concealed... 'I loathe your hat with a passion,' he said with an effort at lightness. 'It's the worst hat I ever saw in my life.'

'It can't possibly be the worst hat you ever saw. This is London. Horrible hats must be ten a penny. Isn't there even a man who goes around with a model of a ship on his head?'

'Yes, Joseph Johnson, an old sailor and ballad singer. I've met him and spoken with him, and he wears a cleverly contrived model ship, not an ordinary hat. And it still looks much better than that misshapen monstrosity.'

'Really? I quite like it. I think it gives me an air.'

'An air of being deeply disreputable, certainly. An air of having found it in a gutter in a low part of town, and picked it out directly from the mire and put in on your head.'

'Nonsense. It belongs to Robert – he's loaned it to me, and warned me that I'll have to replace it if I lose or damage it, which is quite fair, because it's his second-best one.'

'I hate to think what his other hats must be like, then. I will compensate him – in fact, I'll pay to destroy it. Pounding it back into the dirt where it belongs would relieve my feelings nicely.'

'Perhaps later,' she said, 'when our business is done. I am sure a guinea or two would reconcile Robert to his loss, and God forbid that a dandy's tender sensibilities should be offended.' He could hear the laughter bubbling up in her voice, even though he was trying hard not to look at her and mostly succeeding.

The distraction wasn't really working, though. All this nonsense about hats – was he flirting with Meg? Of course he was, and unless he was truly losing his wits she was flirting back. They were passing along Brook Street now, Jack Fishwick a silent presence at his other side. Just because his old groom wasn't saying anything didn't mean he had no thoughts on this whole misbegotten project; Dominic could practically hear him thinking that his master, normally so calm and controlled, showed every sign of having run mad. God knew it was true.

It was only just over a mile to their destination, and walking had seemed more sensible, for purposes of concealment, than taking a hackney carriage. Past Piccadilly, the streets they made their way through grew rapidly less respectable and less safe. If anyone looked closely at them as they passed, they'd seem an odd trio indeed, but nobody seemed inclined to do so, at least not yet. The streets and leafy squares of Mayfair had been quiet enough except for a few carriages – too late for parties to be starting, too early for them to have finished – but as they neared Seven Dials, the atmosphere changed, and became undeniably more menacing. The buildings they passed grew shabbier, and the roads were narrower and dirtier, unswept, with piles of noisome refuse that must be avoided. There were groups of men, and women too, some standing still, talking, laughing and drinking from bottles, some moving about, like them, with a sense of purpose. From the corner of his eye, in the shadows, Dominic could see people in pairs, doing things that would be much better done in private if they must be done at all. He hoped Meg hadn't noticed, but he expected that she had – she was wide-eyed and silent at his side now – and he would settle for her refraining from open comment.

There were bodies huddled in doorways, too, for what precarious shelter the small spaces offered, bundles of rags that were people. Some of those bundles were heartbreakingly small. After a little while Meg said, all traces of amusement gone from her voice, 'There are children here. I knew, of course, that there must be... While I have been dancing, and driving in the park, and enjoying wearing Maria's outrageously expensive clothes, there are adults and little children living on the streets, so close, starving. At the mercy of those bigger and stronger than themselves. Selling themselves, perhaps, in order to eat.'

'It's all too true, and it can seem overwhelming,' Dominic told her soberly. 'Hopeless. But it isn't, not entirely. There are people who care, and who are trying to do something. My father was one of them – he saw what you see, and it was the children above all who elicited his pity and concern too. The Foundling Hospital takes babies, of course, but older children who have fallen through the cracks and are scraping a precarious living on the streets had been sorely neglected except by a few religious organisations. He wasn't religious, but he bought a building not too far from here, set it to rights, and endowed it with money. Though he died ten years ago, his work continues.'

'You continue it?' Was that disbelief in her voice? It shouldn't sting – they barely knew each other, after all.

He said lightly, 'He left money and instructions in his will to make sure I did.' He did not say that he had added to it; that would sound like boasting. 'Money is the easy part. Time is much more precious. I don't give much of that, and actually, it has always been an enterprise run mainly by women. It is better so. It's hard enough for women to win the trust of those who have been betrayed by the world, perhaps abandoned or cruelly mistreated by their parents; for men, it is almost impossible. And to teach the children that fine young gentlemen in fashionable clothes – men who have gold to offer them – might be persons they could place their reliance on is not, in fact, necessarily a useful lesson. Better they stay wary.'

'I can see the truth in what you say,' she answered sombrely. 'But I am very glad to know that something is being done. Perhaps—'

He interrupted her. 'Forgive me for being uncivil, but you may see for yourself that efforts are being made, as well as hearing about them.' They had almost reached their destination – they were in Bedford Row now. 'Do you observe those two women there, surrounded by children, and the tall man standing somewhat apart from them?'

A little ahead, just before the left-hand turning into Henrietta Street, a curious scene was playing out. A handcart had been set down, and ragged children – a few of them disturbingly tiny, most of them apparently in their teens – were crowding around it. Some of them were clamouring excitedly, others were silent and wary, darting glances about them as though they feared some trickery or ambush. They held steaming mugs, and clutched paper wrappings from which savoury smells reached the observers, even at this little distance. Dominic had not been surprised to come across the cart – he knew that this was one of Angela's usual nights, and he'd been looking out for her, knowing she was as regular as clockwork in her patrol and could, perhaps, be of some help with his mission tonight.

A tall young African man stood to one side, surveying the scene with a frown between his brows. Two women were handing out the food and drink to the children under his watchful gaze. They were both past their first youth, perhaps in their forties or so, warmly dressed against the evening chill. One of them was white, short and stocky, and the other, a woman of above-average height with an impressive figure, was also African, her head wrapped in a colourful cloth in place of a bonnet.

The watchful man moved closer to her, and spoke a few words, and she glanced up sharply, a warm smile dawning on her face. 'Dominic!' she said. Her eyes darted to his companions, and she nodded at Jack Fishwick in obvious recognition, but if she thought Meg's presence odd – whether she'd guessed she was a girl or not – in this place and at this hour, she said nothing of it.

Dominic strode forward and took her hand. 'Angela, well met,' he responded, pressing it. 'I wondered if we might find you here, and hoped we would. This is no time for formal introductions, but Angela, this is a friend, who had best remain nameless just now. This is Angela, known to all as Mother Jones, and her companions Susan and Aaron.'

'I'm very pleased to meet you all,' said Meg politely, trying to sound manly. She said nothing more, and Dominic thought she must be somewhat stunned by everything that she was seeing. Lord knew what she made of it.

The children still crowded about the two women, careful to avoid coming too close to the newcomers, and Dominic said, 'Can I have a word or two with you, Angela? I know you're busy, and I won't keep you a moment; I just want to ask you something.'

'Of course,' she said, brows raised, and stepped aside from the cart, leaving Susan to continue handing out provisions and speaking with the livelier of the children; some of them were silent, and did not answer her when she addressed them, but they were all eating and drinking with ferocious attention. Aaron continued to keep watch over them all, his vigilance unrelenting.

'Jack, which house is it?' Dominic said. They'd moved forward and were almost at the junction with Henrietta Street, so that they could see down it towards the piazza. There were still knots of people about, crowding around the doors of a rowdy tavern nearby, but nobody approached them or appeared to pay them any mind. This was a place where ordinary standards of dress and behaviour could not be said to apply, certainly not during the hours of darkness, and far stranger sights than their little group could no doubt be seen here every night of the year.

'That one on the right at the end – the far corner,' Fishwick said. 'There's a cove on the step standing guard, can you see, sir, Mrs Jones?'

'Thank you. What do you know of that particular house, ma'am?'

It was so pleasant not to have to engage in endless explanations. Angela replied readily, her deep, lilting voice making music of the stark words, 'It's a brothel, of course – but I assume you knew that – much like any other. Run by a woman, as they mostly are, a woman my age, goes by Sally. It's no worse than most, and better than many. That is to say, the girls there are usually fifteen or upwards, and I've heard nothing of them being held there against their will, or having their clothes taken from them, or any such unpleasantness. They even have a doctor in to check them over every now and then, for all the good that does. I hope that answers your questions, Dominic?' Her ironic tone said that she was consciously refraining from asking questions and that he should be appropriately grateful for her forbearance.

'Thank you – that's good news, as far as it goes. We've been told about a runaway abigail we believe is staying there, a girl by the name of Jenny Wood. And a young lady, perhaps, a blonde, might be there too. Not the sort of woman you'd generally expect to see in such a place. We have no reason to think that either of them is being constrained in any way, but they may be taking refuge there.' It was a long shot, but he had to ask. Angela and her two helpers were out on these streets several nights a week, rain or shine – it was just possible they might have seen something.

She shook her head. 'I don't know any of the current inhabitants. If they're full grown, or more or less, you know I don't concern myself with them overmuch. I have enough to do. There's church ladies who try sometimes... Good luck to them, I say, for all their moralising.' She sounded exhausted for a moment, depressed and unlike herself. It was as he'd told Meg a moment ago – even Angela, who'd devoted her life to helping London's most vulnerable, couldn't kill herself by trying to rescue everyone, so great was their number, however much they might need it and deserve it.

Jack cut in, 'Mrs J, begging your pardon, young Jenny's got a suitor, if that's the word, been making her life a misery. He may be the reason she's here, assuming she is – he's forced her out of a comfortable situation with his attentions. We know he's followed her here, tried to gain entry to the house, but failed. It'd be nice if someone could have a quiet word with him sometime soon, teach him the error of his ways.'

The woman who called herself Mrs Jones smiled, her eyes bright and lively again. 'That sounds like the sort of thing Aaron might just be interested in. It's none of my affair, of course, but if you were to give him a description of the man...'

'That I will, ma'am,' said Jack. 'Thank you.'

'Thank Aaron, not me. Do you need his help, though, with this mysterious business of yours, Dominic?'

'I don't think so,' he replied. 'We're not forcing our way in.'

She surveyed him measuringly. 'No need, I'm sure. Look at you, so fine as you are – they'll welcome you with open arms. But they won't like it, you know, if you start asking too many questions.'

He shrugged. 'There's always bribery.'

'There's always robbery with violence, Dominic, if you start flashing the cash.'

'I'm armed.'

'Still, be careful, my dear. We'll be here for a little while longer, and then we'll move into the piazza for a time. We'll keep our eyes open for you as long as we can, but then we'll have to head off home.'

'We don't plan to make a lengthy stay. If Jenny's present – it's really too much to hope that the other girl I mentioned might be hidden away there – we just want to talk to her for a moment.'

'That'll be a novelty for her.' She reached up and touched his cheek lightly. 'Well, I've told you to be careful. You'd best get on. But tell me, before you go, how's my lovely Davey doing? I hear you're a terribly strict employer.'

He grinned. 'He's the strict one. No man is a hero to his valet, you know. But I try to live up to his expectations. It would be a crime to disappoint him.'

'I'm glad to hear it. He's one of my great successes, you must know, and the children are always so excited when he visits us and tells us stories of his life. And that reminds me, I was going to send you a note to tell you, I've just had word Annie will be back in London very soon; the regiment's moving. I'll let you know when she arrives. I know she'd love to see you – they all would.'

He smiled at her, his worries forgotten for a moment. 'That's good news. I'd like that.' He could feel Meg's silent, curious presence at his side. She must have overheard, she must be wondering what it all signified, but it was a long story, not his secret but that of others, and besides, there was no time. They needed to get inside that house, and out of it again, without any trouble. They needed to get Meg home safe. No more delaying.

14

Meg was puzzling over all she'd heard and seen as she stood in Covent Garden. Sir Dominic hadn't said so explicitly, but she assumed that the people she'd just met were a part of, or in charge of, his father's charitable foundation. Perhaps, if they could be persuaded to trust a little, some of those lost children would climb wearily into the cart or walk at its side and accompany the women home tonight, wherever home was, to find a safe, warm bed to sleep in, on top of the hot meal they'd already had. Maybe even a chance at a whole new beginning, if they wanted it. That was a good thought.

He was plainly more involved than he had claimed to be in the project. These people all knew him well, and had for many years. His valet, it seemed, was someone who'd been saved from the streets long since and given a new direction in life. Gentlemen's gentlemen were well paid and highly esteemed, among the very highest rank of servant, so this was no small thing. That much she could decipher. The rest of it – Annie, and the regiment, and other people concerned somehow – she could not make head nor tail of at all. Except that there was a closeness there, a warmth in his voice, and in Angela's when she spoke to him. She didn't know Sir Dominic at all, she realised afresh. He was her sister's betrothed – for now – he'd agreed reluctantly to help her, he'd almost kissed her, they flirted and teased each other... and that was all. But the intimacy they sometimes shared could only be fleeting and illusory. It would be better not to forget that, and not to imagine that there was anything more substantial or meaningful between them.

'We need to set about this, and be done with it,' he said now. They had moved away from the little group of people, closer to their destination. 'It's not too late for you to step aside, Miss Nightingale. You can wait in the square, with Angela and Aaron. Help Susan give hot pies and warm chocolate to the urchins. I hope that doesn't sound patronising – I assure you, I don't mean it so. You'll be quite safe with my friends. Much safer than you'll be inside that cursed house, you must realise. I'm sure I won't be long, but it would ease my mind a great deal if you would stay outside, out of harm's way, and wait for me.'

'I know it would,' she answered, moved by his concern for her once more, but still resolute. 'And I'm excessively grateful for all that you've done, and all you're prepared to do. I know you think me headstrong and perverse, and perhaps I am. But Maria's my sister. I have to come with you, even if it's one chance in a thousand that she's in there. You must see that. I owe her that much and more.'

He sighed. 'Very well. No sense in delaying, then. If anything does go wrong, Meg, get out by any means you can, please don't wait for me, and run to Angela. You know she'll be close by, and you can trust her with your life – she and Aaron will make sure no one pursues you or hurts you. Promise me you'll do that, at least.'

'I swear I will.'

They walked further along the short street and stopped before the end house. 'Wait here, Jack,' he said. 'Keep your eyes open for trouble. We shouldn't be long, all being well, and I have my pistols.'

'So do I,' said Fishwick, turning back and melting into the shadows. His voice was a grim whisper. 'Let's hope we neither of us need them.'

The door was still guarded, and as they approached it the man who'd been watching their approach stood and barred their way with his thick body. He was tall and massively built, and his face was heavily scarred, especially about the eyes, and his nose bent from some previous blow. A boxer, Meg thought. His cloudy gaze ran over them both in a hard, lewd way that made her profoundly uncomfortable. 'This is no molly-house,' he warned them, turning his head and spitting, not quite in their direction but not so very far away either. 'You'd be better off round the corner, with your own kind. I'm sure you know the way well enough, my fine backgammon fellows.'

Meg didn't know what a molly-house was, nor a backgammon fellow, though perhaps she could guess, but apparently Sir Dominic did. 'You misunderstand our intentions,' he said coldly. 'We do not seek merely a room for our own use, but congenial company too. My friend and I are looking for a young woman.' As he spoke, coins clinked heavily and invitingly in his palm, and the man took them and pocketed them with astonishing swiftness.

'Treat yourself, sir,' the man said expansively, stepping aside and grinning broadly as he pushed the door open with a loud creak. 'Beg pardon for the misunderstanding. Young women is what we has aplenty, and fine ones, too. Have two. Or three. Perhaps it's a-watching of the young shaver setting to it with a bouncing wench that tickles your fancy, in which case, fill your boots, as they say – all tastes, within reason and nature, is catered to here, my lord, as you will soon discover.'

'How kind,' said Sir Dominic in arctic tones. He couldn't be shocked, Meg knew – he must surely be a man of some experience, and this was, after all, a brothel rather than a young ladies' seminary. But she could tell that he was horrified, no doubt on her behalf. She tried, and failed, to suppress a giggle. He heard it and swore under his breath, grasping her arm and urging her over the threshold.

'He'll just think you're over-eager,' she murmured provocatively.

There was, perhaps fortunately, no time for him to respond to her teasing. The door opened into a wood-panelled hall with several more closed doors leading out of it, and they had scarcely had chance to look about them when a woman approached them, confident and smiling. Perhaps this was Sally. She was lavishly dressed in bright silks and skilfully painted in a fair approximation of youth, but her eyes were old and infinitely wary. Once again Meg was uncomfortably aware of swift, assessing scrutiny. But clearly the light was better here, or the observer more astute, because the woman said shrewdly, 'I'm happy to see you, sir – my lord? – but I must tell you, this isn't the sort of house where it's customary to bring your own female company, however… charmingly unconventional. Normally, we provide the charming company, and I assure you, it's all you could wish for. Perhaps you will come in, and see if you care to make some new friends? If Sweet Polly Oliver, dressed in her brother's clothes, is the tune you like, as I see it is, that too can be arranged here. But if your tastes are a trifle more unusual, of course – both of you – that can also be catered for, up to a point.'

'I'm happy to pay,' Sir Dominic replied, and Meg was aware,

though his voice was casual and his manner languid, of an underlying tension in his tall body as he stood protectively close to her. 'But it's a specific young woman I'm seeking, one I have reason to believe is staying here, and I'd just like to speak to her for a few moments, nothing more.'

'That,' said the woman, becoming markedly less genteel, 'is what many of them say. You're the second one this week, in fact. And those that say such things are generally looking for trouble.'

'I'm not, I assure you. Trouble is the last thing I desire. I'm just looking for Jenny Wood.'

'And what do the likes of you know of Jenny Wood?' Her tone sharpened further, and her stance was undeniably belligerent now. It was no wonder, really, that she was so suspicious, after the other man had tried to force his way in to see Jenny and been rebuffed. They should have realised this might happen. And this was her house, and she was in control. Some primitive instinct for danger made Meg suddenly conscious of other eyes watching them too, other ears listening, from the rooms deeper inside the house, with no friendly intention.

Sir Dominic said coolly, 'I know little of her, in the sense that I've never met her. My name wouldn't convey anything to her, either, since I am a stranger to the young lady. But I do know that she was hounded out of her former post by a fellow servant who would not cease importuning her, and I know too that he saw her here, a few nights ago, and attempted to gain entrance but was refused. I have nothing to do with him, or with her former employer. I just want to assure myself that she is well, and ask her a question or two about a mutual acquaintance of ours. And I'll compensate her for her time, naturally, and you for yours.'

He raised his voice a little, and Meg realised that he too

knew that others were observing them, judging them. 'I have arranged for Miss Wood's pursuer to have a little private chat with a friend of mine – a man from the West Indies by the name of Aaron, with whom you may be familiar, at least by sight. If you do know him, you'll be aware he's not one to be trifled with. He doesn't care for bullies, Aaron, especially not bullies who play their tricks on defenceless women, and I have a notion he'll be quite effective in persuading this fellow to go away and never trouble the young woman, or perhaps any young woman, any more.'

'You know Aaron?' Sally was incredulous.

'Very well indeed. And Angela – Mother Jones, if you recognise her by that name – even better. She'll vouch for me. She vouches for you, up to a point – she says this is a decent house, where women aren't kept against their will. So I'm hoping you'll allow me to speak to Jenny, if she's still here and will grant me a few minutes of her time.'

'I'm here all right.' A girl was standing on the stairs, her hand on the banister, looking down at them. She was tall and dark, with strong, handsome features and untrusting eyes. 'But who are you, and what the hell do you want with me?'

15

Seeing them together, and seeing the older woman's alarmed reaction to Jenny's presence, it was suddenly obvious that they were closely related. She's no orphan; Sally's her mother, Meg realised, and she just prevented herself from blurting it out.

'I'd rather not give my name in front of so many interested listeners,' Sir Dominic said. 'And we really do just want to talk to you. Nothing more, I promise.'

Jenny came down the last few steps with deliberate casualness, cocking her hips, mistress of the scene, but as she grew nearer and the light in the lower hallway revealed Meg's face, the girl started, and subjected her to a much closer scrutiny. 'Well,' she said, 'I know who *you* are, at any rate! At first I thought you was Maria, but you're not, are you? You must be the sister, Meg. The wild country bluestocking.'

Not Miss Maria, or Miss Nightingale, but Maria. And this was a woman who could tell the twin sisters apart at a glance, when her close friends noticed nothing amiss and when her own father sat down at table with her and could not. Perhaps, against all the odds, they'd come to the right place after all. 'Is she with you?' Meg's voice was unsteady, now that it came to it. 'Please tell me she is. I've been so worried about her.'

'Let's have some privacy so we can talk,' Jenny said, frowning a little. 'It's fine, Ma – they don't mean me any harm. I think I know why they're here. I'll take them in the back parlour, and we won't be long. Five minutes, no more. Don't fret!'

Sally still seemed reluctant to admit them, and her posture remained defensive, but she made no objection as Jenny passed her and led them further into the house. The girl didn't speak again before they came to a closed door at the end of the passage, opening it and preceding them into a small, scantily furnished wood-panelled room. There were two young women lounging there in flimsy, transparent gowns, playing cards in a desultory fashion at a small table, but she dismissed them with an abrupt jerk of the head, and a brief, 'Kindly fuck off, would you?' Meg supposed she should be shocked again, but she knew Sir Dominic would be appalled afresh that she'd overheard such terribly unladylike language, and the impulse to laugh caused her to bite her lip to restrain herself.

The girls pouted as they dawdled from the room, their avid eyes on Sir Dominic – his handsome face and figure, his immaculate, expensive clothing – and one of them, a short brunette, reached out and trailed her hand slowly across his broad chest as she passed him, looking up at him meltingly. He didn't move or react in any way, his expression quite impassive, but Jenny said menacingly, 'Unless you want to feel my boot up your arse, Lily...?'

Lily didn't appear to be in the least abashed; she was grinning saucily. 'Maybe later, if it's a slow night,' she shot back pertly as the door closed behind her. 'But I'd rather feel his...'

Perhaps mercifully, the door cut off her words, and Jenny

sighed and gestured towards a tired-looking satin sofa. 'Ignore her. You might as well sit down, but you won't be here long, you know. She's not here, your sister, and I don't know where she is. I take it she's run away?'

'A week or so ago,' Meg said urgently, subsiding into the grubby cushions, her heart sinking as she absorbed the impact of Jenny's words. 'But you don't seem surprised. You were obviously quite close, if she's told you about me. Are you sure you don't have any idea at all where she might have gone?'

'Close...' replied Jenny musingly. 'You could say that. We were, once upon a time, but I haven't seen her since I left that damn depressing house of your father's, which is a couple of months ago now. So I'm sorry, I wish I could help you, but I don't know anything. Ask her friends, is all I can say to you, the ones she was at school with. That red-haired one, maybe. They're thick as inkle-weavers, those two, or used to be not long since. I'd wager she knows all Maria's secrets.'

'Lady Primrose?' Meg said in surprise. 'Really? We've seen her, but she could tell us nothing.'

'Told you nothing, I believe. Could tell you nothing? I'd not be so sure. She's a knowing one, she is, and sharp-eyed. I'd wager she realised at once you weren't Maria, just as I did. Really, you should talk to her.'

Meg didn't want to reveal to anyone that she was masquerading as her sister unless she was obliged to, even if this strange girl might have guessed that she must be since Maria was missing. So she didn't respond. It seemed their visit here had been a failure, save for this one tiny, fragile clue. Jenny said suddenly, 'Maria used to read your letters out to me sometimes. I liked that. You have a proper way with words – I could picture it, how you described it all. Your house and your village, all the animals and the changing of the seasons. I've never been in the country, though I went to Kensington Gardens once. So much green, it made you dizzy! It was like going again, or better, hearing what you said about it. And the other parts too. Climbing out of the window in your breeches in the moonlight so you could go on an adventure, I remember that one in particular...'

There was a mischievous glint in the girl's eyes, and Meg knew she was blushing. She'd rather Jenny said nothing more, given the precise nature of her adventures and the fact that Sir Dominic, close by, also had sharp ears, and a sharper brain. Her emotions were in turmoil, but she could not take time to dwell on them now, in this place of all places. She said hastily, 'I'm glad you enjoyed it. If you really can't tell us any more, we should thank you and go, I expect. You must be busy, and we interrupted your evening.'

Jenny laughed. 'Am I giving away all your secrets to your fine gentleman? I'm sorry!' She didn't appear to be sorry in the least. 'Yes, you should go, but don't worry about me. My ma's not the sort would put me in her business here; that's why I ended up as a lady's maid. More respectable, you might say, than making your living on the town. But it hasn't quite worked out that way, has it? I'm not going back and having that canting hypocrite of a footman pawing at me day in and day out. At least here they have to pay for what they fancy, rather than getting it for free. I'm grateful you warned him off, but his type don't stop. And there's always more where he came from, in my experience. The gall of him, sneaking off to bawdy houses every chance he gets, and then smearing *my* reputation just because I wouldn't bump giblets with him!'

'I don't know if it will be any consolation, but the rest of the servants in the house were furious with him, and have made his life a misery ever since you left,' Sir Dominic said unexpectedly.

His concern for this woman who could mean nothing to him gave Meg a warm feeling, and she was feeling quite heated enough already. Her breeches felt tight, constricting suddenly, and she tugged at her cravat.

Jenny shrugged, apparently unimpressed by his words of consolation. 'It's nice to hear, but not one of them stepped in and did anything – none of the men, anyway, though the housekeeper gave him a piece of her mind more than once, for all the good it did. That fubsy-faced old butler was happy enough to wink at his behaviour – he wasn't going to rock the boat by telling his master or mistress, not him. No, I'm done with that life, at least for a while. I'm going to take some time and look about me.'

'I said I'd pay you and I will.' Sir Dominic put a small pile of golden coins down on the table. 'Thank you for your time, Miss Wood.'

'I told you, I'm not a whore,' she said. 'No disrespect to whores, since my ma was one, as must be plain to see, but I'm not.' She didn't sound angry, just weary.

'I'm not implying that you are, nor is it any of my business either way. You didn't have to talk to us, but you did. And if you've lost your position through no fault of your own, and lost the back wages you were owed too, you should be sensible and take it. It'll give you a little longer to decide what you want to do next.'

'You're right.' She scooped up the coins and they vanished into some hidden pocket as she opened the door to let them pass. As Meg drew close, she said abruptly, 'I hope you find her. Good luck. I'm sure she's safe, though – she's awake on all suits, you know, even though she seems to have her head in the clouds. People often don't reckon with her as they should.'

'Thank you. I hope you're right.'

'I am, I'll go bail. And,' she said, grinning, 'you're a cunning enough one yourself, aren't you?'

'What do you mean?' Meg wasn't at all sure she really wanted to know, but the words escaped her nonetheless.

Jenny leaned forward, with a sly look up at Sir Dominic, and whispered in Meg's ear, 'I see you've moved on – and up! – from country boys and larking about in barns!'

16

There was no reason to linger once Jenny had told them what little she knew, and Meg and Sir Dominic made their way swiftly out of the house, ignoring the surprised looks they received from the doorkeeper. Obviously he'd expected them to stay much longer, given what he believed they'd come for. Dominic found himself in an uncomfortable state of arousal that he could only hope was not obvious to others as he blessed the relative darkness of the street. Meg's cheeks had flooded with fiery colour at the girl's final words, and she raised no objection when he suggested they find Angela and take their leave of her, so that she would be reassured they were safe. Clearly, Miss Margaret had no desire at all to be questioned over the outrageous things Jenny had said to her as they left, and no wonder. The atmosphere between them had grown heavy with a particular type of tension and he was positive they both felt it with equal force.

Fishwick fell in beside them, appearing silently out of the shadows as they headed off into the piazza, but soon left them after a brief exchange of words – a farewell to Angela and her companions – which Dominic afterwards could not have recalled at gunpoint.

A few minutes later, Dominic and Meg were quite alone in a hackney carriage, making their way back towards Grosvenor Square. He'd procured the vehicle on Bow Street with efficiency and speed and told the driver to set them down on Davies Street, a little way short of their destination, considering the convenience worth the risk. If he also had a deep desire to be private with her in a small, dark, intimate space, he pushed away the treacherous thought. He needed to get her home safely, and he would.

'If Jenny was right,' she ventured, plainly made uncomfortable by the silence that was thickening between them, 'it seems we may have had the answer in our hands, days ago, without knowing it. I thought she was telling the truth, as far as she knew it, didn't you?'

'Yes, I did,' he said gruffly, shifting in his seat and trying to focus, which was difficult when she was so close that their bodies were almost touching. Were touching, when the wheels jolted over a pothole and her thigh brushed his. Hell and damnation. 'And I can't help you with this part of it. I think you're going to have to call on Lady Primrose on your own, and press her more strongly than we were able to at the ball. A morning call between good friends – what could be more natural?'

'And do you think I should reveal to her who I am?' Her voice was soft, troubled, and good God, he wanted to take her in his arms and drive all those worries from her mind, and his. Embracing her would be crazy, and it would solve precisely nothing, but how badly he wanted it. He didn't want to *talk*.

'If Jenny has the right of it,' he said with a concentration he could only marvel at, 'she knows already, which must mean she also knows that your sister is gone, even if she doesn't know where she is right now. And even if she is ignorant of whatever the bloody hell is going on, there can be little harm done – she's a close friend of your sister's, everyone keeps telling us, and therefore is hardly likely to spread the news of her disappearance far and wide.' He paused and then said, almost despite himself, 'But Meg, at this point it scarcely matters.'

'What do you mean?' It seemed she would force him to say it in plain words.

'I mean that if we don't find your sister very soon, it'll all have to come out in any case. You know that the damn wedding is barely two weeks away.'

'If Lady Primrose indeed knows where Maria is, it may all be set right,' she said optimistically.

He gritted his teeth. 'How? How may everything be set right?'

She didn't answer him. She didn't know.

He went on, his tone deep and intense, 'I feel as though I've said this to you before, but it bears repeating – you cannot possibly think that your sister has any intention of marrying me, or that it would be a good idea if she did. Nor can you believe I have the faintest desire to marry her. I won't say she's the last woman on earth I'd wish to marry, but – no, actually, she is. The very last.' He felt the truth of it bone-deep as he said it.

She was still silent. His heart was racing and his blood pounding in his ears. The carriage felt very small suddenly, and yet not small enough. She was close, but he needed her closer. 'Aren't you going to ask me why?' he said. His voice was ragged, hoarse, and very low. He scarcely knew what he was saying, apart from the fact that it was dangerous and forbidden, wrong and so perfectly right, and he could not stop it for the life of him.

'Is it because you almost kissed me in the park?' There. She'd said it.

'No,' he said. 'It's because I'm going to kiss you now. Shall you like that, Meg Nightingale?'

'No,' she responded, astonishing him, 'and you shan't do it, because I'm going to kiss you first.'

17

Meg turned to look at him properly at last. There was an inevitability to what was going to happen, now that they came to it. They were very close to each other – had they moved, drawn together by some irresistible force? – and the naked hunger in his face took her breath away, so closely did it match her own. No wonder she was shaking. It was odd, disturbing, to feel so strongly connected to someone she barely knew – she'd admitted as much to herself, not an hour since – and who barely knew her. She had secrets, and no doubt he did too. He must. She'd glimpsed the edge of something important earlier tonight, she thought: Annie, the regiment. And apart from all that, he was engaged to be married to her sister, however little he wanted it, and however little her sister seemed to want it. What a terrible coil they found themselves in, and he couldn't see a way out of it, any more than she could. Perhaps there was no way, and they were all bound for disaster. But just now none of that seemed to matter in the least. Not compared with the irresistible temptation of touching him at last. Had she only admitted what she needed from him this morning? It seemed much longer; it seemed to have settled into undeniable fact.

'Are you, now?' he asked. His deep voice was amused, and there was something delicious in the way the warmth of that combined with his desire. And hers. They were alone, in a precious, fragile little bubble, as they jolted over cobblestones; the world seemed very far away and entirely unimportant. My cap over the windmill, she thought. How right you were, Mama. Here goes.

He was waiting for her, and she liked that too. It was a little awkward, here in the carriage, but on the other hand she was wearing breeches, which ought to make it easier. She leaned forward, steadying herself with her hand on his shoulder, and brushed his lips with hers. It was a tiny, brief contact, but it set a bolt of electricity jolting through her, and she made a soft little sound and deepened the kiss. He tasted so good. His hands came out to hold her then, and this allowed her to put her arms about his neck and press herself to him in the darkness. She knew he wouldn't let her fall.

She might have started it, but he was a most enthusiastic participant. His hands were under her jacket, strong and tight about her ribcage, linen and silk sliding under his touch. Not many layers covered her skin and came between them: just three – chemise, shirt and borrowed waistcoat – but that was still too many. She knew it would be glorious to be naked, with his hands exploring her and hers exploring him. That was impossible here and now – she was not quite so reckless yet – but there was no time to regret what they could not have, because he was tasting her lower lip, sucking on it, drawing it into his hot, wet mouth, and it felt wonderful. She anchored her hands in his glossy hair and returned the favour, then let her tongue slip into him, meeting his. God, it was good. Somehow they knew instinctively how to please each other, fitting together like pieces of a puzzle.

It seemed impossible to be close enough, no matter how she tried. She climbed onto him with clumsy urgency, one knee set on the carriage seat, her thigh pressed to his, her other captured tight between his spread legs. He must have felt that this was a precarious position in a moving vehicle, because his hands released her, but only to slip down her body and anchor themselves on her buttocks, holding her hard and strong against him, pulling her into his body. So good. His legs trapped hers, a most welcome pressure which she returned, gripping him with her thigh muscles. Heat grew at her core, and spiralled through her. She moaned against his mouth and pressed herself closer to him. She wasn't sure how much could be done in a moving carriage in the darkness – her previous experience had all been sadly stationary – but she'd love to find out.

But a loud banging, sudden and shocking, dragged them rudely from their absorption in each other. The carriage was no longer moving. An impatient voice: 'Davies Street, guvnor, like what you asked for!'

'I wish I'd told him to drive to Dover!' he whispered, the breath feathering across her lips and making her shiver.

18

Dominic looked down at Meg as the hackney carriage rattled away, leaving them standing close together on the pavement. The houses just here were silent and shuttered, but people were spilling noisily out of a mansion further up the street; carriages were waiting to meet them, and link boys with flaming torches stood ready to light their way home. Some of them would probably be heading in this direction soon enough. They were a few minutes' walk from Grosvenor Square, and her father's house. No more than that.

That ridiculous hat of hers had come off in the carriage – and no wonder – and she'd almost left it behind, scrambling back inside in a panic to get it as he'd paid the jarvey. She was clutching it now, looking dazed, dishevelled, her lips swollen from his kisses; he didn't suppose he was in much better case. Probably worse, because at the start of this evening, which felt like several months ago, he'd been immaculate; she'd called him a dandy, but in reality he'd been a Corinthian ready to take on the town, while she, however adorable she looked in jacket and breeches, had never been anything remotely close to that.

He couldn't say, in fact, what she might look like to others – a scrubby schoolboy, an urchin, or very obviously and shockingly a beautiful girl in disguise? He was far past telling. All he knew was, he wanted, needed, to pick her up and carry her home with him. When they got there – it was a good twenty-minute walk, probably more if carrying someone, but he felt equal to anything just now – he'd bear her straight up the stairs and take her to his bed. It was a large, comfortable bed, which he'd never before shared with anyone, and perfect for what he had in mind. He wasn't sure if he'd then strip her of jacket, waistcoat, shirt and breeches quickly, in his eagerness, or very, very slowly, to prolong the delicious, forbidden experience, but in either case, they were coming off and staying off. And she was getting in his bed, naked, and staying there, possibly for a couple of weeks. Months.

None of this was truly going to happen, of course. Not now and not ever. He'd walk her home like a gentleman and see her safely inside, and then he'd... go and throw himself in the Serpentine? That should cool him down nicely. Was it deep? Presumably he'd find out.

He had to say something. 'I'm sorry, Meg.' She'd ceased being Miss Nightingale to him some time ago, it seemed. This abrupt apology hardly demonstrated his perfectly polished manners, his icy self-control, but it was a start, he supposed.

'Are you, really?' she said, her voice still warm and intimate. *She* didn't seem to be. He wanted to kiss her again. To eat her up. Perhaps he could kiss her while he was carrying her home. Perhaps she could wrap her legs around his waist...

'No.'

'No? No, you're not sorry after all, or no to something else?'

He sighed raggedly. 'No, I'm not sorry, but I should be. No to... all the crazy ideas in my head. I took advantage of you, I told you quite unforgivably that I wanted to kiss you and you were understandably agitated by all that had occurred...'

'I kissed you first.'

'I know you did, I'm hardly likely to forget it, but that doesn't help at all! I'm trying to take the blame, Meg. As a gentleman must. It shouldn't have happened. And we shouldn't be standing here talking. Drawing attention to ourselves. I dare say I am acquainted with the residents of half these houses, not to mention the people leaving the party, some of whom are about to drive straight past us and get a good look at our faces.'

'You're right.' She set off at a fair pace in the direction of Brook Street, her long legs making short work of the pavement, and he caught up with her. They walked for a while in silence, but it was a silence that hummed with tension. If they hadn't been interrupted, if the carriage journey had been longer because her father had lived in Kensington or Hampstead, where would they be now? He didn't want to dwell on what might have happened next, however wonderful it would have been. It wasn't as though he could, as he should in all honour, offer to marry her to save her reputation. He'd be perfectly happy to do it, if it weren't for the inconvenient fact that he was already bloody well betrothed to her sister.

She said, 'You didn't take advantage of me – I won't let you say that, or even think it. I knew exactly what I was doing.'

'I'm glad to hear it. But I don't think either of us knew what we were doing, or we wouldn't have done it.'

'It felt as though we did.'

He groaned. She was making this much harder than it needed to be, with her damned inconvenient honesty, which he was now obliged to match. He might wish that what had just passed between them had never happened, but he couldn't let her think that he hadn't wanted it. He'd wanted it more than anything he'd ever experienced in his life, and he wasn't prepared to lie about that, least of all to her. 'I know that. I know it felt right. More than right.'

'Necessary.' She said it softly, matter-of-factly, but it pierced through him like a blade. It was so exactly what he felt himself. Trust her to put it into words that shouldn't be uttered. Naming things made them more real, and so much more dangerous. 'It felt necessary.'

He wouldn't admit quite so much to her. What good would it do? 'We've had a difficult few days, we've been forced together, and we spent time in that damned bawdy house, where everyone was looking at us as if we'd gone there together for a purpose quite different from our actual intentions. The whole atmosphere was overheated, you must have felt it. In fact, I know you did. I'm sure that's partly to blame.'

'Did it excite you, then, being in that house with me, having everyone think...?'

'No,' he said again, when he wanted to match her candour and say yes. Yes, I wanted to demand they give us a room we could lock ourselves away in for as long as we both wanted.

'You can admit it, you know. I won't be shocked.' After a moment, 'It excited *me*. It felt wicked, forbidden, and I liked it. If we'd been left alone there...' He groaned at the thought, and at the piercing knowledge that she shared it. It was all too easy to picture what might have happened. His self-control was a fragile thing just now. 'Although it began, I suppose, when you took hold of me and almost kissed me in the park. Or even before that.'

They were back at the mews now, the narrow street as dark and deserted as it had been a few hours ago. Nothing had changed, except that they'd kissed. Would undoubtedly have done much more than kiss, if they'd not been so rudely interrupted. And now they were talking about it. It was thrilling and terrifying in equal measure. He was supposed to be a gentleman of honour. He *was*.

'I've been unsettled ever since I came to London,' she told him, moving a little further ahead, into the deeper shadow. He followed her. Of course he did. He'd follow her anywhere in this seductive darkness. 'I used to have a lover – well, no, that's wrong: I had a sweetheart. We used to meet, and kiss…'

'You climbed out of your window in the moonlight.' He remembered what Jenny had said, and he could easily imagine her doing it. He could imagine her coming to meet him, rather than another. He'd be waiting for her, eager and impatient for her touch. He'd take her in his arms… His imagination was doing a great deal of work tonight.

'You heard and understood what she was saying? I was afraid you had. I did do that. More than once, many times. And I liked it. The adventure, and the kissing and all the rest. It's natural, isn't it? But we've stopped now, he and I. A few months back. He didn't break my heart, nor I his – we just drifted apart, I suppose. I'm sure he'll marry soon, before he's twenty-one; people often do, in the country.'

'You didn't want to marry him?' Though it was none of his business, he could not help but ask.

'It never occurred to me. Maybe it did to him, but he must have realised it would be a mistake. You shouldn't have to marry someone just because you want to kiss them in a barn. Or do a great deal more than kiss them. You need a better reason, or you should.'

'You're a dangerous radical, Meg Nightingale.' It was so intoxicating to talk so intimately with her, here in the warm night. She was intoxicating, that was the truth.

'Do you disagree with me? I wouldn't have thought you

were a hypocrite. I expect you've kissed people, and done much more than kiss them, and yet not married them. I won't believe you, actually, if you tell me you haven't.' He had to laugh – he had no defence against her devastating frankness. She went on matter-of-factly, 'It's not as though my parents' marriage made me want to rush into matrimony with the first man I met, so I could be miserable just like them.'

How could he raise any honest arguments against that? 'You told me theirs was an arranged marriage. Like my parents' was; a family decision, not theirs, such as so many young people were obliged to submit to, twenty or thirty years ago. And that match wasn't particularly happy either, for that matter. Not at the start, and certainly not for long.' There was much more he could have said, but it was not his secret to share.

'So you thought you'd make yourself unhappy with my sister in exactly the same fashion, even though times are changing for the better and arranged marriages are no longer so common. That makes no sense at all.'

'You're right, of course. That was a terrible mistake too. I sleepwalked into it, I thought it didn't signify what I did, because… well, it doesn't signify why. I hope it's not too late to put it right.'

'Dominic…?'

'Yes, Meg?' She hadn't called him by just his Christian name before, while he'd been making free with hers for quite a while, it seemed. Odd that it should matter.

'Why are we still talking? It doesn't seem to be resolving anything, and all the while you could be kissing me. Holding me.'

'In this alleyway?' He took her in his arms, not needing to be told twice, and she relaxed into him with a little sigh.

'Well, there's no barn available. Or private room. The plain truth is, I'm confused, Dominic. I'm worried about Maria, and a little angry with her too – why didn't she write to me, or to Mama? I still don't understand that. I'm beginning to wonder if I ever really knew her, and if others, like Jenny and Lady Primrose, know her much better, because she has allowed them to. I think she must have secrets, when I never kept any from her, however discreditable they might be considered to me, and that hurts. I don't know what's going to happen to any of us. If we can't find her, I wonder if it'll be because she's perfectly safe and well but just doesn't want to be found. A little part of me is thinking she might just be very selfish and careless of others' feelings. And if she does choose to come back, on another whim, what then?'

'I'm not marrying her; I can tell you so much. I know men don't break off engagements, that they can't. Well, I'm breaking this one off, no matter how much scandal it will cause.'

She gave a little hiccup of wild laughter, presumably at the thought of the new horrors his words called up, and rested her head on his shoulder. 'My father might challenge you to a duel! Can you picture him calling you out?'

'I cannot. Your half-brother might, I suppose, if he felt the family's honour was at stake. But no, he wouldn't, not if I explained all the circumstances to him. I've no intention of fighting him, or anybody else – matters are difficult enough as it is. Nobody can be expected to marry someone who runs away from them and hides and sets everyone in an uproar rather than simply talking. I'm not an ogre and I won't be treated as though I am.'

'No, you're not. Of course you aren't. You don't deserve this either. But what I meant to say, Dominic, was that I feel I don't know anything – not where I'll be or even who I'll be, Meg or Maria, by the end of the week – but I do know I want you to kiss me again. For much longer. And I think you want to kiss me too. In fact, I know you do.'

He drew her deeper into the shadows, his hands tight on her waist, and said, 'I'd like to do a great deal more than kiss you. You must be aware of that.'

'Of course I am. I've told you that I'm not entirely inexperienced. But there is no barn, no place we can be private, and perhaps it's just as well. Life is complicated enough right now, don't you agree? To be completely alone with you with no checks on our behaviour but the ones we can manage to put there is more temptation than I need tonight. I don't trust myself to resist you. But I don't believe kissing and taking some comfort from that will make things any worse – do you?'

He pulled her closer still, which was answer enough, and in the darkness their mouths found each other again, and there was no more talking. They held each other tight and lost themselves in each other, for a little while – a precious oblivion. His hands were under her coat, seeking her warm, soft skin and finding it, beneath waistcoat, shirt and chemise, and soon enough they had pushed the fine fabrics aside to cover and caress her breasts. Her nipples were hard buds of desire and she pressed herself into his hands, filling them, urging him on; God, this was so good, so wonderful, and more would be better, more would be everything.

But even as he kissed her and held her, took pleasure and comfort from her warm, responsive body in his arms, and gave pleasure in return, he wasn't sure she was correct in what she said. He feared that every moment he spent with her, every caress he gave her or she gave him, every single smile or confidence they exchanged, drew him deeper into a place of sorry confusion, where his desires and even his hopes warred against what he knew to be right, and what the obligations of a gentleman must be.

Dominic had never considered himself to be a man ruled by sexual desire, certainly not to the extent of losing his senses over a woman; he'd seen others do it often enough, and failed each time to understand what had driven them to it. That was a temptation he'd never known and had, previously, struggled to imagine. A brief, intense infatuation with a bold-eyed young woman of the town when he'd been in his late teens, at Oxford, had been as close as he'd come to making any kind of fool of himself, and really, that had been nothing to speak of; he'd known even when he was enmeshed in it that it was bound to end soon, and not in marriage, despite his youthful posturing. There'd been embarrassing scenes with his parents over the whole business, but it had not been genuine deep feeling on either side, nor anything close to it.

He was experienced enough, but all that experience had been more a matter of physical release and physical sensation – of taking and, he hoped, giving pleasure with a willing partner who did not treat the matter any more seriously than he did. He'd always been careful, had taken no risks with his health, his reputation, or his heart. As a result, he knew he had the reputation in society of being a cold fish with little interest in women. In the past, he'd shrugged when his friends accused him of being heartless – why should he deny it? Excessive emotion was so tedious, and such bad ton, he'd drawled with languid affectation, almost convincing himself that it was true. Some of them had laughed, and some of them had shaken their heads and told him he was sadly mistaken.

He'd never even fancied himself in love, not really, and a part of him had been glad of it, while a smaller, quieter part had been sorry, aware that he was missing something important, unsure what he could do about it. But it was foolish to harbour regrets, he'd told himself. He'd seen men – his own friends among them – take ruinously expensive mistresses and lavish fortunes on them that they didn't have, he'd seen married men run away with other men's wives and wreck the lives of dozens of people, including innocent children. His own father… Sir Thomas had whispered to him once nine years ago, very close to the end of his life, every word a perceptible effort, 'I know you don't understand the choices I've made, Dominic, in the name of love, and perhaps you judge me harshly for them. But you're young. One day you'll know. I pray for your sake, my dear boy, that you will know. Otherwise you won't really be living.' His father was long dead, his dangerous decisions and human inconsistencies buried with him as far as the world knew. How could this belief in overmastering love sit easily with Sir Thomas's wish to arrange a marriage for him? He'd never know now, he supposed, for it was far too late to ask. But for himself, in his father's terms he'd never truly lived in all these years; he'd never lost sleep over a woman, still less been tempted to throw all at hazard for the prospect of a joy he'd never experienced and had been unable even to imagine.

Until now. Now, when he was betrothed to her sister.

19

It was terribly late when Meg crept back into her father's house again, and even then sleep was a long time coming. It was impossible to find rest when so much was uncertain. She was aware that, despite her brave words, her deeper entanglement with Sir Dominic was probably a reckless mistake. It wasn't that she regretted it precisely – she remembered how happy and how safe she had felt in his arms and could not help but smile even as she sighed with frustrated desire and a wicked wish that he could be in her bed with her now – but there was no denying that it made an already tangled situation more complicated. What could possibly come of it? She had no idea, but suspected that the answer was: probably nothing but regret. She fell into an uneasy slumber just before dawn and rose late and heavy-eyed.

Mrs Treadwell told her that her aunt was feeling a little better, and wished to see her. Aunt Greystone was to be found reclining limply on a sofa in her bedchamber, still in her dressing gown, with handkerchief, smelling salts and hartshorn close at hand, in case of emergency, but not currently in use.

Meg was sorry that she had no positive news to give her, apart from the fact that Mrs Greystone's own former maid, Jenny Wood, had been interviewed and was of the strong opinion that Maria must have found shelter with one of her schoolfriends. If Meg allowed her aunt to assume that Jenny was still to be found under Lady Purslake's respectable roof, she thought that was a forgivable deception, considering the alternative of telling the unvarnished truth, which would surely bring on a relapse – more spasms – and do no good to anyone.

Mrs Greystone was excessively grateful for all she was doing to help, which was agreeable, but ended the conversation with a renewed plea to keep the matter from her father at all costs, which was not. Meg might with justice have reminded her that the wedding was now little more than two weeks away, and gone on to reveal Sir Dominic's fixed determination not to go ahead with it even if Maria did reappear – but that too would scarcely be helpful or constructive, she felt. Instead, she shared her intention to visit Lady Primrose that afternoon and talk to her in private, a plan which her aunt approved.

She had a more open and honest conversation with Hannah, who was glad to hear that Jenny was in good health and not under any duress. The old nurse shook her head when Meg told her that it was her opinion that Jenny, far from being an orphan, had grown up in her mother's brothel from childhood, judging by her easy familiarity with the place and its inhabitants, and certainly did not need rescuing from it or from them; possibly, given Jenny's forceful personality, the reverse was true. 'I dare say her letters of recommendation were not as truthful as they should be,' Hannah said, 'which is very bad, I suppose, but she was a good maid and a hard worker, for all that. It's hardly her fault, where and to who she was born, and she has her living to make, same as any poor girl.'

Meg assented whole-heartedly, adding a trifle tartly that she had enough to worry about without concerning herself with such peripheral issues, and that it was her further opinion that what Mrs Greystone didn't know couldn't hurt her. There was no need, surely, to cause her any further upset regarding a matter that could be of no possible significance to her in the greater scheme of things. It was hard to see, she said, how they were all to be extricated from this imbroglio without a great many much more shocking revelations and distressing scenes, in which her poor innocent aunt was almost bound to be involved, and Hannah was obliged to agree.

She armed herself with another of Maria's fashionable muslin gowns and a corded blue and white pelisse to cover it, tied a modish blue silk bonnet with a great many feathers securely over her short curls, and set off resolutely for Lady Primrose's house in her father's carriage. She could only hope that the Duke's daughter would be at home, and willing to see her. It would be a dreadful anticlimax if she were not, obliging her to come home directly.

The Duchess of Fernsby, who was now sadly deceased, had presented her husband with a great many pledges of her affection before expiring, presumably from exhaustion, which could not be wondered at. There were twelve or more Fernsby siblings, Sir Dominic had told her, mostly daughters. Luckily the Duke could not be said to be short of space to accommodate his large family, living as he did in an enormous, decaying family mansion of great antiquity in a most unfashionable part of town hard by the less than fragrant River Thames. It wasn't, in terms of mere distance, so very far from Covent Garden, where she'd been last night.

Meg was admitted to the ancient building without delay, through a sort of turreted gatehouse, and conducted along dusty, damp-smelling corridors to what the butler described to her as the Young Ladies' Parlour. This proved to be a panelled chamber of Tudor date or earlier, which contained to her relief a great deal of rather shabby old furniture but only one young lady at the present moment – Lady Primrose, pretending to leaf through a journal.

The door closed behind her, and the two women regarded each other in silence. Meg had suddenly had more than enough of beating about the bush and said, 'Lady Primrose, I do not wish to be discourteous, but you know perfectly well I'm not Maria. I'm assured by one who knows her well – and clearly better than I do – that you'd have realised that the moment you set eyes on me, even if you don't actually know where my sister is. But I'm hoping you do, and that you'll be so good as to tell me. You're my last hope, in fact, unless I want to go around London revealing my masquerade to every person Maria is even vaguely acquainted with, and probably causing a huge scandal that will ruin her reputation forever.'

Lady Primrose didn't appear to be in the least surprised by this bald statement. 'Of course I knew instantly who you must be. Maria had told me that your aunt was bound to summon you and beg you to take her place, and that you would certainly agree. I was very glad to see, when I met you, that her plan was working to perfection.'

'Has she been staying with you?' Meg asked a little unsteadily. 'I think, if you know so much, she must have been. Is she here now – will you let me see her?'

Lady Primrose had no chance to supply any answer. A section of the worm-eaten linenfold panelling that lined the stuffy little room creaked as it swung open, resolving into a door that had previously been concealed, and behind it – after five long years of painful separation and all the recent fear and anxiety – Maria.

It was so very strange. Meg knew with her conscious mind that Maria must have changed and grown during their years apart, just as she had, and she knew too that they were still identical, or nearly so – similar enough, at any rate, that they could be mistaken for each other by one who did not know them well, or did not care enough to look closely. And yet the face she saw in her thoughts and dreams each night was not the face in the mirror, the face (more or less) she saw before her now, but the thirteen-year-old Maria she'd last seen sobbing piteously, being held and comforted by Hannah Treadwell on the steps of Lord Nightingale's house as they'd been torn apart by their mother's desperate need to claw her way to freedom and their father's intractable refusal to let her take both her beloved children with her.

Meg wasn't conscious of crossing the space between them, but she must have done so in a couple of long strides, because her sister had scarcely moved, but a second later they were embracing, clinging to each other, both weeping copiously. Lady Primrose, without uttering another word, left the room in a more conventional manner and closed the door securely behind her. Meg was only dimly aware of her departure.

'Maria, Maria, where have you been?' she sobbed.

20

'I'm so sorry,' Maria managed at last, when they had both ceased weeping quite so hard and clinging to each other as though they might be torn apart by violence once more. She took off her spectacles and cleaned them rather ineffectually on her handkerchief, then set them aside on a table, smiling anxiously and myopically at her sister. 'I realised – when it was too late to stop it – that I must be causing you, and my aunt, and Hannah, a great deal of anxiety. But then it also struck me that, even if I'd wanted to come back, it was impossible for me simply to reappear at home, since you were taking my place.'

'Mama was most worried too,' Meg said. There was a great deal to untangle in what her sister had said, but she could not help but notice this glaring omission and address it. She feared their mother's actions would always be a bone of contention between them – for the first time it occurred to her that perhaps her father had intended it so when he forced her to make her terrible choice.

'Was she?' There was a hint of bitterness in Maria's voice. 'That will be why she has rushed to London to help you in your search for me. Has she even written to enquire about me since you arrived? I can see the answer in your face: no, she has not. I knew my aunt would summon you, and that you would come immediately – I don't think I ever believed *she* would. And I have been proved right, have I not?'

Meg said defensively, 'Mama is obliged to finish her novel by the agreed date so that she can be paid. We need the money to live, though it is little enough in all conscience. You must know that Father does not... But I don't mean to fall to pulling caps with you, Maria, over Mama or anything else. I'm just so glad that you are safe and well. I've been excessively worried about you; increasingly so as time passed with no word.' This was as close as she meant to come to pointing out that if it was true that Maria could not have reappeared without causing a great bustle, she could, surely, have sent a message quite easily. Just a short letter by an anonymous messenger would have made an enormous difference. She wouldn't have had to reveal her whereabouts, even, merely that she was in good health and under no duress. It would have meant a great deal.

'You're angry with me,' Maria responded instantly, her face troubled, oddly defenceless without her glasses. Meg should have known she couldn't hide any part of her feelings from her twin for long. 'You think I should have told you that I was here, with Primrose, or at least that I was safe.'

'You must have known how concerned I would be. I'm not angry, truly I'm not, though I must admit I have had moments of... exasperation at how hard you had made it to find you. But I don't care, really, and I won't upbraid you. I'm sure you had your reasons.'

Maria took her hand and squeezed it, drawing her to the sofa. 'Let's sit down. We won't be interrupted, and I do owe you an explanation for dragging you into the middle of such confusion and leaving you alone to deal with it. It's true, I know – I could have written to you before I left, even, and explained what I meant to do. Asked for your help.'

'Why didn't you? That's what's hurt me, Marie – the fact that you've been keeping secrets from me, when I have kept none from you. At first I was annoyed with you, and then I began to feel that I must have been a very poor sister all these years, if you believed you could not share...'

'Never that!' Maria said swiftly. 'I promise you, never. I know our father has done his best to drive us apart, and our mother put her own interests above ours – above mine, certainly. But I have never blamed you for any of it. You were as much a victim of their selfishness as I was.'

It was hard to know what to say. 'Mama would tell you that it was more complicated than you will admit; that, however difficult it was for you to live with him, and however much you have believed yourself abandoned by her – she knows you feel that, Marie, and it pains her greatly every day – it would have destroyed her, and done me almost as much harm, to live with him and constantly be at outs with him. You cannot claim she broke up a happy home – you must remember that it was never that, when we all lived together. The endless arguments that you above all of us hated so much. I remember you begging me in tears not to provoke him so, instead to behave meekly, as you did, and I recall too telling you that I did not know any other way to be.'

Her sister sighed deeply and said, 'I do understand, Meggy. I have felt abandoned – that is the perfect word – but just lately I have gained a new perspective on it. It is hard, I suppose, to acknowledge that one's parents are human beings who have their own lives to live. How easy, to arm oneself in self-righteousness and say that they should sacrifice all for their children, and how foolish. We are grown women now, and should know better. I do know better. I could not ask such a sacrifice of her, and more than that, I know she's right to think that you and he could never have rubbed along together in relative peace as he and I have done all these years. It's ironic, really, that it should be so.'

Meg did not have time to ask the meaning of this last rather odd remark, for Maria went on, 'I have so much I need to tell you, and yet here I am, being a coward and putting it off. How did you find me, in the end?'

'We thought we would track down all the servants who have left Lord Nightingale's employ in recent years, and see if any of them might be sheltering you, or at least if they knew something of your whereabouts.' Meg saw her sister's eyebrow quirk at the word 'we', and was aware that she was blushing. Maria must know that she had been spending a great deal of time with Sir Dominic; if nothing else, Lady Primrose would have told her as much. She went on hastily, 'Jenny Wood – you remember her?'

'Oh, Jenny,' said Maria with a little triangular smile and an oddly conscious look, 'of course I do.'

'Well, she ran away from her position in Lord Purslake's house without giving notice, just about the time you disappeared. We thought that the timing of her flight might be a sign that you were together, though it turned out to be nothing more than a freakish coincidence. But we tracked her down to a most extraordinary house in Covent Garden – a brothel, Marie, can you credit it? – and she told us that if anyone would know where you were, it would be Lady Primrose. She said that even if she had appeared to know nothing, I should question her more closely, for she was sure to be in your confidence. So I came to see Lady Primrose, alone, as she suggested. She was my last hope. And Jenny was right.'

Maria showed herself quite willing to be side-tracked, and Meg could not fail to notice it. What could her secret possibly be that made her so very reluctant to reveal it? 'Sir Dominic took you to Jenny's mother's bawdy house, Meg?' she said, her eyebrow quirking once again in the way Meg remembered so well. 'How shocking, and how interesting! I must say, you do appear to have grown excessively close to him in the short time you have been in London. I thought you would have to tell him the truth of your identity, since you could not know whether he had driven me away by some ill-treatment, and you could hardly go on pretending to be me in your interactions with him when you did not know what manner of man he is. But I didn't imagine he'd actually be helping you so actively, least of all taking you to brothels!'

'Don't exaggerate, Marie! You know perfectly well why he went there, and why I had no option but to accompany him. And does all that matter, in any case? You still haven't told me why you ran away, and surely that is more important just now.' Meg had no desire to discuss her feelings for Sir Dominic, and really, they could be of no relevance to the coil, of Maria's own making, that they found themselves in.

'It could matter a great deal. It could be the perfect solution to all our problems, in fact – yours as well as mine – if you think you might like to marry him in my place.'

21

Meg was speechless. 'I might…?'

Maria said urgently, clasping her hand, 'Please hear me out before you fly up into the boughs, Meggy. I must tell you that I wasn't consulted at all in advance about this match my father made for me; I didn't have the least idea that he had any sort of scheme in mind. You know what he's like, so you won't be at all surprised. He didn't even condescend to tell me himself – he informed my aunt, and she, poor thing, was obliged to pass on the news that I was to be married quite soon, to a man of my father's choosing, and one I had never met. She was distressed for me, but she is so greatly in awe of him, and so dependent on him for the necessities of life, that she will never stand against him – I learned long ago that there is no point imagining she will.'

Maria paused for a moment, then went on with a little difficulty, 'Aunt consoled me by pointing out that Sir Dominic is a great catch: one of the most eligible men in London, in fact. I must admit it's true. He is not yet thirty, handsome, and rich, from a good family, has excellent manners, appears to be both intelligent and amiable, and for a wonder there is no breath of scandal attached to his name. How many other young gentlemen in society can claim as much? If he has had mistresses in keeping, which you'd imagine he must have done, he has been admirably discreet about it. Our father might easily have chosen many a worse man than such a paragon of perfection, Aunt said, and even in my shock and anger I could see that this was true. Someone old, like the man they made her marry, someone perhaps diseased, or otherwise highly disagreeable in person or reputation. I do not delude myself that Father cares a button for my wellbeing, since he loves nobody but himself. But still...'

She jumped to her feet and took a restless turn or two about the small, stuffy room. 'I suppose I have always been so conformable to his wishes – or so he has always believed – that it never occurred to my father that I might object or cause the least difficulty. He doesn't care, naturally, what I actually feel about the fact that he has the right to dispose of me, and my fortune as he chooses; I am a woman, and women count for nothing in his eyes. Less than nothing. It's merely that he has a great dislike of confrontation – he would as soon argue with his horse, or a piece of furniture, as with any woman. And you know, Meggy, for a while, I actually thought I could do it. Marry Sir Dominic, with all that that implies. God knows I was eager enough to get out of that dreary house and away from my father.'

Meg said, trying to puzzle her way through this when she could see that there was still so much that she did not understand, 'So you agreed at first.'

'I did. I thought, Well, it will rescue me from my father's control, not to mention his bad temper and selfish indifference to my welfare. It could hardly be any worse than the half-life I was living, and might be better. It was to be an old-fashioned marriage, of course, with no talk of love on either side. Sir Dominic would no doubt leave me in peace to live as I wished, once I had given him the child or children he must need to secure the future of his name. I could promise in good conscience never to present him with a brat fathered by another man, or give any such cause for gossip, and we would go our separate ways, live entirely detached lives, as so many couples do, asking nothing more of each other than public courtesy. A cold-blooded arrangement, but one I thought I might be able to countenance. So yes, I agreed when he came and asked me. On my father's strict orders, my aunt was listening, to make sure I said all I should, and nothing I shouldn't. But Father need not have worried, not then. It was all excessively civilised and barely human.'

'What changed?'

Maria was standing by the small Tudor window, her back to her sister, gazing out through the thick, distorted ancient glass, and Meg saw that her hands were clasping the windowsill so hard that her knuckles stood out white against the old wood. 'I could not bring myself to do it,' she said at last. Her voice was constricted. 'As the day of our wedding grew closer, the reality of it began to bite. They had me ordering up gowns and night-rails, and however discreet they were, my aunt and the shop woman between them, it was clear that they were designed to tempt him, to make him desire me. Dhaka muslin so fine you could see your hand through it, the woman was at pains to tell me. Your hand, indeed! And I realised, as I should have realised before, that I *could not*. I simply could not, however much sense it made. So I panicked and I ran.'

'He is so repulsive to you?'

'He is a man.'

Meg leapt to her feet, feeling sick with distress, and went to her sister's side. 'Oh, my dear, you have been hurt, I had no idea and I am so sorry—'

Maria laughed in what appeared to be genuine amusement. 'I promise you I haven't. He has done nothing to give me a special disgust of him, poor man, and nor has anyone else. I have not been outraged or assaulted or anything of that nature.' She turned and looked Meg in the face and said bravely, 'He is a man, my sweet sister, and I am not made that way. I'm not like you, and I cannot pretend to be.'

Much that had been unclear now made perfect sense to Meg, and she felt a fool for not realising the truth of it before. She ought to have been quicker, because she knew – her mother had made sure she knew and understood – that people did not always find love with the people the Church and the dictates of so-called respectable society told them they should. 'Jenny...' she said slowly.

'Jenny, and half a dozen others, I dare say, when I was at school,' Maria replied with a fine show of carelessness. 'I have been a sad rake, Meggy, a Sapphic rakess, and I fear I have left a trail of broken hearts in my wake, though I have met my match now in Primrose. She... she knows who she is, Meggy! Perhaps you have seen that in her, though your acquaintance has been so brief. She is very strong and good and determined, and I need that strength and goodness. I would be lost without her – I was lost, before, and courting disaster. We love each other, and you are to wish us happy, if you please. We plan to live together, to make a life that suits us both in a house of our own, far from my father and her family, and with your help I believe we can do it.'

'Of course I wish you happy! But why didn't you tell me? Marie, why didn't you?' She put her arms around her sister and hugged her, and after a moment of stiffness Maria relaxed into her embrace, and they held each other in a blessed moment of silent sharing. 'Oh, if you thought I would be disapproving, and that is why you did not tell me, now I really will be angry with you! I promise you, I am not so censorious. Whatever you think of Mama, do her the justice of believing that she would have never brought me up to believe in the conventional morality that has caused her – and us – such unhappiness. You must remember that about her, surely!'

'I didn't think you'd be disapproving, but I... I meant to tell you a hundred times, I began to write the words, but when it came to it, I could not set them down on paper. If I had been able to see you, to tell you in person, it would have been different. Of course I remember Mama's views, and her writer friend Miss Spry, who has lived with Lady Louisa Pendlebury for so long. But this is *me*, not some stranger. *My* life. Meggy, I think when I began to enjoy myself with girls, at school, I decided to say nothing of it because... Because if I didn't actually have to explain it to you, I could choose to think it was mere trifling that had no greater significance. For some of them, probably most, it was nothing more than that. An interlude, a safe way to gain pleasure and release without putting oneself in danger.'

'I can understand that,' said Meg, thinking of Will.

Maria smiled wryly. 'I thought you might. But as time went on, I realised it was much more than that for me. That it is nothing more or less than the way I am made, and cannot be changed. I suppose it had not truly occurred to me that grown women outside school might live their lives that way, or at least try to. I should have known that, I had reason to, but somehow I could not apply it to myself and to my own future, until I was obliged to face it at last. With Jenny – it was so exciting! We had been flirting for months, little stolen glances, caresses as if by accident, her hand brushing my neck, or straying a little as she laced my gown for me. The night she first came to me in my chamber, my God... We took so many risks, if we hadn't been living with such imperceptive people as my aunt and my father, we would have been found out a dozen times. I felt so alive, and I knew I wasn't just passing the time before some man came along.

'And then Primrose... We had been no closer than friends at school – she had seen what mischief I was about, and wanted no part of it. But at last she declared herself, and gave me an ultimatum: I could sport with half the girls in London, or I could have her, but not both. I had thought, and so did she for a while, that marrying Sir Dominic might be the answer to our problems, if I could only be patient and endure it. Perhaps one day, in a couple of years, she could have come to live with me as my friend and companion, and nobody would have cared or thought it in the least odd. But I realised in the end that it was not possible, that I could not endure to live a lie till then, with all the disagreeable intimacy that it would entail, and naturally she could not wish me to do violence to my feelings. I would not ask such a thing of her if our situation was reversed.'

'Jenny was jealous of Primrose as you grew closer,' Meg realised among all this tangle of emotion.

'Yes, that's why she left my aunt's employment. And I think perhaps Lady Purslake...'

'Goodness.'

'But perhaps not, since she has left there too. I don't know. But in any case, I realised I could not marry Sir Dominic, and Primrose and I are determined to find a way to be together without having to wait in suspense and uncertainty for years. What if I did not give him an heir, what if I could not have a child at all? It was too bad to be thought of. And there is my fortune, left to me and not to my father, if only I can lay my hands on it and use it.'

'I quite see why you cannot marry Dominic, and I will do all I can to help you, but to take your place, that is quite another matter, Marie! What about *my* feelings?'

'Really? So you are telling me now, Meg Nightingale, that you do not care one whit for Sir Dominic, though I notice he is simply Dominic to you already, as he never was to me? You have only been in London a few short days, and yet you have become so shockingly and so swiftly intimate with him! I must say, I am delighted to hear it.'

Meg was blushing furiously again. 'I have not the least notion how you can claim to know whether I do or I do not care for him, or speak of intimacy. Even if I did... did like him, you cannot have known that I would when you conceived this crazy scheme! And yet you talk of me taking your place with such breathtaking ease! I do not mean to be unsympathetic, but you do take a good deal for granted!'

'Meg, perhaps I do, but it is not so mad as it sounds. I knew – for you had told me so often in your letters – that you dream of a life outside of Mama's house, and I cannot wonder at it. You want to travel the world, have adventures, meet interesting people, and write about it all. Have people read what you have written. But you will never be able to do most of those things as long as you stay in Somerset. You no longer spend time with Will, which I must say is just as well, but you will never become acquainted with anyone you would care to marry, living in that tiny village and seeing the same dull people year in, year out. What is to become of you? I thought if my aunt brought you to London, if you took my place, at least you would have a chance to look about you and perhaps, just perhaps, you might see the sense of a match with Sir Dominic.'

Seeing that her twin was gazing at her in mute astonishment, Maria went on persuasively, 'All the excellent reasons my aunt evinced for me to marry him do not apply to me, and you now understand why, but Meg, they *do* apply to you! I realised as soon as I made his acquaintance, and you must see that I was right!'

As her sister still made no response, but only stared, a frown creasing her brows, Maria continued, 'Is he not all the things I said – handsome, rich, eligible, intelligent and amiable? Is he not even – though I was in no mood to appreciate it – amusing? For I know you set great store by that.'

Meg said faintly, 'Yes, he is all those things.' And so much more, she thought but did not say.

'I could not know, of course, that you would be attracted to him, but I confess I hoped you would be, and now I see by your blushes that my plan has worked much better than I could ever have dreamed, and that you are strongly drawn to him! And he to you, I would wager.' Seeing her sister's embarrassed face, Maria asked gleefully, 'Have you kissed him? Oh! I see you have wasted no time, you wicked jade, and that you have! Well, then. I make you a present of him, and all you have to do is thank me politely and say you will take him, and we may all be comfortable. How excessively well it has all worked out, even better than I could have hoped! Primrose will be delighted; I cannot wait to tell her!'

Meg spluttered, '"Thank you politely!" You can't just... just pass me a man as though he were a parcel of cheap muslin or a pair of gloves that's been misdirected and say, "Take him, for I don't want him!" He must be supposed to have some say in the matter!'

Her sister shrugged and replied ruthlessly, 'He was content enough to marry me, when we scarcely knew each other and there was not a spark of interest between us. If you and he like each other, which I well perceive you do, why should he not marry you instead? He needs an heir, of course, which was my great concern, and if you are to tell me that the getting of one with him would be a grievous hardship to you, as it must have been to me, I must say that I shall not believe you! Why, I daresay you are halfway there already.'

'Maria Nightingale, we are not!'

'But you very easily could be. Come now, would this not be a great deal better than sneaking around in draughty barns with a farmer who – at best – would tie you to the village forever and have you spend your precious life in labour for which you are excessively ill suited? Sir Dominic will ask no such sacrifice of you! And take it from me, Meg, swiving is much, much more comfortable and enjoyable when performed in a bed, at leisure, without an audience of farm animals! You will be a lady of great consequence in the world besides, if you care for that, you will be able to do all the things that you have been dreaming of and more; you will even have time to write, without the disagreeable necessity of making a living by it, which you have so often told me is almost impossible. I have had very little proper conversation with him, it is true, but I know he does not in the least disapprove of women writing, for he told me so once. He spoke with genuine admiration of Madame D'Arblay and her works – said she was a good friend of his father's. For your purposes, I consider him close to perfect. All you have to do is decide forever more to be me, and I will be you. What could be simpler?'

Meg found her voice at last in the face of all this torrent of persuasion. 'I had understood that you wanted me to marry Sir Dominic instead of you. I didn't realise that you actually wanted me to... to take on your identity, and for you to take on mine!'

'But of course! It makes perfect sense, and nothing else would serve half as well,' Maria said with terrifying casualness. 'I am the elder daughter, and heir to our grandmother's fortune; you are not. I have made my come-out in society; you have not. Nobody knows you, and therefore not a single soul will ever notice you are not me. If Maria Nightingale marries Sir Dominic De Lacy, everyone will be delighted. Nobody will care if soon afterwards humble and impoverished Meg Nightingale goes off to live quietly in the country as Lady Primrose's companion. I will share my fortune with you, which indeed is what should justly have happened to it in the first place, and we shall be happy and free of both our parents. What could be easier? It is quite our father's own fault, for giving us these ridiculous names, which I dare say is what put the idea in my head. When you are married, all you need to say in church is "I, Maria Margaret" instead of "I, Margaret Maria". If you stumbled over the words, even, and said your own name, I dare say nobody would notice. You must admit, it is an excellent scheme!'

It was a highly alarming scheme, and all the more so because Meg could see that Maria was right – it could so very easily work. They *were* all but identical still, and she, as the second, poorer daughter, was much more obscure as far as the world was concerned. There ought, she thought, to be many, many rational objections she could raise, and the fact that she could not at the moment think of any more than one scared her more than all the rest.

'It would be living a lie,' she said unsteadily. 'Asking Dominic to live a lie too, for that matter. Deceiving his family, his friends…'

Maria smiled a little sadly at her words. 'Well, you see, I have been doing that for a while, and must do so for the rest of my life, even if Primrose and I do contrive to be together, so perhaps it does not seem at all out of the way for me. Tell me truly, *is* the idea of marrying Sir Dominic displeasing to you? For despite all my joking and my strong desire to persuade you, I can quite see that if it is, I cannot be so selfish as to ask you to do it. You might wish to kiss him, and do a great deal more, he could be ideal for you on paper, and still you might have no desire to marry him and live with him for the rest of your life and have his children, I quite see that.'

'No,' Meg said after a moment. 'No, I cannot say in all honesty that it is displeasing. I am attracted to him, and yes, he is attracted to me, even though we have known each other for such a short time. It would be idle to deny it. And although your scheme seems crazy – is crazy – I can see that it could work, and nobody would ever be any the wiser. But quite apart from anything else, I have not the least reason to think that he would agree to it. Why in heaven's name should he?'

'Why don't you ask him?'

22

Eventually, Meg was obliged to return home – or to her father's house, which was after all not her home and had not been for five years. She had no desire to go back, but she was afraid that if she lingered too long she would be missed, by her aunt and by Hannah, if by no one else. Even more than that, she feared that if she didn't pluck up the courage to tell Sir Dominic all she had discovered soon, she never would, and yet obviously she must, and without delay. She could see that the Duke's household operated along such casual, ramshackle lines that another young lady residing there would make not a bit of difference to anybody but the overburdened servants, and to stay with Maria after their long, cruel separation was tempting – but she could not.

Her sister had given her permission to reveal her secret to Sir Dominic, since Meg herself was adamant that he could and must be trusted, but to nobody else, so the interview with her aunt that she was obliged to have when she returned to Grosvenor Square inevitably held some difficulties. Mrs Greystone was greatly relieved to hear that Maria was safe and well, but she still could not understand why she had fled, and was much inclined to call up the Nightingale carriage, go instantly to the ducal mansion and beg her, on bended knee if necessary, to return and continue with her interrupted engagement. Meg, she said, could not possibly have been persuasive enough in the representations she had made to her twin. Had she cried? Mrs Greystone engaged herself to cry a great deal, and otherwise exert every possible pressure on one who had – before this curious new start of hers – always been excessively biddable. Meg answered truthfully that she had indeed cried, and that Maria remained fixed in her determination not to marry Sir Dominic nonetheless.

She did not currently feel equal to revealing Maria's rather startling solution to the problems they faced, fearing that her aunt would embrace it with enthusiasm and urge her to go through with it without complaint. So when that lady commenced wringing her hands and saying rather wildly that she had no idea what was to become of them all, Meg could only sigh in sympathy and leave Mrs Greystone alone to bathe her forehead in lavender water and lament the selfishness and wilfulness of modern youth in the shape of Miss Maria Nightingale. Did anybody imagine, she wailed, that she, Susan Nightingale, had actually wanted to marry Mr Greystone, who had been quite thirty years her senior and had resembled nothing so much as a creature that resided under a damp rock? No, she had not, but she had obeyed her parents! The fact that he had quite providentially died five years later was immaterial. And Sir Dominic, by contrast, was young, charming and *handsome*!

Meg would very much have liked to lock herself in her chamber and seek temporary relief in breaking things and stamping on them, but instead she sent Hannah to Sir Dominic with a letter asking for an urgent meeting, expressing herself in such emphatic terms that she was unsurprised to see his high-perch phaeton at the door a short while later. She was ready and waiting in a smart green pelisse and bonnet – it was astonishing how much of her time currently was spent dressing very finely in order to have extremely awkward conversations – and greeted him in a rather subdued fashion once she was handed up to sit beside him. 'I collect,' he said, looking down at her with a frown between his strongly marked brows, 'that your mission was unsuccessful, since you appear somewhat downcast.'

Meg darted a glance at the impassive groom who stood perched behind them. 'Oh, no,' she responded. 'I've found her. She was... where we suspected she might be. But I promise you, sir, we really can't discuss the matter while you're driving.'

It seemed to her that his careless response cost him some effort. 'You dare to doubt my skill, Miss Nightingale?' he said with forced lightness, avoiding a heavy dray wagon by a matter of inches as he spoke, as if to prove her wrong.

'I doubt anybody's skill to hear what I have to tell you without making some involuntary reaction to it,' she said frankly. 'I'd rather not test your prowess so severely this afternoon, if you don't mind. I've had a very trying day already and I am in no mood to be overset. And also, we really do need to be private for this particular discussion.'

'In that case, I believe there is a tree in the park with our names upon it,' he replied with a wry little smile, and after that he said no more until they were alone, concentrating upon his driving for the next few minutes and leaving her prey to a conflicting turmoil of emotions. Telling him the first part would be hard enough, though she could not predict his reaction – but the rest of it... It would be so much easier if she were clear in her own mind as to exactly what she wanted.

Fishwick took the ribbons with his usual impassivity and drove away, leaving them to stroll for a few moments in silence, an electric awareness humming between them. It was a fine late afternoon and the park was busy enough, but they avoided the most frequented areas and Meg, her hand on Sir Dominic's arm, had the odd sense once more that they inhabited a little bubble of their own. Last night, they'd kissed, caressed – her body still tingled at the thought. Could it all really be as easy as Maria asserted? The idea of marrying Sir Dominic herself was so unexpected and so extraordinary that she had not yet begun to take the measure of it. She said abruptly, 'Maria is quite safe, and always has been. She has been with Lady Primrose all this while.'

'And yet that lady told us nothing when we encountered her, and gave not the least sign that she realised who you were. She must have known that you were deeply anxious – frantic – about your sister's disappearance and her wellbeing. Did she also know that I was aware of the substitution? I think she must have done. That is all... most curious.'

'Maria had strictly enjoined her not to reveal anything to us, but merely to observe us and report back.'

'Even more curious. You saw your sister?'

Meg smiled rather mistily. Whatever she might regret, however confused and uncertain she was, at least she could never regret the reunion with one she had missed so badly for so long. The pain of their separation had been like being torn in two, and now they were whole again, despite all their problems. 'I spent several hours with her, talking. She admitted me fully into her confidence at last. And I have persuaded her that I must be allowed to share her secret with you. She could see that, after the way she has treated you – though indeed she could not help it – you are owed an explanation.'

'And yet you hesitate to give it,' he noted with brittle courtesy. 'Please, I beg you, go on. If you fear to wound my self-esteem, you should not. Once I apprehended that a young woman has found the prospect of matrimony with me so hideous that she flees her home to avoid it, all further considerations of *amour propre* must be foolish self-indulgence.'

Meg stopped and turned to face him. This anxiety at least she could remove. 'It's nothing to do with you, nor anything you have done or said. Nothing at all, I promise. Not even a lack of trust in you, or not precisely. Her heart was not free to give to you, and if she could not give that…'

'Your sister does love another man, then, though she has not gone so far as to elope with him?' She could not tell from his voice whether he was glad or sorry at the thought. They were standing quite close together, the sounds of the park having receded to a distant hum in the intensity of their conversation, but in this moment his face was shuttered and she could not read him. She feared what he might say when he knew the truth. Perhaps she feared above all being sadly disappointed in him, if he reacted badly. Few people had had her unconventional upbringing, she must remember. But still she had no option but to tell him.

She took a deep breath, and said very low, though in truth there was not the least danger of their being overheard, 'She loves another, Dominic, yes. Someone she wishes to spend her life with. But not a man. Gretna Green offers her no sort of solution to her predicament.'

He was silent for a moment, but his voice was surprisingly calm and level when he answered her. 'Ah. I see.' And then, 'Is it Lady Primrose?' Whatever he was feeling in reaction to this most unexpected news, at least he did not appear to be angry or disgusted, which was a huge relief. If she had put him on a pedestal, he had not fallen from it yet.

'Yes. They hope – their plan is to set up house together, far from town, like the Ladies of Llangollen.'

'She didn't think to tell you all this before? To write to you?' Now an edge of exasperation did enter his tone.

'I asked her that, of course. She said she tried, but could not bring herself to set down the words on paper. There was so much of her life that she had not shared with me, so many important things, she simply did not know where to begin. You can surely see how hard it has been for her.'

He sighed. 'I suppose I can. And that girl last night – Jenny…'

'Yes,' she said again. 'This is no sudden start or moment of madness. It is her life, her true nature. I think you must understand, therefore, why Maria accepted your offer at first, and why she realised she could not go through with it after all.'

He seemed reflective, and perhaps a little sad. 'It is all much clearer now. Indeed it is. And I cannot be surprised that she did not feel able to tell me, of all people. Such a dangerous secret is no small matter to entrust to another person, and that a virtual stranger. I must consider that it is very much for the best, for both of us, that this marriage does not happen, even supposing I had never set eyes on you, my dear Meg.'

'It would have made you both deeply miserable, whatever else happened. I do not see how it could have been otherwise.'

'It would,' he acknowledged. 'And more than just the two of us, I'm sure. Do not think for a moment that I am not sympathetic to her situation. But what was she about, leaving you to pick up the pieces without a word? I presume she foresaw that your aunt would call on you and that you would find yourself obliged to take her place? She planned all this, in short?'

'She did.' There was no point trying to deny it.

'With what possible object in mind? Surely not just pure mischief and a selfish disregard for others?'

There was no dodging it. 'Not that. She hopes that I will take her place. That was her object, in fact, in ensuring that I came here and met you, and all the rest. She wanted to... to force us into proximity, even intimacy, I suppose.' She did not say, she thinks you perfect for me, and I for you; she could not put him the position of feeling obliged to say yes, or insulting her and saying no, or...

'She did all this in the hope that you would marry me?' His voice was very low and intimate, and she shivered, remembering last night. So tempting, so dangerous, to give in to the undeniable attraction that flared between them...

'More than that. Much more than that, Dominic. She wants me to become Maria, and she will become Meg. An exchange of identities, unknown to anyone but those closest to us. She offers to split her fortune with me, so that she can live as she pleases with Lady Primrose, since nobody will care what the apparently penniless younger daughter does. She thinks that if you were happy enough to marry her without knowing her, it can make no matter to you if you marry me instead.'

'"It can make no matter..."? That's crazy.'

'Is it? I don't know,' Meg said dully. 'I feel I've lost the ability to judge. My head is simply whirling, and although it was my hope that a little time would allow me to make sense of it all, I cannot say that I feel any clearer in my mind than I did when I left the Duke's house.'

Sir Dominic reached out and clasped Meg's hand. 'I would have you understand me properly,' he murmured, his voice low and intense. '*My* mind is clear, and has been for a while, despite the coil in which we find ourselves. The idea of marrying you instead of your sister is not at all crazy. On the contrary – it has taken possession of my mind and my heart, these last few days. It began that first evening I met you, and has grown stronger every day since. A fierce conviction that I have been offered a chance of happiness, beyond hope or expectation, that I would be very foolish to let slip from my grasp. For the first time in my life, I know what I want, and it is you. Will you marry me, Meg Nightingale?'

23

'Dominic...' He was gazing at her so very warmly, he was standing so close. They were back under the shelter of a tree again, this one a huge old weeping willow, the branches with their fresh green leaves sweeping close to the ground and offering almost total concealment. They were as alone as they well could be in such a public place. It was extremely tempting to move closer yet, into his embrace, and rest her head on his shoulder for a moment, to gain strength from the sensation of his arms about her, and then, then to raise her head and lose herself in kissing him, and ignore the confusion of feeling that was raging inside her. But he would take that as tacit acceptance, of course he would, and she must not. She must resist, and more than that she must make him understand.

'Yes, Meg?' Anticipation and anxiety were warring on his face, along with the ever-present desire that mirrored her own. She knew he wanted her, but she was deeply unsure if that could be enough.

She continued with an effort, 'I don't think you can properly have understood me, and indeed I cannot wonder that you have not. It's not merely – merely! – a matter of you marrying me, me marrying you. Maria's plan is that I take her place, and she takes mine. Forever, Dominic. She proposes that the wedding continues, just as it was planned, and that I stand beside you in church and lie before everyone and say that I am Maria Margaret as I become your wife.'

He said slowly, 'I had realised that that was what she meant, but she cannot be serious in suggesting such an outlandish scheme, nor you in contemplating going through with it. I know you are her sister, and would do a great deal to help her, but to ask that of you…'

'I said as much,' she told him. 'I said that it would be living a lie – for the rest of my days! – and asking you to do the same. Deceiving your family and your friends and, if you care for such a thing, lying in church, too.'

'What did she say?'

'She said that she had been living a lie for years, and must always do so; that she was, therefore, not asking me to do anything for her sake that she would not have to do herself. That if I would lose my identity forever, she would lose hers too. Dominic, I am in such a sad state of turmoil, I do not know what to think!'

'Meg, my dear, you realise, of course, setting aside all other considerations for a moment, that if you and I agreed to this plan of hers, we would never be legally married? If anyone should discover the imposture, or if she herself should change her mind and want to be Maria again, even if it were years later…'

'I cannot think she would ever do so, but it's quite true, the consequences if we were to be found out would be quite terrible.'

'For us, and even more so for our children, who could never

be legitimate. It is no light matter, to commit oneself to such a dangerous deception, and I still do not understand why she thinks it necessary. Do you?'

'I'm afraid I do; that is the worst of it. I have had a little time to think of it, where you have not, and I discussed it with her at great length once she had told me all. She needs at least some part of her fortune, to make her plan possible, since Lady Primrose is sadly impoverished. And she is sure that if we told the truth, or some manufactured version of the truth – said perhaps that you and I had met each other and realised that we liked each other better – my father would be so angry at being made a fool of, as he would see it, that he would make sure to deprive her of his mother's legacy, at the very least, and cause a great scandal besides. I cannot doubt that she is right in believing so. And if he found out about Lady Primrose, about what they are to each other, he could make their lives impossible, even dangerous. He could have her locked away, perhaps, in an asylum, Dominic, if he cared to be so bitter and vengeful. Who could prevent him? I could not, nor could Mama, in sober truth, and I do not think you could either. You would have no standing in the matter. Would we not all be entirely powerless? She is not of age, we are both three long years away from being so, and he is her father, her guardian, and a peer of the realm. He would have the full weight of the law on his side, and public opinion too, I dare say.'

He was frowning now, his face grim. 'You truly think him capable of such villainy towards his own child?'

'I do not know him well enough to be sure of it, but Maria does, and she must be the best judge of what he will or will not do. You can see why I am so very uneasy in my mind!'

'I can. I had not realised the full difficulty of her position, and of ours.' He broke off for a moment, frowning; his eyes were on her face, but she wasn't sure if he was really seeing her.

At length he said, 'I can also see now that it would be very wrong in me – unconscionable, in fact – to press my suit at such a time. What I want above all things to do, but must not yet, is ask you if you would accept me, if only we could resolve these matters so that your sister stands in no danger and is able to live her life as she pleases; if such a perilous scheme somehow became unnecessary, and you could choose freely.'

She looked up at him. His words kindled a warm glow within her, but she should not allow herself to be melted by it. 'Dominic, I can't say... don't ask me to. I cannot put all this trouble out of my mind for long enough even to consider such a question. I am aware that we are in such a bind that it paralyses all thought, and furthermore the nature of our acquaintance has been so very short, and so peculiar...'

'I know it,' he said, smiling reassuringly. He took her hand and pressed it, and she squeezed back gratefully. 'It has only been a few days, has it not, and now this fresh start? Forgive me – I should not even have mentioned it, since to mention it is to assert it and to urge it upon you.'

She shook her head. 'There is nothing to forgive. You have had a great deal to bear, and now this. What shall we do? I cannot puzzle it out now – my head is spinning so – but in the meantime, is there anything to be done? Oh, how I wish my mama was here to advise me. She is so wise, and it seems to me that we have great need of wisdom.'

'Should we summon her – or, better yet, since such matters cannot safely be set down on paper, shall I go and fetch her? It would be a matter of two days only that I would have to leave you, I dare say, or just a little more.'

'It is kind of you to offer, but I do not think we should. She still has her book to write – the urgency of making a living does not, unfortunately, go away just because of the extraordinary difficulties we find ourselves in. And I must think it weak in me not to try harder to find a solution for myself.'

'For ourselves,' he said. 'You are not alone in this, my dear. And I think, you know, now that you have put the matter in my mind, I must speak to my own mother. Not seek her advice, necessarily, but certainly to tell her.' He saw that her face was clouded with yet more anxiety and said gently, 'I would not dream of sharing your sister's secret, I promise you. I would not tell her *why* your masquerade has been necessary. But even if we should in the end decide to go through with this lifelong imposture – and my mind misgives me greatly over all the serious implications of it – I cannot countenance deceiving her in this fashion. Not forever. I have not always been entirely honest with her, our relationship has not been the easiest, and I do not wish to create further barriers between us now. I must believe your sister does not ask that of us – I'm sure, for one thing, she would not expect you to attempt to hoodwink your own mother in such a way.'

She sighed in agreement. 'No, even if it were possible, which even Maria must admit it is not. Mama would never be deceived for as much as a second, and I would never think to attempt it. She has not deserved such treatment from me. Having said that of my mama, how can I ask such a deception of you, towards yours? It would be beyond cruel and unfair.'

'Thank you! I will go and see my mother directly – there is no sense in delaying. And we should leave this place, in any case. Have you some engagement tonight?'

'I expect so, but I am not going, even if my aunt feels well enough to accompany me, which I doubt she will. She knows that Maria is safe now, but nothing more, and so she is most distressed at her refusal to return and set all to rights, as she sees it. I will plead the headache, should it be needed. Indeed, I am almost sure I feel one coming on.'

'I'm not surprised. I am conscious of a great sense of oppression myself. I'm sure you will be the better for some rest. Shall I call for you tomorrow, early – shall we ride together? Perhaps things will seem clearer in the morning once we have both slept.'

They agreed that they would meet again the next day, and Sir Dominic escorted her home, kissing her hand as he left her and giving her a very speaking look. She smiled tremulously at him and hurried to seek the sanctuary of her chamber. Unfastening her pelisse and throwing off her bonnet and half-boots, she flung herself onto Maria's bed and gazed unseeingly at the faded silken canopy above her.

Her head was pounding in earnest now; there would be no need to feign a headache. Rack her heated brains as she might, she had no idea what in the world they should do. Could it really be true that there were only two options open to them: to commit themselves utterly to a lifetime's deception and a sham marriage, or to reveal some version of the truth and thus betray her sister, with all the grave consequences that might bring? If there was a solution for this riddle – and her mama had brought her up to believe that there was always an answer to be found for any problem, if only one applied one's sense and intelligence to the matter – she could not imagine what it might be. She groaned, and rolled over to bury her face in the soft pillow and seek the blessed oblivion of sleep.

24

Dominic, meanwhile, made his way to Clarges Street, and was fortunate enough to find his widowed parent at home. She was delighted to see him, and not in the least surprised when he rather firmly requested a private interview, without the awkward presence of poor Cousin Sarah. He was fond of his cousin, and grateful for her unstinting devotion to his mother, but in these highly unusual circumstances they would do much better without her. That lady was quite sure they must have private matters to discuss – she would not think of intruding on the sacred filial bond – not the least need in the world to beg her pardon – so kind and considerate always to one who scarcely merited or expected such attention – and thus gently twittered herself out of the room.

'I trust Miss Nightingale is well?' Lady De Lacy said as the door closed, smiling fondly at her only child. 'Does she require my chaperonage once more this evening? You know I am only too happy to oblige her in any way – so soon she will be a member of our family, and I am sure I could not be fonder of her if she were my own daughter.'

'Mama,' he replied, his face serious, 'there is no easy way to tell you this, so I beg that you will hear me out while I explain. I am afraid what I have to tell you will be a great shock, but I have no choice but to share it. Since our engagement party, the young lady you have assumed – quite naturally – to be Miss Nightingale has in fact been her younger sister, Margaret. Meg.'

'Dominic, do not tease me so, I beg! I don't have the least idea what you're saying to me,' his mother said, her expression blank, only the restless movement of her thin hands betraying the extent of her agitation.

'Miss Nightingale found herself unable to face the prospect of marrying me.' Here he was saying it again for what seemed like the hundredth time in the last few days, but now he knew the reason it did not sting any longer. 'It does not matter why. She ran away, in fact, and Mrs Greystone summoned Miss Maria's sister – you will recall that they are identical twins – and induced her to take her place, to assume her identity. In case you should judge either of them harshly, I should tell you, if you do not know it already, that Mrs Greystone is quite in awe of her brother, frightened of him, in fact, and would do almost anything to avoid incurring his wrath.'

'And you... you have known this for how long, Dominic?' His mother's voice was rising, both in volume and in sharpness.

'Since that night of the engagement party,' he said a touch wearily. 'Miss Margaret revealed her identity to me immediately. She thought, unsurprisingly, that her sister's flight might be laid at my door, through some ill-treatment or discourtesy that I had offered her after our betrothal. Miss Margaret challenged me, in fact, to explain myself. I was able to convince her that she was quite wrong in her supposition, and we have been busying ourselves in trying to discover Miss Nightingale's whereabouts ever since. There is no point going into detail, but

I think you must be able to see that, whatever happens, my marriage with Miss Maria cannot now go ahead.' He drew a breath, glad to have the matter off his chest, and considered how best to convey some part of Maria's plan and their qualms about it, but he was not to have the opportunity to do so.

'Cannot go ahead?' his mother repeated shrilly. 'Cannot? Dominic, it must!'

'Ma'am, I know you have become greatly enamoured of the idea, but you must see how impossible it is, that I should marry one so reluctant. Even if she could be forced to accept me by some disagreeable form of pressure to which I could never consent, my own feelings would not allow me to continue, knowing her extreme dislike of the match. If you are concerned that there will be a scandal—'

'My God!' she burst out furiously, much to his astonishment. 'There will be a scandal on a scale you cannot imagine! We will be ruined!'

'I cannot think that matters are so very serious, ma'am. There may be a little gossip when it is known that she has cried off, but it will surely soon pass over, as such things always do.'

'Dominic,' she said heavily, her face pale and set, 'I see that I must tell you all. There are machinations of which you are ignorant, but I fear the time for concealment is long past. My dear son, much as it pains me to say so, I too have been deceiving you. This marriage, which I presented to you as your father's fondest wish, was in fact nothing of the kind!' She paused, as if to see the effect her dramatic words had on him.

He was silent for a moment, his thoughts shifting and falling into place. 'I had wondered...' he said slowly at last. 'It seemed so unlike Papa, to make a plan, and such a plan, behind my back. I have been struggling to reconcile the idea with my knowledge of him; it has given me sleepless hours. But good

God, whyever would you say such a thing? I cannot think it right of you, ma'am, to deceive me so! Were you so desperate to bend me to your will that you must lie to me, on such a subject?'

She blenched, and said tragically, 'It was a ruse. I admit it gave me grave qualms to practise on you so, Dominic. You are not the only one who has had sleepless nights over this, I promise you! But I dare say you still cannot possibly suspect why I should have taken such a grave step, my poor ignorant child?'

Dominic could not doubt the genuineness of her emotions, but as always the manner in which she chose to express them put him so greatly in mind of Mrs Siddons in one of her less successful roles that he struggled to be sympathetic. 'Clearly not just because you have a great fondness for getting your own way, which I might otherwise have suspected,' he responded with a little pardonable asperity. 'I am sorry to be excessively brusque, ma'am, but really, we are in such a sad coil, I wish that you would cut line and tell me what precisely it is that you mean, and lay off these Drury Lane airs while you do so.' When his mother made no response but rather looked at him with an oddly shame-faced expression, he felt sorry for her despite his irritation, and said more gently, 'It cannot be so very bad. Tell me, and we will find a way through it together.'

She looked at him in silence for a moment longer, and then said baldly, as if exhausted, 'Very well. I am being blackmailed.'

25

It was the last thing he had expected to hear. 'Blackmailed,' he repeated, unsure if he had heard her correctly, or if she was still indulging in her fondness for exaggeration.

'By Lord Nightingale,' she said. Now that she had cast off the theatrical mannerisms that had always irritated him so, he could see that she was genuinely frightened.

'I don't understand. You can have done nothing...'

'Oh, indeed not!' Lady De Lacy spat out. 'I have done nothing, and nor, my dear son, have you. But we would be the ones who would be made to suffer for it.'

He was silent for a moment, at a loss, then a sudden burst of unwelcome illumination struck him. 'My father,' he said. It was not a question; it was all becoming clear to him now.

'Your father,' she agreed with deep and abiding bitterness. 'Using his precious charity, his great reputation for philanthropy, as a cover to meet that shameless woman, to live with her, to make a fool of me!'

There was no point, Dominic knew, in attempting to defend

Angela Jones, his father's long-term lover, to his mother – it would be cruel as well as useless. There was little point, for that matter, in attempting to convince her that Sir Thomas's charitable impulses had been genuine, whatever consequences had sprung from them. He and Angela between them had saved dozens, perhaps hundreds of children from the dirty and dangerous streets of London, and made life a little easier for many more they could not save. But if Lady De Lacy had ever given a fig for any of that, she did not now. 'I didn't know you knew,' he said gently. 'I had thought it could be kept from you, so that the knowledge would not hurt you. Whatever else you believe of my father, however justified your anger with him might be, please do believe that he never set out deliberately to wound you.'

'He may not have intended to, but still he did it. I always knew,' she whispered, her voice vibrating with pain and anger. 'Always. I knew where he was going when he left me alone, time after time. And I knew about the child.'

Dominic passed his hand over his face for a moment, then rose from his seat and went to take his mother's hand. 'I'm sorry, Mama,' he said. 'I truly am.'

She clung to him with a pressure that was almost painful. 'He had to drag you into it too,' she went on, 'and for that I really never will forgive him.'

'I swear I didn't know while he was alive,' he said steadily.

'You played with her. His shameful brat. Your half-sister!'

'I did,' he acknowledged, 'when he took me to the house. I became fond of her, it's idle to deny it. Our ages being such, just three years between us...' Best not to go there, perhaps. Certainly best not to say her name. 'But I did not know who she was, I promise you, Mama. If there was a conspiracy to deceive you, you must believe that I was not part of it. Not then. I had no idea of her identity, or of their relationship, until he died and I read the private missive he had left me.'

'And when you discovered the truth, you did not tell me.'

'At his urgent request. He was convinced you knew nothing. He wanted to protect you from the knowledge – begged me to do so in his letter. He wouldn't have told me at all, Mama, if it hadn't been necessary to appoint someone whose discretion could be relied upon to have a care for their financial wellbeing once he was gone.'

He wasn't being honest now. Not completely. But stark honesty could only hurt her even more. He had kept this secret for nine years and he would keep it as long as she lived. He would never reveal to his mother the details of that final deathbed conversation he'd had with his father, Sir Thomas's slow, painful confession, in rasping breaths that each cost him a little piece of precious life, that the only woman he'd ever loved had been Angela, and not the lady from his own class and background his parents had pressured him to marry. Of course he'd clasped his father's thin hand as he died and promised he would look after Sir Thomas's lover and their child, as long as they and he lived and beyond. He'd done it gladly, not as a mere matter of duty. He loved them both, had always done so since his early childhood as a lonely little boy with – as he had always believed – no siblings, and few playmates. But why tell his mother? The truth could be a mercilessly cruel thing.

'You see her still. You see *them*. You are intimate with them.' It might have sounded like an accusation, but it was said so levelly that it seemed more a painful statement of fact.

'Mama, I do, but I have an obligation to them; my father made it so.' It was much more than that, they were family too, but once again, no need to force the painful knowledge on her.

'It doesn't matter if that's true or not,' she said wearily now.

'There's no point in reproaching you for something that is not your fault but Thomas's. And yes, you are right to think me weakly self-indulgent, as I know you do, to mind so much that he never loved me. But whether I am or not, Lord Nightingale somehow knows of their existence. Their identities, everything. Of your father's cruel betrayal of me, and the child that was born of it. The bastard mulatto child.'

'That is not—'

'I will not have you school my tongue, Dominic. Not today. Be silent. The mulatto child. The shameful bastard. That is what the world will say, as they make pious, shocked expressions and laugh gleefully behind their hands, and in my face. That is, if they don't cut me completely. That is what Lord Nightingale will tell them, you can be sure of it, if you do not marry his daughter.'

He could see that there was no use in trying to argue with her, such was the depth of her distress. And though the way she spoke about people he cared deeply for must disturb him, it could not come as a shock. She was concerned only for herself and for her standing in the world, but, the truth, if it came out, would damage Angela and her daughter as much as it would damage Lady De Lacy. More, much more, because they were so much more vulnerable, lacking the protection that her wealth and status brought her.

He rose to his feet and paced restlessly about the room, oppressed by its confines as he always was. 'Good God, ma'am, why? I understand that he is blackmailing you, to bring about my marriage with his daughter – I have grasped as much as that!' he said impatiently. 'But what I cannot conceive is why he should do such a thing!'

'Nor I,' she answered listlessly. 'I asked him, of course, but he would only smile in that infuriatingly smug way he has, and tell me nothing to the purpose. How I loathe and despise him! You are a great catch, I suppose, and by this stratagem he has captured you. Maybe it is no more than that.'

'Even supposing that to be true, why should he care? However generous my arrangements might be, he will not lay his hands on a penny. I have not made him a trustee of his daughter's marriage settlement; he is far too advanced in years. And Miss Nightingale herself is a substantial heiress, is she not?'

'You know she is. But what does it matter? Maybe he merely does it because he can, to enjoy having power over us. Maybe he's mad. I think he must be. A madman with the means to ruin us, that's a comforting thought. But you see now why the wedding must go ahead, Dominic. I implore you to think of me, of my standing and my pride, and how humiliated I would be, if you have no care for your own reputation!'

He could see why *she* thought the marriage must go ahead. It would be unreasonable, he supposed, to expect his bitterly hurt mother to have any concern for the other potential victims of Lord Nightingale's cruelty, or understanding of their situation. And he didn't have to agree with her motives at all to understand that they were in a terrible bind, even worse than before. 'To give in to blackmail is to encourage the blackmailer to try again,' he said. 'Or so I have always understood, not having any previous experience of such matters.' He was struggling to regain his customary insouciant manner.

'In normal circumstances – if there can be said ever to be normal circumstances when one is being blackmailed – I cannot doubt that you would be correct, Dominic!' said Lady De Lacy tartly. 'But surely not in this case. Our scandals will become Nightingale's too. I cannot believe he intends to expose us to public censure and mockery once his purpose has been achieved and our families are inextricably tied together. He will have got his wish, the dreadful creature, his daughter will be Lady De Lacy – what more could he possibly want from us?'

'Perhaps you're right,' he said noncommittally.

He could only be glad that he had never had the least intention of revealing Maria's secret to his mother. She was plainly at her wits' end. He would not put it past her, in her desperation, to try a little blackmail on her own account, by threatening Lord Nightingale that she might spread the details of his older daughter's unconventional private life far and wide. Things were ugly enough as they stood without making them worse in such an incendiary fashion. They were in dangerous waters, he thought, more dangerous by the day. There was a great deal to think on here – not least the knotty problem of whether he could in all decency betray his father's confidence, and Angela's, to Meg. He must, if he were to tell her that Lord Nightingale was more despicable and far more ruthless even than she and her sister had imagined. That seemed like something she should know, and Maria too, for their own protection as much as anything else. But it was not his secret...

26

Meg, despite the fact that she had gone to bed so excessively early and without her dinner, did not wake until the early morning. The much-needed slumber brought a little counsel, though she was not sure if she should trust it, since it was a low, seductive voice, sounding very much like Sir Dominic's honeyed tones, that whispered in her ear and said, *After all, why not*? Perhaps Maria was right – perhaps she, as an outsider, saw more clearly. Meg had never had a distinct idea of her own future before, but she thought she could picture herself married to Dominic. Making love with him, getting to know him, building a life together, writing, one day travelling with him. He was a good companion, she knew that already. She didn't care at all for being a great lady, or for fortune and luxury, but they could be happy, she thought. They might be happy together, and share that happiness with others.

Was she really going to say yes, next time she saw him? She thought she was, but she felt shy, still unsure – as though the idea of a life with him was a present she had been given unexpectedly; something so precious that she dared not show it to anyone else yet, but needed to keep as a secret while she examined all its contours. A shining globe of possibility, a velvet temptation. Riding with him today... she couldn't do it. It was too much, too raw. If she saw him on a horse, in breeches and top boots, she'd want to drag him off and throw herself upon him shamelessly. In Hyde Park!

And it was not as though this decision of hers solved all their problems at a stroke. Was she saying she was prepared to take up the masquerade as Maria, for the rest of her life? She thought she was, but... She would write to him properly later in the day, when her thoughts were more collected, and say yes, and they would face all these difficulties together. And if she saw him – and she hoped she would – it would be in private, an idea which lit a flame deep inside her.

She wrote him a brief note now, revealing nothing of her feelings but crying off politely from their arrangement to go riding together, and stayed in bed, thinking of him, imagining their future, smiling to herself despite all the obstacles that still stood in their way.

It occurred to her as she lay there that she had no idea – never having needed to consider such matters previously – whether the banns had been read in St George's in the normal manner over the course of three weeks, or whether the ceremony was to be carried out by expensive special licence. Could church weddings be organised in such a manner and, if so, would it even be possible for her to take her sister's place under her own name, assuming that was what they ended up deciding to do, or would they have to begin the whole business of application again, and give a great many awkward explanations besides? She let out a little hiccup of wild laughter at the thought of Sir Dominic disclosing urbanely to some mystified reverend gentleman that he had, in fact, somewhat confused the precise appellation of his betrothed, even to the extent of applying for a licence at Doctors' Commons in the wrong name, which was, after all, a mistake anyone might make, and quickly set right. It was easy to imagine that all sorts of objections and legal obstacles might be raised to such a switch of brides. To marry him as Maria would be far easier, of course, but should she? Would he agree to that, even if she decided she could do it?

After nuncheon, she went out with Hannah to walk off her fidgets with the excuse of doing a little shopping. She had not the least need to buy anything, and barely any money in her purse in any case, but she was fizzing with restless energy, and it was another fine, bright day. Hannah suggested that, if she had no particular aim of her own in mind, they might browse in a new bazaar she knew of in Soho Square, where all manner of things, from sewing supplies, fabrics, accessories, even children's toys and books, might be purchased at reasonable prices. It might be crowded in the afternoon, she warned, but they were perhaps less likely to encounter anyone of Maria's acquaintance there than in the more fashionable shops of Bond Street. Meg agreed energetically that this was a good notion, and they set off. The walk through London's most fashionable streets was less than a mile, and to stride out in the fresh air was more to Meg's taste than sitting idle in her father's carriage for the short journey. She was largely silent on the way, nervous of sharing her thoughts with anyone, even this woman who'd known her as a baby, and Hannah appeared to be aware of her mood and did not attempt to coax her into speech. This morning she'd told her old nurse that she'd found Maria and that she was safe, but had not had permission to share any more, and so had left her guessing.

Once at their destination, Meg couldn't summon up any

interest in the colourful rolls of fabric sitting ready to be taken down, cut up according to patterns and made into gowns. It would require an effort of imagination that she simply could not summon at the moment – who would she be, by the time some piece of material she bought now was transformed into a gown? And admitting that she didn't know, how could she be expected to look at muslins and silks and take them seriously? Maria Nightingale – the future Lady De Lacy – had gowns enough, and Meg Nightingale, dowdy country bluestocking, didn't need them, unless of course *she* was to be the one to marry. It was exciting, she must acknowledge, but all still so uncertain.

They wandered aimlessly about the stalls, with Hannah trying and failing to engage her restless companion in this trinket or that pair of evening slippers, when she suddenly became aware that her companion had stopped dead in her tracks and was pulling hard at the sleeve of her pelisse. 'Miss Meg!' Hannah hissed. 'Don't say anything, but look! Over there on the left!' As she spoke, Hannah, most extraordinarily, dragged her with some force and speed into a place of partial concealment behind a tall glass cabinet of goods.

She couldn't conceive what possible reason there could be for such urgency, but she raised her eyes impatiently and looked in the direction Mrs Treadwell had indicated. The object of her attention was an establishment selling children's toys, she saw. It made a brave show with its bright colours and varied stock, enough to delight any child's heart, but it could be of no possible interest to her. She was about to say that she didn't even know any children, certainly not well enough to wish to buy them trinkets, when she saw why Hannah had called on her with such insistence, and why she had been so quick to make sure that they were not seen into the bargain. As she watched in horror, she felt the blood drain from her face, and thought for the first time in her life that she might swoon.

Meg and her companion beheld a pretty family scene. A tall, young lady, who was dressed with great neatness and propriety but not, perhaps, in the first stare of fashion, was laughing as two bright-eyed, curly-haired little boys in identical frilled shirts and nankeen trousers tugged at her hands and begged her to help them choose. It was sufficiently obvious that they had been told they might have one gift each, and to pick carefully. The poke of the lady's modest chip-straw bonnet was moderate in size and did not conceal her glossy dark ringlets, expressive brown eyes and smooth brown skin. Meg judged her to be rather older than herself, maybe in her mid-twenties. The boys, a handsome pair of perhaps six and five years old, were made in her image and plainly her sons. The gentleman who accompanied them, who was laughing with them and teasing them with the ease of long familiarity, was known to her. Very well known to her. It was Sir Dominic De Lacy.

She wasn't sure she'd ever seen him so carefree. The worries that still oppressed her seemed to have left no mark on him, she thought bitterly, as she watched him engage in earnest debate with the smaller child about the merits of a miniature cricket set over a box of toy soldiers. The little boys plainly stood in no awe of him, and when at last their choices were made and Sir Dominic paid for their prizes, they at first thanked him politely, as prompted by their smiling mother, and then flung their arms about him, as high as they could reach, and hugged him fiercely. She could see that he protested at their boisterous show of affection, but in a joking way. He was very good with them, loving and patient, and why should he not be? Clearly, he was their father.

Meg was frozen in astonishment, still as a statue, and there was not the least need of her companion's whispered admonition to keep silent; she had no idea what she might say if she spoke, and she certainly had no desire at all to attract Sir Dominic's attention to her presence. Could anything be more mortifyingly embarrassing than such an encounter? Yesterday, he had asked her to marry him, had come close to some sort of declaration of deep feeling, if not of love; today, she beheld him, happy, smiling, intimate, with his mistress and their two young sons. He might be famous for his polished ease of manner and habitual cool self-possession, but even he, surely, would struggle to navigate such a situation. What could he possibly say, to either wronged woman? The books of etiquette could be small use in such a situation. There would scarcely be a chapter on How to Introduce One's Mistress and Natural Children to the Lady to Whom One Has Just Proposed Marriage.

As the shock subsided a little, and as she watched the family make their way towards the exit of the building, the older child clutching Sir Dominic's hand securely, chattering away to him nineteen to the dozen, and the younger jumping excitedly at his mother's side, showing off his new toy, Meg realised one more nightmare detail: the woman was familiar in appearance. It wasn't so much her pretty, animated face as her tall frame, good shoulders and queenly bearing. She'd last seen her mirror image in Covent Garden, a few nights ago, by the handcart that dealt out food and succour to the children of the street. Angela Jones. Mother Jones. And now she recalled the woman's words, and a name: Annie. 'She'd be so pleased to see you. They all would.' And Sir Dominic: 'That's good news. I'd like that.' It seemed so strange to her, that Mrs Jones had been easy and friendly with Sir Dominic, who must be the aristocratic seducer of her daughter, the father of her illegitimate grandchildren. But perhaps he provided handsomely, perhaps there was some story behind it all of which she was ignorant... It seemed she was ignorant of a great deal. What a naïve fool she was. It hurt more, she accepted, because of her tentative decision this morning. She'd been so happy. She'd thought they could have a future. He would never know it, she would make sure of that, but he had betrayed her most cruelly.

Hannah said significantly, 'Well, I never did! And I thought so highly of him when I met him, and you too, I'll be bound. That was a sight I didn't expect to see this fine day, Miss Meg, I do declare!'

'Nor me,' Meg replied levelly, though it cost her an effort to retain her fragile composure. She could say no more just now, and hoped Hannah had no further desire to discuss the subject and exclaim over Sir Dominic's shocking secret. There was a pain, somewhere inside her – not a sharp, stabbing pain, but a dull one. An ache she did not care to put a name to, lest naming and acknowledging it made it worse. Foolish girl that she was, she had thought, hoped... She felt sick, all of a sudden, she realised, heavy, and very tired. 'Let's go home,' she said. 'Let's hail a hackney and go home directly. I've had more than enough of shopping.'

27

Yesterday, Meg would have sworn, as she lay on her sister's bed contemplating the canopy above her and wondering what in heaven's name she was going to do, that she could hardly feel worse; today, the problem that had loomed so large had in a sense been solved for her, and yet she was much, much more distressed. She realised that she was weeping, had been weeping for a while, and wiped away her tears with an unsteady hand.

She couldn't possibly marry Sir Dominic, that much was crystal clear. Whether under her own name or her sister's, she could not invest her happiness and all her hopes for the future in a man who kept such grave secrets from her and was so irrevocably committed elsewhere. Not even for Maria's sake could she do such a thing. She was quite prepared to accept that he had a past – he was a man of almost thirty, of course he did – but what she had seen today had not been past but present, and indeed future. Those innocent, trusting boys needed a father, and would till they were grown, and she needed a husband who would share his whole life with her, not some small part of it, some meagre corner. It wasn't a matter of infidelity – he hadn't been unfaithful to her, as he'd only known her a few days, and plainly this woman had been a presence in his life for many years. It was a matter of commitment and of honesty. What other secrets might he be concealing? Above all, it was a matter of trust.

And there was more. If she was an acceptable bride because she was of noble birth and had blonde hair and blue eyes, and Annie was not because her mother was an African, and yet she was good enough to share his bed and bear his children, that didn't reflect terribly well on Sir Dominic either. She had thought better of him. She was, she acknowledged, profoundly disappointed. Hurt. She'd though the electric physical attraction they shared was something special, perhaps – now she admitted to herself, now that it was too late – a sign that something deeper could develop between them. But she must face the fact that he had shown himself to be promiscuous, and not to be trusted. He hadn't lied to her, he hadn't explicitly said, I am free to marry you, free of all ties and able to commit myself to you utterly. Free to love you. But she'd thought that was what he was promising. It was what she would offer, if ever she married anyone. Herself, all of herself, without reservations or nasty little secrets. Or big secrets, for that matter. This was a big secret.

Damn him, with his insinuating charm and his captivating smile and his air of being someone she could depend upon for honesty, when plainly she couldn't. She supposed, sniffing, that she'd had a lucky escape. Her heart was bruised but not broken. She wouldn't allow it to be. It had only been a few days. Damn him.

She would tell him, in dignified words with no unbecoming show of emotion, that she had reflected upon the matter and had come to the conclusion that the idea they should marry was not feasible. Not even to help her sister could she do it. She'd tell him that she could not entertain those sentiments for him that a woman should feel towards her husband. That his was not a character that could ever inspire such sentiments in her, and he could take that however he liked. If he didn't have a guilty conscience, he should – think of those little boys looking up at him so trustingly, and their mother, so relaxed and happy in his company, and Meg herself, who'd been beginning to think that... But no point going down that road. Not now.

Meg was looking forward to telling her sister of her decision even less than the necessary encounter with Sir Dominic. She was under no obligation to reveal her true feelings to him; she could tell him as much or as little as she cared to, and by all the rules of honourable behaviour he could press her no further. With Maria, the case would be different. She'd tell her how wounded she was, and perhaps find comfort in doing so, but the upshot of it all would be that she could not help her. Maria's ingenious plan for both their futures would be in ruins. Their restored sisterly relationship was still so new and so fragile that it might easily be damaged by the revelation; she hoped her sister would not think her selfish. But now that she knew the truth, she felt she had no choice. Perhaps she was selfish, then, to put herself first.

The thought that Maria might think that she was concerned only with her own future happiness to the exclusion of everyone else, even her twin, hurt her, and if she couldn't do anything about Sir Dominic, could she perhaps do something about that? It occurred to her now that there might be some other way that they could puzzle out between them that would allow Maria to live the life that she wanted. Could they perhaps swap identities somehow in any case, so that Maria could be with Lady Primrose as Meg, and Meg remain in her father's house as Maria? She could easily do so much for her sister, if it wasn't a matter of marriage – and just now, she felt sure that it would be a long, long time before she'd contemplate trusting another man enough to marry him. The engagement could be called off – there would be gossip, but the world did not need to know a reason, and *she* would be the one facing down the stares and the whispers, not Maria, which she was quite prepared to do. This fresh idea, of course, had the drawback that it would not enable Maria to lay hands on her fortune – but might that detail be overcome? Her mother had taught her to break down a knotty problem into its component parts so that they appeared less overwhelming: she would do that. She felt as though some faint glimmering of an idea was lurking deep in her brain, and could only hope that it would emerge into the light in time to be of some use.

She'd speak to Sir Dominic first, though. It was all very well for him to say that he wouldn't pressure her or renew his suit while matters remained so confused and uncertain, but all the while the day of his wedding grew closer and closer. It was time, she thought, to put a stop to that nonsense. She was not going to stand in a church and commit herself irrevocably to someone on whom she could not place her reliance. Thank God she had realised in time exactly what he was.

28

Meg scribbled a hasty semi-discreet note to Maria, telling her that she had made discoveries about A Certain Person's life and character that made it impossible for her to contemplate tying herself irrevocably to him. She was going to see him, she explained, and tell him so, and then would visit Maria as soon as she could to explain matters more fully and to see if they could puzzle out some new solution between them. The money was the chief problem, she wrote, and as she did so the infuriatingly elusive idea seemed to nibble at the edge of her conscious thoughts once more, only to dart away, like a fish in a stream, when she tried to capture it.

A colder, more carefully considered and formal missive went off to Sir Dominic, asking him to call on her at his earliest convenience, and once it was despatched Meg could only wait. She realised – once it was too late to do anything about it – that Sir Dominic might easily not be in, sitting idly around waiting for a summons from her; was it not excessively likely that, after the touching family scene she had observed, he had accompanied his mistress and children to wherever they were staying, and that he remained there still in domestic bliss. Domestic bliss, and yet yesterday he had offered for her! 'He could be gone for days!' she said aloud to the empty sitting room, pacing up and down it. 'Days!'

However, Meg's worst fears were not realised; a surprisingly short while later, her anxiously straining ears caught voices in the hall, and Sir Dominic was announced and ushered in without any greater ceremony; the butler knew, of course, that she'd sent a note to him not an hour since and that he must be calling on her in response to it. He knew, too, as all the senior servants did, of Maria's disappearance and her own masquerade, and so it was no wonder he showed her visitor directly into the room rather than enquiring if she was at home. Of course she was at home to her supposed betrothed and co-conspirator.

Sir Dominic was as immaculate as ever in snowy cravat, blue coat, pantaloons and shining hessian boots with jaunty gold tassels. (Those damn boots.) There was a warmth in his eyes as he greeted her that would have been highly gratifying in other circumstances; now, though, it angered her. No doubt he is attracted to me, she thought. I can hardly take it as a unique compliment! No doubt, like many a man, he thinks he can have everything he wants, including several willing women at once at his convenience. Well, he can't. Not me, not this time.

'Sir,' she said coldly. 'Won't you sit down? There are urgent matters we must discuss.'

A little frown appeared between his brows, and the ardour in his gaze was replaced by a searching regard. Whatever you might say about him, however untrustworthy he was, he was far from stupid. He knew instantly that something was wrong, though he could not have the least idea what it might be.

'Has something happened, Meg?' he said. 'Some more bad news?'

'No, but I have been considering, and I have come to the conclusion that I cannot marry you – whether in my sister's name or in my own. I thought it only right that I told you so directly.' Meg was proud that her voice barely wobbled as she said this. The new, chilly version of herself was unfamiliar and not particularly likeable, but she wasn't trying to be likeable just at the moment, and to speak so correctly and emotionlessly served as a sort of armour, she was discovering.

'And yet you say that nothing fresh has happened to bring you to this decision?'

'Nothing. I have reflected deeply on the matter, and I am resolved that I am right. To marry you in the guise of my sister is clearly impossible, for many excellent reasons. If I cannot so help her, to marry you as myself would serve no useful purpose at all. The wedding must be called off without loss of time.'

'"Serve no useful purpose"?' Sir Dominic mused. His face was almost expressionless, but there was a spark of something in his eyes – Meg could not tell, and should not care, whether it was hurt, or anger, or some combination of the two. His feelings could be of no possible significance to her, and no doubt it would do him good not to get his own way for once in his life. 'That is a curious choice of phrase. I confess that when I so maladroitly pressed my suit – was it only yesterday? – it was not because it "served some useful purpose". Nothing can have been further from my mind than any considerations of sordid practicality.'

'That cannot be so,' she said steadily, her anger at his hypocrisy giving her strength, 'because you have made it quite clear to me in the past that your main reason for seeking my sister's hand was to obtain a legitimate—'

'Your sister's hand, yes,' he cut in impatiently. 'I've never denied that. But not yours. Be damned to legitimate heirs and the requirements of the family and all that nonsense. Marrying you would be quite a different matter, for me at least. I thought you knew that, Meg.'

It was cruel, she thought, to offer her the possibility of happiness and snatch it away. 'I thought I knew it too,' she said half to herself. 'But I was wrong.'

'Meg, my dearest...'

He had risen from his seat and was coming towards her; she feared he meant to put his hands on her, even kiss her, which ought to disgust her. And yet she was forced to admit that it still struck a fugitive spark of excitement in her. Despite all she had seen such a short time since, despite knowing that he belonged to another – or should, if there was any decency in him – the thought of him holding her, caressing her, still made her heart leap and her pulse race. She knew that if she let him touch her, she would be lost to herself. Her every instinct screamed at her to move away to safety, to put some distance between them, but she held her ground, though it was a struggle. 'Mere physical attraction is no basis for marriage. I'm sure it's more than a lot of people have, but it's still not enough for me.'

If she'd thought that would check him, she was wrong. 'I entirely agree with you,' he said. He was very close to her now. 'I am well aware that we've only known each other for a short while, and in these cursed awkward, impossible circumstances, but I had thought, had hoped, that something was growing between us that you were as aware of as I.' His voice was very low and intense. 'To say that I want above all things to kiss you, to make love to you, cannot be news to you, and you are right, such a connection can hardly be unheard of. Until today, I had thought that we shared that awareness, yes, but beneath it a deeper and much more important feeling that—'

She could not let him say it, odious, lying hypocrite that he was. 'No. No, you are mistaken. Will you not believe me when I tell you so?' She was aware that a note of desperation rang in her voice, which, if he heard it, could hardly serve to convince him that she was utterly indifferent to him. But it was so hard to be cool when hurt and anger threatened to overwhelm her.

'As a gentleman, I should take my rejection, and leave you,' he said drily. 'You will say that you owe me no explanation, and it is true, you do not. You can owe me nothing, this situation is none of your making, and if you ask me to leave you, I must take my dismissal and trouble you no more. But every fibre in my being screams out to me that that would be the worst mistake I have ever made – that something is horribly wrong, and I must set it right before terrible damage is done that I would regret for the rest of my life. Someone has wounded you, has told you something untrue and greatly to my discredit. I can only think that. And if you believe ill of me with no good cause, should I not try to defend myself, in a matter so vital to both of us and to our chances of happiness?'

'No such thing has happened. No one has traduced you; I have heard no rumours or gossip. I would not listen, in any case, if someone I did not know and trust – and who else could it be but someone I did not know and trust, given the nature of my acquaintance in London? – spoke ill of you.'

'Then I can only assume that your own doubts have preyed upon you and driven you to this decision. Is that correct? I think it must be. And what can I say to you to convince you that we can find a way through this so that we can be together in honour and honesty?'

Enough of this. While a great part of her wished to send him away and never lay eyes on him again, then to curl up and weep till she was exhausted, another part of her was furious, and would like to see his reaction to the truth when he was faced with it. Let him try to wriggle his way out of this! If it would hurt her to speak, it would hurt her more to keep silent. Honour and honesty, indeed! She had not meant to say it, but it seemed, since he pressed her, that she must. 'Sir Dominic, I saw you myself, this morning, in the bazaar. You say I should not listen to gossip, but I presume you will allow me to credit the evidence of my own eyes. I know what I saw, and it can have only one explanation, which has nothing to do with honour and even less with honesty.'

She looked at him, expecting to see guilt and horror written plainly across his handsome features. Panic, even anger, since members of the male sex, her mother had cautioned her, often became enraged and even violent when confronted with the incontrovertible evidence of their own bad behaviour. But unbelievably, astonishingly, he was smiling. Grinning. He appeared to be entirely at his ease, even amused. She could have slapped his face. Good God, were men truly so different, were they all of them utterly devoid of all human feeling?

'You saw me in the bazaar, with Annie and the boys?' he asked.

'Yes,' she said stiffly, offended by the ease with which he said the other woman's name to her. 'I saw your happy little family scene. And how you can stand there and smirk at me—'

'Meg, she is family – they all are. It's perfectly true, I assure you. But not in the way you think. My dear, she is my sister.'

29

'Your sister...?'

Dominic took her hand and drew her to the sofa. 'Annie is my half-sister,' he said. 'My father's natural child. Angela is her mother. You must have noticed the great resemblance between them, now that you have seen them both. I would have told you all, once I'd had a chance to ask Angela for her permission to share her secret with you, but I've had no chance to speak to her. I hope she'll forgive me now – I hope they both will – but I can't let you labour under such a misapprehension any longer. It's too important to me.'

Meg sat, suddenly weak-kneed, and he joined her, saying urgently, 'I must tell you the whole story, so that you may understand. Angela was no kept woman, and he no careless seducer. They loved each other till he died.'

He hesitated, as if revealing his family secrets cost him something, and then went on, 'My parents' marriage was arranged, as you know, and it was no happier than your parents' union, though there was no such open breach between them, just a growing coldness. As they grew further apart, my father devoted more of his attention to his charitable foundation. The energy he expended on his beloved project was a greater and greater source of friction between them, since my mother disapproved of it and saw it as an unbecoming way of spending his time, and so their estrangement increased even more – it's hard to tell at this distance which came first, and perhaps it scarcely matters now. In any case, it was there that he met Angela – she was a nurse, a very good one, employed to look after the children, and very quickly she became vital to the success of the whole endeavour, and the real head of it. Annie is three years younger than me, and by the time she was born my parents were all but separated, though they lived under the same roof still. It's not my place to justify my father's infidelity – it's none of my business and I have no right to judge him – and I must always feel sorry for my mother, but Annie is my sister, and her boys, Toby and Nick, are my nephews. I am very fond of them, rascals though they are. I'm sure you could see that, though you misinterpreted the cause of it.'

'Her husband was not with you, though, or I suppose I could not have jumped to such a foolish conclusion...'

'He's a lieutenant in the militia. Tom Gilbert, a very good fellow. He grew up in the children's home, playing with Annie and falling in love with her, but was later adopted by a prosperous Anglo-Portuguese merchant family who paid for his education and helped him commence his military career. His regiment has been posted in the north until now, but they have just been transferred to Hertfordshire, and so Annie has brought the boys to town for a while to spend time with their grandmother, and with me. We haven't seen them for several months – as you can imagine, it's hard for Angela to get away for long, so this move so much closer will be a boon to her, and to Annie.'

It was a great deal to take in. 'Does your mother know of their existence, then?'

Dominic said sombrely, 'Until yesterday I would have sworn that she did not. But I know now that she does – she tells me she has always known, and that she was aware of Annie's birth too, and felt, still feels, great bitterness and anger. My father only told me all when he was dying, nine years ago, to make sure that I would have a care for them when he was dead. I have kept his secret from her ever since. But I knew them well already, since my own childhood. He took me with him often, when he went to visit the foundation, and that was another source of conflict between him and my mother. Now, of course, I know that it was not just a concern for my safety or even a desire to keep me far away from children she considered low, unsuitable playmates; no, she knew that I was spending time with Angela and Annie, and growing close to them. She was jealous, and I suppose I cannot blame her. As with your parents, mine did not bring out the best in each other, but always the worst. It is a sadness to me to see this continuing even now that my father is long dead. I would hope my own life and marriage could be very different.'

Meg was astonished, but it did not occur to her to disbelieve him. She could see how it all fitted together, and Angela's words and her friendly attitude to Dominic, which had previously puzzled her so much, now made perfect sense. She felt almost faint with relief. 'I gravely misjudged you. I owe you an apology, it seems.'

'And I you. You would have been spared this anxiety if I had told you sooner, and I should have done, Meg, because I learned something yesterday from my mother that is of great importance to both of us. I knew I should tell you, and we must tell your sister too, but I hesitated to do so, and that was wrong.'

'Tell me...' she said instantly. 'Do not fear to hurt me. I was foolish not to come forward when I saw you this morning, but instead leapt to conclusions that were unjustified. I had almost decided – no, I had decided to marry you, despite all the troubles that still beset us. I was going to write to you and tell you so, and then I saw you...'

He took her in his arms, and she sighed and snuggled closer. 'You were jealous,' he said, and she could hear the satisfaction in his voice.

'I suppose I was, but more than that – I felt I could not trust you. Not that you had betrayed me precisely, for you had made me no promises of fidelity, but that you were not the person I thought you were. I was happy, Dominic, and excited, thinking of a future with you, and then... it all melted away from me, and I felt so sick and foolish.'

'I will make such promises,' he said, his hands warm on her body, smiling down at her tenderly. 'I do make them, very gladly, and will keep them. There are women in my past – a few, not many – but in my future there is only you. You're all I want and need.'

'Oh, Dominic...' she sighed. She pulled down his face and kissed him, a sort of fierce claiming, and he matched her in passion and in certainty. Despite the many difficulties they still faced, they had chosen each other, and this long kiss sealed it.

After a while she pulled away a little and said, 'I am beginning to know you, and I can tell that you are still troubled, and cannot quite forget it even as you kiss me. Tell me, my dear, whatever it is, and we will face it. All these secrets are so dangerous, it seems to me. They eat away at one's judgement and cloud one's vision. Let us be completely done with them.'

'Yes, I think that's right, though perhaps sometimes easier to say than to do.' He grimaced, but went on, still holding her, taking comfort and giving it, 'Very well, my dear. You are right, of course. My mother told me yesterday that the marriage was no plan of my father's – that was a lie she concocted to persuade me. And the scheme was not hers either; instead, she felt she had no choice in the matter, and was desperate to bring about the match for the most disturbing reason. I am sorry to say that your father is blackmailing her.'

Meg remained silent for a moment, aware of Sir Dominic's eyes on her face. Her brain was whirling, struggling to fit all these pieces together to form a coherent picture. 'He had learned your father's secret,' she said at last, once she had digested this most unexpected and unwelcome news and made some sense of it.

'Yes, exactly that, though I still have no idea how. I have realised since yesterday that perhaps he did not actually know the full truth, but was guessing based on some rumour he happened to recall, and my mother's horrified reaction only confirmed his suspicions. It scarcely matters, after all. My mother is extremely anxious that it should not be spread abroad, and so complied with his insistence that she press the match on me. He certainly cannot complain that she has not done exactly as he asked. But I doubt that will be enough to satisfy him if the marriage with your sister does not go ahead.'

He sighed, letting her go at last and running his hands through his immaculate honey-brown locks and disarranging them in a way that showed how disturbed he was. Her fingers itched to smooth them back into their habitual order, as an excuse to touch him again, to be close to him, but this was scarcely the time.

'My poor mama does not emerge with a great deal of credit from the crisis. I expect you can imagine her ignoble reasons for wanting to keep matters secret. They go beyond the understandable wish not to be humiliated before all the world by the knowledge that her husband had a mistress and a child. Such illicit affairs and their result are common enough, in all conscience; that is not what she minds. And however little sympathy I have with her motives, it would be useless to deny that Angela and Annie would be the ones who suffered most if the truth were revealed. Not that she cares for that, of course, but I do. I must. For one thing, I imagine it would be nigh on impossible for Angela to continue in her present situation, which is so much more than a job to her, if the fact of Annie's illegitimacy were revealed. It has been hard enough for her in the past, when she was pretending to be a widow. She could lose her position, her home of many years and her purpose in life. Of course I will always support her, but she is a proud woman and places a high value on her independence, as why should she not? And Tom Gilbert's adoptive family would hardly welcome the public scandal and notoriety, even though they do already know the truth of Annie's parentage. A great many people would be hurt, most of them entirely innocent. The poor lost street children most of all, if Angela is taken from them. It's like a stone thrown in a pond – the ripples spreading outwards. Ripples of malice.'

'I am so sorry.' The words seemed sadly inadequate; Meg felt helpless in the face of this new catastrophe.

He shook his head emphatically. 'There is no need at all for you to apologise for your father's conduct. You have been as much a victim of his freakish behaviour as anyone else, as has your sister. But now you see why I hesitated to tell you, and why I knew I must at last. It is most unhappy tidings, and makes matters even more complicated.'

'I suppose I cannot be surprised at anything he does. His motives are always a mystery to me, and I am quite ready to believe him capable of anything hurtful. But Dominic, this explains a great deal, but it does not explain everything. *Why* is my father so anxious to marry Maria to you, and willing to go to such extraordinary lengths to gain his desire? The news of his horrible blackmail scheme makes it all the more inexplicable, really, not less. What possible reason can there be for such desperate urgency? Whatever can he hope to gain from it?'

30

Dominic said slowly, 'I asked my mother as much, and she had no answer to give me other than that that perhaps Lord Nightingale is a lunatic, which may be true, I suppose, but hardly takes us any further. But it's a very good point. Nothing that you have told me about your father and nothing that I have seen in my short acquaintance with him leads me to think that he cares at all for your sister's wellbeing, whether he is sane or mad.'

'Certainly not enough to make him seek to blackmail an eligible gentleman into offering for her,' Meg agreed. 'As soon as you say it out loud, it's quite plain how ridiculous the whole idea is. He cares a great deal for his mother and his youngest sister, or the idea of them at any rate, now they're safely dead and can't trouble him with any demands, but he doesn't give a fig for any other woman alive. Not my aunt, not me, and not Maria. And he's not in the least mad, just extraordinarily selfish and in love with the idea of his own consequence. It doesn't make any sense! If he was so eager to see Maria well bestowed – which honestly I can't believe he has ever been – he needed only to approach your mother like a normal person and suggest the match. It *is*, on paper, an excellent idea. I'm sure she'd have been ready enough to agree, since you've told me she was already eager to see you married. My sister's a great heiress! Why should anything so extreme as blackmail be needed?'

'You're right, my dear. The curious nature of his behaviour is clearer now that we know about the coercion. Can we puzzle it out, do you think? It feels as though we have almost all the pieces, could we but put them together in the right manner.'

Meg jumped to her feet and began to pace up and down the small room, her skirts and petticoats swishing emphatically with every turn she made. 'I keep thinking I know something!' she exclaimed. 'I keep thinking that the clue to it all is almost within my grasp, but then it slips away from me when I try to seize hold of it. What can it be?'

Dominic regarded her with fond amusement. 'I hope you'll forgive me on this occasion if I don't get up and join you. There really isn't room for both of us, and I should feel foolish standing watching you. Does the pacing help you think?'

'Not so far, but I can't be sitting still – I feel so restless. My mother has always taught me to break problems down into their separate parts, and deal with them that way. Can we do that, Dominic? What do we know for certain – I mean things that we are absolutely sure of, rather than things we merely suppose to be true?'

'The main thing we know,' said Dominic seriously, 'is that your father is extraordinarily keen, one might even say desperate, to have your sister marry me. Not just anyone who might be equally eligible, but me. And we also know he has, or thinks he has, a hold over my family.'

'That's very well put. We do know both these things as facts. Can we say, then, that he is desperate for Maria to marry you in particular, just because he has a hold over your family, and no other?' Meg asked. 'I know that isn't certain, not like the other two points, but can we test it as an idea for a moment?'

'Of course. So, my extremely obvious eligibility lies, we may suggest, not – as one might have expected – in my many sterling qualities of person and character, nor even the numerous favours nature and circumstance have blessed me with...'

'But only in the stark fact that my father has power over you,' she finished for him triumphantly. They were both grinning. 'Really, Dominic, it's beginning to seem to me that apart from that you could be almost anybody.'

'I'm sure it's good for me, you know, to endure these constant blows to my self-esteem and nobly rise above them,' he mused. 'I might have been wandering around London at this very moment thinking myself the devil of a fellow if I hadn't been drawn into the orbit of your family. Your sister flees from me as if I had the plague, your father doesn't care what the hell I am as long as he can blackmail me, you jump to the worst possible conclusion...'

'You'll get over it, I'm sure,' she said, blushing a little. 'You don't appear to me to be suffering noticeably from a deficit of self-esteem. But anyway, to prove the point sufficiently, it's not all about you, you know. It's not about *who* Maria must marry, it's about *why*.'

'Why your father needs your sister to marry someone who is in his power?'

'Exactly.'

He frowned in concentration. 'Logic suggests that the marriage itself might not be his end goal. There must be something further. In truth, he gains nothing financially from your sister's union with me. It could be argued that he gains socially, of course. If his estrangement from your mother has somehow damaged his reputation, or the reputation of your family, and he wishes to rehabilitate it though this connection…'

Meg shook her head vigorously, still pacing though more slowly now. 'I'm not sure it has been damaged, or not very much. Many married people in your world live apart. Many married people are notoriously and frequently unfaithful, for that matter, which my parents aren't, and as long as they are reasonably discreet in their amours, nobody cares much. And according to Maria he never goes into society, and only spends time with scholars like himself, who barely know what century it is. The latest scandal they concerned themselves with probably involved the Emperor Commodus. I really don't think it can be that.'

'Very well, then. In which case, the power must be the important thing. The power that the marriage gives him over me, and my family, even after the wedding. I put this to my mother, in slightly different terms, and she disagreed. She thought that a threat to expose our secrets would be toothless once our families were inextricably linked, because the gossip would hurt him too.'

'But that's not true, is it, Dominic?' she said excitedly, pausing and gazing at him. 'If my father doesn't care at all about being the subject of scandal, which I don't think he does, he could very easily threaten to spread rumours about you at any time, and mean it.'

'Spread rumours unless we do what, or to prevent us from doing what?'

'That's the point, isn't it? How can we know?'

'What if he has a secret of his own, one which might be revealed to me – or must be revealed to me – once the marriage has gone ahead? And one which I might otherwise be tempted to expose, only I won't be able to, because of the hold he has over me. Imagine if your sister married anyone else, someone uncompromised, how would they react on finding out whatever it is? That's a good question to ask, I think.'

'If he has a secret, Maria does not know it. I'm positive of that…' Meg said pensively. 'If she knew it, she would surely have told me, and in any case I think she'd hold it over him in order to obtain what she wants from him: the freedom to live as she pleases.'

And then, 'Oh, Dominic, my goodness, I think I know what it is.' She looked at him without really seeing him, the cogs in her brain meshing together and turning one upon the other like the mechanism of a mantel clock that was about to strike noon. It all made sense now – the blackmail, her father's urgency to see Maria married, and married to Dominic of all people in particular – everything. It was so elegant and nasty a solution that it surely could only be correct. 'What it must be. If I'm right, this explains everything. And if I am – it's a dreadful thing, but I hope I am right! Because then he can be stopped. And we can all be free.'

31

Meg said animatedly, 'Dominic, I am horribly afraid that he has stolen all her money. As well as being her father he is her trustee, though I do not know if she has others, and I do not think there is anyone who would question his right to invest her money as he chooses. Not now Mama is gone from his house. I am perfectly confident that he has shared no details of my sister's fortune with her – you've met him; you have seen how he is. I fear he has taken it and spent it all, and that is why he was so keen for to marry you.'

'A man he thinks is in his power,' he responded slowly. 'Someone who would be unable to object, however furious he might be when he learned the truth. My God, Meg, you must be right!'

She was in a curiously ambiguous mood, both energised and troubled, eyes sparkling, and her intelligence was exhilarating to him. 'What I do not know,' she said, 'though perhaps I can guess, is what he has done with such a fortune. Look about you – he certainly hasn't spent it on interior decoration.'

'No,' he said, 'and from my experience of the wine he serves his guests, he isn't spending it on that either, and God knows he can hardly have had a new coat this century. Well, I am not one of those men – though I would go bail your father is just such a one – who cannot endure to think that his wife is more intelligent than he is. I stand in awe of your superior intellect, and I believe you truly have got to the bottom of the matter at last, and will shortly puzzle out all the rest. Yes, I can see that you are quite puffed up with your own consequence as a result, and I cannot marvel at it. But if we were indeed married, madam, I can think of many enjoyable means I might employ to remind you that intellect is not quite everything.'

'Really? How intriguing.' She seemed most willing to be diverted from these serious matters now.

He rose and came to her side. 'Oh, yes,' he said, looking down at her, smiling wolfishly. 'I might, for instance, shower you with kisses till you cannot distinguish your head from your heels and admit that in some matters I may have the upper hand. That's while you still remember how to speak in coherent sentences, of course, which presently, I assure you, you will forget.'

'Try me.'

'That's a most tempting offer. Rather in the nature of a dare, perhaps, if you imagine for a moment that I will not do it.' They were standing very close together now, and Dominic in reality had very little idea what he was saying. God, he wanted her. This flirting and teasing was all very well, it was delightful, but underneath it all he was always aware now that he wanted her so badly.

'I think you probably will do it. I'm sure you're quite capable of it. The question is, will it achieve its object and make me submit to you?'

'The beauty of my plan,' he murmured, reaching out and

running one long finger very gently down her cheek as she closed her eyes and swayed towards him, as caught up in the moment as he was, 'is that it doesn't matter. Whether you do or you don't, I'll still have kissed you. There's nothing I want more in life just now – or at least, nothing I can have. I need to forget everything else in the world, all of our worries and our uncertainties, in the sheer intoxicating pleasure of your embrace. So how can I lose?'

'Must I be the loser then?' She turned her face to where his hand still rested, and found his palm and pressed a kiss into it. The intimacy of it almost overset him. He shivered, the intensity of emotion she aroused in him still new and strange and wonderful. He'd unhesitatingly trade all the sex he'd ever had for one soft touch of her lips on his palm. She pierced him to his core. Which didn't mean that innocent little caress was enough for him; far from it, he was hard for her, here in her aunt's drawing room in her father's house, with only a closed door – not even a locked one – between them and the danger of discovery. It was all so tangled in confusion. He wasn't sure if anyone in the Nightingale household would mind enormously if they were discovered in a compromising situation, since the woman she was supposed to be would – if nothing occurred to stop it – be his bride in a week or two. But it would make it so much harder for Meg to cry off, to refuse to become Maria forever, and that would be damnably unfair. It would be just another, softer form of blackmail, and he could not countenance it, tempted though he was.

'I hope you will never be the loser by any action of mine. I want to give you everything.'

She chuckled, her breath whispering across his sensitised palm and sending a bolt of electricity leaping and fizzing through him. 'I can't believe you really want to give me... everything... here and now, in this room, sir.' The tip of her tongue darted out and licked the tender skin, and he groaned. She was tormenting him, and it was delicious.

'Of course I do. My idea of everything encompasses a great deal, I should tell you.'

'So does mine,' she breathed, and then that dangerous, wicked tongue of hers licked its way slowly up his long finger to the end, circling it, before she drew the tip into her hot, wet mouth and began sucking on it. He gasped and stroked the inside of her lip very gently, and in response she sucked harder, drawing his whole finger inside her and moving up and down upon it in a manner highly dangerous to his composure. His other hand, sadly neglected, jealous of its more fortunate fellow, sought her breast and cupped it. Through the thin fabric that covered her, he felt her nipple harden under his touch, and brushed the pad of his thumb across it. It was her turn to let out a low, inarticulate sound of pleasure that vibrated enticingly around his wet flesh. It was searingly erotic in itself, and as a taste of greater pleasures to come it left him breathless. To imagine her moaning in just such a fashion, to imagine not only hearing the delicious sound but feeling it, while she...

But she released his finger with tantalising slowness and said against it, 'Your clever plan to kiss me into helpless submission... how's that working out for you, Dominic? Do you feel I'm on the brink of breaking down and acknowledging your superiority in this matter?'

'What plan?' he growled, only half-joking. 'I can barely remember my own name, let alone what I wanted to know. And as for being on the brink, good God... Don't stop, Meg. I have no idea what you were going to do next, but I'm very sure that I was going to like it. Or I could do something – perhaps it's my turn, as is only fair – that you would enjoy enormously.'

'I was enjoying that.' He hadn't moved his hand away from her face – whyever would he? – and she kissed his palm again. But he was highly attuned to her every mood, and he was afraid that it felt like an end rather than another beginning.

'We do need to stop,' she said, confirming his fears. 'We must have been alone here for a great while, and quite apart from observing the proprieties, we need to gather our wits and see how best we can arrange to meet my brother.'

Her words made no sense to him, dazed with desire as he was, but he released her instantly, though he did not quite have the strength to step away from her. 'I don't give a fig for the proprieties, and I give less than a fig for your brother. What in heaven's name has Francis to do with anything? I scarcely know the fellow, apart from recognising him when I see him.'

'Nor I, in truth,' she said, smiling up at him, his frustration echoed in her face. 'I couldn't tell you how often I've met him in my life, but certainly it can't be very many times. I'd much rather stay here, lock the door, and see who can reduce whom to helpless submission. As you said, there really could be no loser in such a contest. But you know it won't do. It's not that I care what anyone would think – what the servants are thinking right now, for instance. I don't, really. But we still have a great deal we need to arrange, and Francis is the key to it all. Or at least, I hope he is. He is the only person who has the right to question Lord Nightingale's finances.'

'You think he may be privy to your father's disreputable secret?' Dominic tried not to let the doubt creep into his voice, but wasn't at all sure that he succeeded.

Meg laughed. 'Oh, no. I'm sure he isn't. I understand from Maria and from Hannah that they have very little to do with each other from one year to the next. They could never be described as close; you must have observed that Francis was not at the engagement party, though I believe my aunt might have invited him even though my father would not have done so. I would wager that he knows nothing at all. But he may be able to find it out quite easily.'

'From what I have seen of him,' Dominic replied drily, 'I find it much easier to believe that he knows nothing than that he will be able to find out anything at all. He seems a good fellow, if a trifle reserved, and has a reputation for being most amiable and easy-going – excessively so, even – but a searching intellect I fear he is not.'

'I did not know,' she said calmly. 'All that I do know of him, really, is that he has as little to do with our father as possible, which I must count as a strong point in his favour. If they lived in each other's pockets, I would be wary of the strength of their connection and would not think of approaching him for help. I might even consider it dangerous. But as matters stand, that is not a concern. If Francis cannot look into things directly himself, which I can quite see he may not be able to if all you say of his character is true, he will easily be able to employ someone to do so. Indeed, it must be greatly in his own interests to take such action, if I can persuade him that there is even a slim chance my suspicions could be correct.'

'Of course he is the perfect person to ask, if you are reasonably certain he can be trusted not to reveal all to your father,' he said, taking her hand and pressing it. 'How can I help?'

32

Not for the first time since her arrival in London, Meg cursed the restrictions that her age, unmarried status and position in society placed on her movements. She told her sympathetic audience of one that it was immensely frustrating to be so constrained by propriety, and not at all what she was accustomed to. She was excessively tired of being obliged to have almost all life's important discussions al fresco, and wondered if the haut ton was even now whispering about her conduct. For herself, she went on to say, she wouldn't have cared what people thought of her, but Maria simply could not afford to gain a reputation for eccentricity – not when her private conduct would bear so little scrutiny by the censorious and her future remained so uncertain. But where to meet her brother was a puzzle.

It was obviously impossible to ask Francis to call on her at their father's house – the world would not think it in the least odd, but Lord Nightingale certainly would if he came to hear of it, and he was almost always at home in the daytime, though closeted in his library, which his female relatives were forbidden to enter. It did not feel safe to have such a conversation with him present in the building; the thought of being the cause of an accidental encounter between father and son in the entrance hall, before she had had a chance to speak properly with Francis, made her feel quite cold and sick.

Although it ought surely to be unexceptionable for a young lady to call innocently upon her brother at his lodging, apparently it was not, unless she was accompanied by a parent or some other older relative. A gentleman's lodging house, it seemed, such as the one in St James's Street that Meg had heard that Mr Nightingale inhabited, was a scandalous, tainting sort of a place in and of itself. Such a den of iniquity was not to be entered by a young lady without very visible and efficient chaperonage to preserve her fragile virtue. A maid would not do; maids could be so easily bribed. Meg thought of asking her aunt to accompany her, but swiftly discarded the idea. Mrs Greystone was surely respectable enough for anyone, but the outing was unusual, and would entail explanations. If those explanations were at all honest, they would provoke a return of spasms and palpitations and complete nervous collapse. Nobody wanted that.

Sir Dominic told her that his escort to Francis's residence – though he was perfectly willing to give it – would make matters worse rather than better. He explained that it might be thought by anyone who observed such an unconventional visit that Francis was in some manner colluding at a private meeting between his sister and her fiancé from which he would, naturally, immediately absent himself. When Meg understood what he was implying, she said hotly, 'It seems to me that the people of the haut ton have all of them extraordinarily filthy imaginations! They could with advantage find other ways to fill their precious time, rather than spend it in putting the worst possible construction on every harmless encounter!'

Sir Dominic appeared to be amused, saying, 'They – I will not say we, for I have always prided myself on the elevated tenor of my mind, you know, Meg, even before I fell under your good influence – do have such an enormous amount of leisure time, and so very little to fill it. Such is their cruel fate, butterflies that they are rather than worker bees. Gossip is highly useful in that regard, and the thing about gossip, of course, is that it doesn't need to be true, or even remotely credible, to be believed. One might even say, the more outlandish it is the better, for people will enjoy spreading it about so much more, and it will have all the success of novelty. So it really is better not to risk it unless we are absolutely devoid of any other alternative.'

They found themselves at a standstill until Sir Dominic proposed that his mother could help, if he informed her that he needed her assistance to get to the bottom of the blackmail she was enduring. It was perfectly permissible for him to take his betrothed to visit his parent, so that they might take tea together in an unexceptionable fashion. And if Mr Nightingale should happen to call in Clarges Street shortly afterwards, why, Francis was a close member of one of the two families which would quite soon be joined, the bride's own brother, and would be admitted to Lady De Lacy's presence as a matter of course. Meg agreed that this was a capital notion, and her only concern was how precisely Francis was to be induced to cooperate with it.

'For you must admit that it is a very odd thing to suggest to him, quite out of the blue!' she said. 'I can write to him – in fact, I must – but I am sure he will think it very strange in me to initiate a correspondence, when we have had so little to do with each other up till now.'

'I think,' Sir Dominic replied soothingly, 'it is best if I seek him out in person on your behalf, not revealing that you are Meg and not Maria at this stage, since we are not sure yet if we can trust him with that particular delicate matter. I could perhaps take your letter to him, and explain it – not your real purpose in arranging a meeting, of course, but merely the fact that you would very much like to see him. I dare say he will not find anything so very odd in that. Is it not natural? He is your brother, you have no other, and you are not likely to acquire one, I assume, at this stage in your parents' lives.'

She agreed that such an eventuality was extremely remote, which could not be a matter for regret in the circumstances. 'And I must admit that I would indeed like to know Francis better,' she mused. 'It would be a pleasant notion, to feel I really had a brother. Perhaps it may turn out that he feels the same about having a sister. It is an uncomfortable sort of thing, to have so few relatives one can be on good terms with.'

'That rather depends on the relatives, I find. My mother has a dreary set of cousins I'd run a mile in tight shoes to avoid. You met them at the engagement party, did you not, and must have perceived how excessively dull they were? But yes, you may well be right. I would not wonder if he turned out to be delighted to establish a more human sort of relationship with you. We will have to tell him that you are not Maria soon enough, I suppose? It scarcely seems avoidable.'

'Yes, I think we shall be obliged to. But I would not share any more of her secrets with him until we see how he takes that news. I can only hope he is nothing like my father.'

Sir Dominic left her now. It had been a long and tumultuous interview, but they found themselves in perfect accord at the end of it. He carried with him Meg's letter to her brother, and promised that he would not rest until he had delivered it, and would, furthermore, supposing his mission was successful, arrange a meeting at his mother's house as soon as possible.

It was early evening now, and he thought that there was a good chance that Mr Nightingale might be at home, dressing for dinner or otherwise preparing for the evening ahead. St James's Street was, of course, conveniently close to his own residence, and so he would look in there on his way home, and might, if he were lucky, track down his quarry with his first effort and not be obliged to pursue him relentlessly through the clubs and taverns of the West End, like some fashionably dressed Nemesis.

Francis had his lodgings in a most respectable-looking sort of house, he found when he arrived, clean and well maintained, with bright brass fittings to the front door. Meg would have been even more irritated to see it than she had been at the thought of it, he was sure, as nowhere less disreputable could really be pictured and yet as a young lady it was effectively barred to her. He wasn't sure if she knew that her reputation would suffer gravely if she so much as walked down this particular street, which was home to White's and its notorious Bow Window Set of ogling so-called gentlemen, but he could easily imagine her reaction to the news.

The soberly dressed manservant who answered the door did not blink when he received Sir Dominic's *carte de visite*. He would enquire, he said, if Mr Nightingale was at home. A few moments later he returned, and intimated that he was.

Dominic was shown into a pleasantly untidy sitting room decorated with a great many sporting prints; the manservant expressionlessly removed a riding-crop, a dog-eared copy of *Boxiana* and a large sleeping cat from a comfortable armchair, so that he might sit in it. The fellow endeavoured to brush away the copious amounts of hair that its previous occupant had shed, and Sir Dominic reflected that if he had missed any, which seemed quite likely, Pargeter would be absolutely appalled to come across it on his master's clothing, which would do him good. The cat leapt up to sit upon the windowsill, the better to glare at Sir Dominic in massive ginger indignation.

He did not have long to wait; his host appeared in a few moments and stood in the doorway, smiling in an uncertain manner, clearly puzzled by such a caller but too polite to say so. He was tall, well-built and fair, like all his family, but sandy-haired rather than the golden blonde of his sisters. He had the pinkish English complexion that so often accompanied light hair, and his face was open, amiable and guileless.

Dominic rose at the sight of him and went to shake his hand warmly, saying, 'It's very good of you to see me, Nightingale, when you can't have the least idea why I've come to visit you.'

'Not at all,' said Mr Nightingale with polite untruth. 'Won't you have a seat, De Lacy?' He removed another pile of miscellaneous objects from the only other armchair and dumped them unceremoniously on the floor so they could both sit.

Dominic said easily, 'In fact my presence is simply explained; I bear a commission from your sister.'

Francis seemed puzzled for a long moment, but then his brow cleared and he said, 'Maria!'

'Yes. I'm not sure if you know that I am betrothed to her.' Dominic reflected that although this statement was objectively true, more or less, it failed entirely to do justice to the complexity of the situation. But this was not the time to entangle himself in such matters.

'I did know, as a matter of fact,' his host replied a little awkwardly. Dominic was beginning to realise that he was not stand-offish at all, but rather shy. 'Should have written to congratulate you, I dare say. Sorry I didn't, hope you'll be good enough to overlook it! Wish you both very happy! The truth is, it's an awkward sort of situation, but that's no excuse for rudeness on my part. Can't claim to know my sister at all well – either of my sisters, there's two of them, you know. Twins.' Dominic indicated with an encouraging nod that indeed he did know. 'Not much of a one for dancing and that sort of thing, myself, so I haven't happened to come across Maria since her debut. Feel a perfect fool surrounded by ladies who might expect me to partner them, or make polite conversation about the latest on-dits. Ugh! But I'm sure she's an excellent girl. Wish I was better acquainted with her, to be truthful – with both of them. Would you care to take a glass of Madeira with me, De Lacy?'

After ascertaining that his host had no urgent appointment, or if he had one he was too diffident to feel able to divulge it, Dominic agreed to this. The wine was poured, his engagement was toasted, and they sat together in an atmosphere more conducive to the sharing of confidences, especially since Francis plainly had a far better taste in wine than his father. The cat made its way across the room and jumped confidently up into Francis's lap, and he stroked it absently. Dominic imagined that Meg would see her brother's obvious love of animals as a good sign, and was inclined to take it so himself.

'Miss Nightingale is also sorry that circumstances have prevented you from becoming as close as siblings should be,' Dominic told him. 'She would like very much to mend matters, if possible. She thought, though, as you did not attend our engagement party, that you also might not care to call on her at your father's house…'

'Dashed right about that!' Francis agreed with emphasis. 'I

remember she seemed clever, back when I used to see her every now and then. The fact is, I don't see eye to eye with the old man, never have. Very few people do. Can't imagine what a time of it the poor girl's had, living there all these years. I know people might have expected me to take Lord Nightingale's part when m'stepmother left him, but not a bit of it. Wasn't in the least surprised, hated to see the way he treated her. Couldn't stomach him for as much as a sennight, myself. Pompous old windbag, cares for nobody and nothing but his dusty old manuscripts. Not at all the thing to say about one's father, and I wouldn't run about the town saying it to just anybody, naturally, but I don't hesitate to tell you, old fellow – you're one of the family now, ain't you?'

'Almost,' Dominic said with a small smile.

'If you don't know what he's like yet – dare say you don't – I expect you'll find out soon enough.' And then, abruptly, 'D'you know what my middle names are, De Lacy?' Dominic, rather surprised, confessed that he did not.

'I'm telling you in confidence, would ask you not to spread it about, but should let you know, so's you realise the sort of creature he is. First name Francis, after his father – nothing too terrible about that. Lucky escape, really, though fellows will insist on calling me Fanny every now and then, teasing, you know. Middle names, though, devil of a mouthful: Marcus Aurelius Antoninus Augustus! I swear it's true. What do you have to say about that?' Francis Marcus Aurelius Antoninus Augustus Nightingale leaned back, apparently satisfied with the impression his revelation had had upon his visitor, and took a healthy swig of his wine.

'That's... unusual,' Dominic said rather inadequately, feeling grateful for the first time in his life that he'd been named Dominic Justin in a reasonably innocuous fashion for his father's cousin and close friend, his godfather, rather than for a Roman emperor and philosopher with at least two too many excessively grand sobriquets.

'I'll say it is! Cursed unusual, sort of ridiculous name a street mountebank or some tumbler at Bartholomew Fair might give himself to impress people. Imagine being saddled with that at school. Every time someone taunted me with it, I knew whose account to set it to: thank you kindly, Father. People seem to have forgotten about it now, and I'd like to keep it that way. Did you happen to hear what he wanted to call the twins, though, before m'stepmother managed to talk some sense into him?'

'Yes,' replied Dominic, wincing at the recollection. 'Maria Major and Maria Minor, wasn't it?'

'Yes, it dashed well was! I was only a boy at the time, but I remember the uproar it caused in the house. And when I was born my poor mother was in floods of tears, apparently, when he informed her of his intention to inflict that horror on me. *She* couldn't get him to think better of it, no matter how much she begged him. Sort of name you wouldn't give to a D-O-G, eh, Tiger?'

After a second's puzzlement, Beau De Lacy realised that his host was not addressing *him* in this curious manner, but had spelled out the word in order not to offend the sensibilities of his pet; the cat made no audible reply, though its expression could be interpreted as sympathetic. Dominic agreed that one would not.

He took out the note Meg had entrusted to him and passed it over, saying, 'Miss Nightingale would like to see you, and since she can't come here and you quite understandably don't care to go to Grosvenor Square, I suggested that I might take her to my mother's house in Clarges Street for tea – tomorrow afternoon, perhaps. You may call on her there without the least awkwardness and without Lord Nightingale knowing anything about it.'

'Ingenious!' Francis's open face was wreathed in smiles as he took the missive, opened it and scanned the few lines inside intently. 'You know,' he confided presently, 'I'm devilish glad you called, Nightingale. Thank you for going to the trouble. Let me know what time tomorrow, and I'll be there all right and tight. It's about time the damage the old monster has caused this family is set straight. One thing I'm sorry about, though, is I won't get to meet my other sister. I understand she's down in the country somewhere with her mother and never comes to Town. I heard a rumour – servants' gossip, maybe – that Father refused to pay for her come-out this year, wouldn't even have her in his house.'

Dominic admitted that as far as he knew this was true, and agreed that it was very shocking and not at all the thing. 'Dreadful, you know, to have such a shabbaroon as a father,' Francis said, his cheerful face clouded again. 'And the worst of it is, it's not even the money – he is a nip-cheese, right enough, unless he's spending thousands on a mouldy old book he wants, but the whole point of it is to punish his own child for her mother's actions.'

'If all goes well,' Dominic consoled him, 'I shouldn't wonder if you are able to meet and become better acquainted with both your sisters much sooner than you might imagine!'

33

Next day, after a flurry of messages, the two conspirators – for so Meg and Dominic felt themselves to be, even if Mr Nightingale was as yet unaware of it – found themselves in Clarges Street, in Lady De Lacy's purplish sitting room. They arrived half an hour before the third guest was expected, and took tea with their hostess and her cousin; it was a rather stilted occasion, upon which mere commonplaces were exchanged and the hideous word 'blackmail' was, unsurprisingly, never mentioned. Meg wasn't sure, since she had forgotten to ask and could scarcely do so now, whether Dominic's mother knew that she, Meg, knew of her father's outrageous threats... Everything was becoming hideously tangled, and she could only hope that today's actions would go some way to cutting through the Gordian knot to the truth; a reference, she thought, worthy of Lord Nightingale.

An awkward silence fell. In other circumstances, Meg supposed, they'd be talking excitedly about the impending wedding, but since nobody but Miss Sarah could be feeling entirely confident that this event was actually going to go ahead, let alone what form it would take, it wasn't the most promising topic of conversation, and soon faltered. Meg felt sorry for the poor little companion, who obviously sensed that something was amiss on what ought to be a happy occasion, but had not the least idea what it might be or what could be done about it.

Mr Nightingale's arrival came as a relief to everybody. Lady De Lacy greeted him graciously, albeit in the manner of one who, though innocent of all wrongdoing, was scheduled to be beheaded in the Tower of London quite shortly, but whose exquisite manners prevented her from mentioning it to anybody. After exchanging a few commonplace words with Francis, she whisked Cousin Sarah away, saying that she was quite sure that the Nightingales had family matters to discuss, upon which she would not think of intruding.

As the door closed behind her, Dominic said, smiling at Meg, 'Although my mother does enjoy an atmosphere of melodrama, she is of course right. Shall I leave you alone with your brother, my dear? I am sure you have a thousand things to say to each other, and my presence cannot be necessary.'

Meg was grateful for his tact, but all at once felt a little shy, and thought she should welcome Dominic's support. How long had she known him – could it really be less than a week? It was a little alarming to think that he already seemed indispensable for her comfort. 'No,' she said. 'Unless you greatly dislike it, sir, I would prefer that you stay. I have no secrets from you, do I?'

He took her hand and pressed it, appearing to understand some part at least of the confusion of her thoughts. Francis said gruffly, 'I want to thank you for asking me to come and see you, Maria. I should have broken the ice myself, but I'm very glad you were braver.'

Meg took a deep breath. It was so hard to know where to

begin. 'I have a great deal to tell you, but I am very glad that you are here. It has been far too long. Shall we sit down and be comfortable while we talk?'

She took a seat, and her companions followed her lead. She said, 'Francis, I would be excessively glad if we could overcome this horrid estrangement, which I know was no more of your making than it was of mine. I would like nothing more than to be a proper sister to you, and although I have had no opportunity to discuss the subject with her, I know my twin must feel the same.'

She had thought, when she began speaking, that this was a mere preliminary to the real reason she had summoned Francis here, something that must be said as a sort of nod to the conventions, but to her surprise sudden tears thickened her voice as she uttered the words, and she knew them to be true. She'd never realised before how much she had missed knowing her brother, and how deeply the sight of him, smiling at her with an almost painful eagerness, would affect her. She stopped, unable to continue for a moment.

Francis reached out and took her cold hand in his large, warm, pink one. He had tears standing in his eyes too, she saw. 'No need to distress yourself,' he said. 'Perfectly understand what you're saying, and quite agree with you. Not another word on the topic after today, unless you want to say it. Not your fault, not your sister's, nor mine. Not Lady Nightingale's, either, for that matter. She was always very good to me, you know, right from the start. She told me that she knew she could never replace my poor mother and wouldn't dream of trying, but that she'd like to be a good friend to me, a sort of aunt or something of that nature, if I wouldn't mind that. Didn't occur to me at the time that she couldn't have been twenty herself when she said it. Just a chit of a girl, really, not much older than you are now, trying to make the best of things.' He cleared his throat of some obstruction.

'I was just a schoolboy, lonely little fellow, would have been glad... but my father wouldn't stand for it, of course. Never could quite see why, still don't know, really, but realised after a little while, especially after you two girls were born, that when she was kind to me, he made her suffer for it in a dozen tiny, petty ways. So... I stayed away. Didn't like to, but felt I had no option. And I dare say you don't recall, but I came round to Grosvenor Square a few times after your mother had gone, thought I'd see if he'd let me be a brother to you, at least. Wanted to take you to Astley's to see the horses, something like that, or to Gunter's for ices. Sort of thing an older brother ought to do for his little sister. Thought we might both enjoy it. But there was no question of it being allowed.' Mr Nightingale still seemed to be experiencing a certain difficulty in speaking; his voice was congested and he was flushed with emotion.

Meg said unsteadily, 'I can see that we have all suffered at my father's hands, and I am very sorry for it. If we can set right what he has done to us in keeping us all apart – for you must know that he has contrived to separate me from my sister too, as well as from you – then I should be very glad of it. But there are things you do not know, and which I must tell you.' She paused and said, 'I think I must be as honest as I can be with you from the start, or what is the point? I'm not Maria, Francis, though I have been pretending to be for a little while – I'm Meg.'

'Eh?' said her brother, goggling.

Meg told him briefly of Maria's flight and her dislike of the marriage her father had arranged for her, and Mr Nightingale shot a rather startled glance at Sir Dominic. That gentleman smiled wryly and contributed, 'Naturally, if I had realised how much Miss Nightingale disliked the idea, I would never have offered for her. But I had no private speech with her and was lamentably ignorant of her feelings.'

'Where is she?' asked Francis, his brows creased with concern. 'I don't like the sound of this at all. My father forcing her into marriage in a dashed shabby way… Is she safe?'

Meg hastened to reassure him that she was, and that she, Meg, had seen her just a day or so ago. She went on to tell him that, once she had realised that Sir Dominic was blameless in the matter and that her sister was in no danger, the situation had begun to seem rather odd to her.

'I should say it is!' her brother said fervently. 'Never heard of such a rum go in all my life! Twins masquerading as each other – not like real life at all, but puts me in mind of a play I once got dragged to, some famous fellow wrote it, can't quite recall his name. I dare say you know the sort of thing I mean. It was funny in parts, but had a lot of devilish tedious songs in it, hey nonny nonny, fol de lol, and so on.'

She was aware of Sir Dominic imperfectly stifling laughter at her side, and said repressively, 'No, I know, but what I ask myself is, why was Father so desperate for Maria to marry Sir Dominic in particular?'

'Dashed good catch, I'm sure,' said Francis politely. 'Beau De Lacy and all that. Eligible, you know.' Sir Dominic was sitting, so he couldn't bow properly, but he inclined his head and upper body in gracious acknowledgement over the teacups. He seemed to be enjoying himself enormously now.

She sighed impatiently. 'Yes, yes, I'm sure we can all agree that he must be quite the most eligible man in London, but why should my father care for that? I don't believe he would trouble himself for so much as a minute over Maria's happiness. You know as well as I do that he doesn't care a button for any of us, nor for what society thinks of him, since he doesn't mix in it. It's not my secret to tell, but please believe me when I say that he has gone to quite extraordinary lengths to make sure that Maria marries Dominic – marries Sir Dominic, I should say – rather than any other man. And I had to ask myself why.'

'Not at all like the old curmudgeon,' agreed Francis disrespectfully. 'So your idea is, there's something devilish havey-cavey going on, eh?'

'There must be,' Dominic said, the humour fading from his grey eyes. 'The truth is that your father has gained a sort of hold over my mother, and has used it to induce her to press the match on me by threatening to reveal the truth to the world.'

'Good God, do you say so, old fellow?' uttered Mr Nightingale, deeply shocked. 'Blackmail, by Jupiter!'

'Precisely so.'

'The more I hear about this,' Francis said profoundly, 'the more I realise that something cursed smoky really is afoot. He must have a strong reason for doing something so rum.'

'We think so too.' Meg knew the time to utter her suspicions aloud had arrived. 'I have been puzzling over the matter a great deal, and I believe that our father has stolen Maria's money – her inheritance from our grandmother. I think he's taken it all and spent it.'

34

'No!' said Francis, shocked. 'Surely not! I know he's a dashed selfish old court card, but he wouldn't do that, would he?'

'I don't see what else fits the facts as we know them,' Meg told him earnestly. She was conscious of a great urge to pace the room in her usual manner, but repressed it in case Francis, not being well acquainted with her yet, should find it alarming. 'Whyever else would he be so keen to ensure that Maria marries a man over whom he believes he has power? Imagine what would happen after the marriage, if I'm right and the money has gone into his pocket. What would anyone else do, on discovering he'd been tricked over the nature of his wife's fortune?'

'He would protest,' said Dominic a little grimly. 'Threaten your father with exposure and public disgrace. Go to lawyers and make a case of it, if threats didn't have any effect. It would all be most unpleasant for your poor sister, of course, or any woman in her situation, but I'm sure it happens all the time, since women are granted so little control over their own money.'

'But *you* wouldn't be in a position to make any sort of protest. You'd be under so much pressure to say nothing, do nothing...'

'I most certainly would.'

Francis had been watching them intently. 'But dash it all,' he said, 'my father is a wealthy man! It's not as if he's addicted to the card tables, or lives an extravagant life. Hasn't bought a new waistcoat for ten years, I dare say. He has vast sums, invested in the Funds, and my understanding is he did well round about Waterloo time, too, when so many people panicked and sold out at a loss and ruined themselves. It all happened by accident, of course. My aunt Greystone told me that by the time his man of business made him understand that there was a battle going on in the present day that he should take urgent notice of, not some cursed ancient Greek affair with lots of chaps running about in skirts and sandals saying poetry, the whole thing was over and Old Boney was defeated and everything went back to normal. Supposing I admit him capable of such villainy, he can't possibly need the money.'

'I think he may have used it to buy books,' Meg told him. She'd been thinking about it, lying awake brooding over the matter, and it was the only explanation that made sense to her. As Francis said, her father's manner of existence was not extravagant except in one key area: his life's obsession, his studies.

'*Books*?' Francis said in utter disgust. 'You think he's stolen thousands of pounds from his own daughter in a dashed dishonourable, not to mention illegal, fashion and spent it on mouldy old books?'

'There was a big library sale six months ago,' Sir Dominic murmured. 'I recall reading about it at the time. Lord Harcourt's collection of ancient books and manuscripts was sold at auction after his death. It was mentioned in all the newspapers, and I understand once everything was disposed of a very large amount was raised for his heirs. There were several unique items of great antiquity that collectors were said to be most excited over. A precious early scroll of Homer was said to be of particular value, and worth many thousands of guineas. If he bought several things, you know, it could quickly add up to an enormous sum that he could not easily lay his hands on by any honest means.'

'Well, I'm bound to say that that sounds exactly like my father,' Francis said robustly, 'getting fired up about some moth-eaten old bits of parchment no normal person would cross the street to pick out of the gutter. Not even in good honest English, I dare swear, but in dashed Greek or Latin or something of that kind! Did the newspapers say who bought the things, can you recall?'

Dominic shook his head. 'Unfortunately not. In such circumstances it is usual to employ confidential agents to do the actual bidding, I understand. The identities of the men behind them would never be revealed without their agreement. They would be under no obligation to make matters public – unless, of course, their intention was not to keep the prizes they had gained for themselves, but instead to donate them to the British Museum, or to some other learned institution, in which case I'm sure they'd be happy to be named and win public approbation for their generosity.'

'Public approbation be blowed. You'd never catch my father doing that,' Francis said positively. 'No, if he'd got his hands on something, he'd mean to keep it, I'm quite sure. Gloat over it in private, maybe show it to a few of his cursed peculiar inky old friends. Perhaps you're right.'

'I believe we are,' Meg replied. 'And the only person who can find out the truth is you, Francis. As Sir Dominic says, it is quite mortifying to reflect how little standing Maria, I, or even my mother, can have in such a matter, even though it concerns all of us so closely. We can be ruined, cheated, and do nothing about it. It is infuriating... but this is not the time for such animadversions, perhaps.'

To do Mr Nightingale justice, it was not necessary to appeal to self-interest to get him to help. Meg had no occasion to remind him that if their father had been playing at ducks and drakes with Maria's fortune, he might easily have done the same with the Nightingale estate. The bulk of the family property, including the Grosvenor Square house and the country estate, was entailed, she knew, and would pass to Francis as next custodian after his father's death; it was no more Lord Nightingale's to dispose of than Maria's inheritance was. But if they were correct in believing him dishonest, heaven knew what he might have done.

Francis showed himself perfectly willing to instruct his lawyer to look into the matter as soon as it might be arranged. 'I have every right to do so,' he said stoutly. 'My father was already past his first youth when his mother drew up her final will, and so she made me a trustee too along with him, even though I was only a boy in short petticoats at the time – looking to the future, you know, as was only proper. I've never been called upon to do anything except sign the odd paper now and again, but I can quite see that I should have been sharper about the whole business. But you don't go about imagining your own father to be capable of such villainy. I'll put my man on it, that's the ticket. He's a young fellow, keen as mustard, name of Clarke, and I dare say there's nothing he would enjoy more than ferreting out a mystery like a dashed legal terrier. It'll cause a scandal, though, you know, when it all comes out, but I do see it can't be helped.'

'I wonder?' said Sir Dominic thoughtfully. 'Public exposure may not be necessary after all, if we keep our wits about us. You're right, Nightingale, when you say that your father, assuming always that our suspicions are correct, hasn't gambled away Maria's portion at the faro tables. If that were the case, there would be nothing we could do but prevent him from causing any more damage. As it is, the money still exists, albeit in manuscript form, and can therefore be restored to its rightful owner. It seems to me that the occasion calls for another great sale of books and manuscripts – this time, the famous collection of Lord Nightingale. You would be well within your rights, I believe, to offer him a choice. He can answer for his fraud in a court of law, and hazard everything – his reputation, his liberty, even perhaps his life, as I cannot imagine him doing at all well in prison – on the uncertain views of a judge and jury, or he can set matters straight without excessive scrutiny by allowing his precious possessions to be sold and every penny repaid. And he would have to relinquish control of all financial matters for the future, of course. He must never be allowed to do this sort of thing again.'

'The items he bought from Lord Harcourt's collection, if indeed he did do so, may not be worth what he paid for them,' Meg said anxiously. 'He is quite obsessive, you know, and not rational, when it comes to his books, or so my mother has told me a dozen times.'

'No, it's quite true that they might not be of equal value to anyone else, but he's been collecting for years, hasn't he? I think you should be prepared to be quite ruthless, Nightingale, in making sure your sister gets her due. And really, I know it's not your immediate concern, but I can't help thinking that if indeed he's tapped into one fund he had access to, he's quite likely to have tapped into another. You should have a care to your own affairs too, and tell your man as much.'

'By Jupiter, I wouldn't be in the least surprised, now you put it like that. And it occurs to me, De Lacy, it would be no more than he deserves, if his precious collection has to be sold and he has to watch it,' Francis agreed energetically. 'Let the blackmailer be blackmailed in his turn! There's a certain poetic what d'you call it about the whole thing, you know? Another of those Greek things, maybe, about the punishment fitting the crime. Like the cursed rum touch of a fellow whose food turned to gold because all he cared about was money. Might quite enjoy pointing that out to the old monster if I get the chance – just goes to show, education ain't all bad, though we see the trouble it can get you into if taken to extremes. Makes you think.'

His companions agreed that it most certainly did, and they took leave of him in great satisfaction, Francis promising to go instantly to his lawyer's office and to report back as soon as he knew anything, however insignificant it might seem.

'A good afternoon's work,' Sir Dominic said, smiling down at Meg, after Mr Nightingale had departed.

'It was, and I am glad Francis proved to be so amiable and amenable, and so happy to be a true brother to us at last, but I need to tell Maria everything that is happening. She must be excessively anxious, and it's bound to take a few days for Francis's lawyer to investigate matters, particularly if my father's man of business is in league with him and throws up obstructions.'

'I am sure Mr Clarke will be on the watch for that. This may all be resolved in a short while, Meg, if all goes to plan.'

'Are you going to ask me to marry you again?' she said, her face still troubled.

'It's not the time or the place, is it?'

'No. Too much is still uncertain, too much could still go horribly wrong. And you can't kiss me here, Dominic – it's your mother's house and she may come in at any moment, or your cousin, or a servant to clear away the tea things. I could not be comfortable.'

He took her hand and raised it to his lips, brushing it with the lightest touch that still made her shiver with frustrated desire. 'It's such a pity,' he said, his voice low and seductive but his eyes full of laughter. 'Although I'm not sure if I wish you to be comfortable, precisely. I had something far more exciting in mind.'

'You are incorrigible,' she said, her voice wavering between sternness and laughter. 'You don't want to reduce me to a quivering wreck on your mother's sofa any more than I wish to be so reduced. Admit it!'

Together they looked at the sofa, which was a fashionable creation in shiny lilac satin, its gilded frame embellished with sphinxes and nameless knobbly Egyptian decorations that might perhaps be intended for stylised scarab beetles. As well as being ugly, it had an undeniably spindly appearance. And it wasn't very large. 'When I reduce you to a quivering wreck,' Dominic said, 'I promise you it will be in private, and on something much more solid.'

'A bed?' she asked wistfully. How wonderful it would be if all this could be over...

'A very large bed, a rug in front of a fire, a couch in my summerhouse at midnight... Meg, I can think of a dozen places. A hundred.'

It was perhaps just as well that Cousin Sarah entered the room just then, to see if Lady De Lacy's guests needed any more tea, or anything else to make them quite comfortable. Since they required nothing that she could provide, nor anyone else, they thanked her for her kindness, and took their farewells.

Dominic drove Meg to His Grace the Duke of Fernsby's house and left her there, promising to return in an hour or so and escort her home. When she emerged, bearing the aspect of one who had been crying at some recent point, she said with a sniff, 'Maria has been in a fever of anxiety over the last few days, and I cannot wonder at it. I was sorry not to be able to give her more definite news.'

'How did she react to your suggestion that Lord Nightingale may have embezzled her fortune? I think you had not shared the suspicion with her before?'

'I had not. She was very angry, of course, but when she had cursed our father in as many ways as she could conceive, and encouraged me to do the same, she agreed that it was all too horribly plausible, and that there can be no other obvious explanation for what has happened. She asked me to tell you that she is very sorry you should have become embroiled in our affairs, especially to the extent of finding yourself subject to something as shocking as blackmail.'

'She has not said anything to distress you, or given you bad news? I know it is not in the least my affair, my dear, though I wish it were, but I cannot help but observe...'

Meg smiled rather damply at him. 'How ungallant of you, to draw attention to the fact that I have been crying, sir! No, I am teasing you. We have been indulging ourselves in talking of the past, and of all the things our father has deprived us of, not least the chance to know our brother.'

'The future will be very different, for all of you.'

'Oh, Dominic, I do hope so.'

35

A few days went by without any news. Mrs Greystone, who still remained in complete ignorance of what was going on, emerged from her seclusion, but was still quite unsteady on her feet, and tearful, and made no protest when Meg said that she had no desire to attend any of the social engagements to which they had been invited, and thus had no need of a chaperon. It seemed safest to avoid public scrutiny, since it was now clear that none of Maria's friends apart from Lady Primrose, who was so much more than a friend, could know of her disappearance or Meg's impersonation of her sister. It was surely best not to risk close scrutiny now that it was unnecessary.

The wedding was now just a week distant. All of Maria's trousseau had been delivered, but it was impossible to know if these magnificent clothes would ever be worn, and in what circumstances.

Meg had little to do all day now but to visit Maria, to ride and drive with Sir Dominic, to avoid her father, and to wait. By tacit consent, she and her sister's fiancé had pulled back a little from the recent intimacy they'd shared. They found comfort in each other's company – she did, at any rate, and she thought he did too. But they spoke of idle, trivial matters, and avoided discussion of serious subjects; particularly they refrained from speculating on whether Francis's lawyer Mr Clarke would be successful in his enquiries. The consequences, if he were unsuccessful, were too horrible to contemplate. Dwelling on the matter could only make her anxious, and serve no positive purpose at all.

Sir Dominic did not renew his suit during this strange time, and Meg was grateful for his forbearance. She tried – and failed – to prevent herself from indulging in daydreams in which matters were magically resolved and she stood at the altar openly as herself and married him, while her mother, Aunt Greystone, Hannah, Maria and Lady Primrose looked on, smiling. In her fantasy, Angela Jones and Annie Gilbert were there too, with the little boys, as an acknowledged part of the family. It seemed most unlikely that this could ever happen, but when had daydreams ever been logical?

She tried too – and failed spectacularly again – to suppress seductive thoughts of what would happen afterwards, when she was alone with her husband, as they undressed each other in laughing haste and fell naked into the bed that he had promised her. He'd kiss his way down her body, his lips worshipping her breasts and then moving further; her hands would fix in his silky honey-brown hair and she'd give herself up to waves of intense pleasure…

But it might so easily never happen. If they could find no ammunition to counter Lord Nightingale's blackmail, if her suspicions turned out to be false or impossible to prove, there would be no way out of their tangled situation without pain and scandal. Even if she quashed her fears and married Sir Dominic under her sister's name – and she still wasn't at all sure if he'd agree to that, or if she should – the fear of exposure must always cloud their happiness. Their children would be illegitimate, and forever vulnerable to discovery. But then if she refused to participate in the masquerade, refused to take that risk on herself, and on Sir Dominic and their unborn children, she'd be betraying Maria and placing her in all sorts of danger... How could she be happy, if she had put her own interests above her sister's and left her in painful uncertainty?

The days passed slowly. Meg's only real recourse was to escape into writing, and she found herself sketching out a fantastical novel in the Gothic style, with two heroines, a pair of twins, Melusina and Marianna, who had long been separated due to the cruel machinations of their guardian. He was a sinister Italian nobleman, who – for reasons presently unclear but which would no doubt reveal themselves in due course, not least to his creator – kept them imprisoned separately, one in a ruined castle, one in a rustic hovel in the middle of a dreary swamp. Meg lost herself in bloodcurdling prose and implausible situations, aware that she was pouring much of her real anguish into the thoughts and feelings of her long-suffering heroines. One of them was presently chained to the wall in a medieval dungeon, dressed in rags and straining against her bonds – no, it was an oubliette, which sounded much better, in the middle of a terrifying storm, and water was rising about her feet, creeping ever upwards. Was it all to end here, leaving her bereaved sister to seek bloody revenge? That was assuming Marianna ever found out what happened, but probably an aged retainer would tell her in a highly touching manner. Or maybe the aged retainer would *think* poor Melusina was dead, when in fact she escaped at the last possible moment...

At this point, a note arrived from Sir Dominic, and Melusina was abandoned temporarily to her watery fate. Meg herself was summoned to tea at Lady De Lacy's house once more; Sir Dominic would arrive to collect her later that afternoon.

She dressed herself with care in one of the new gowns: it had a blue silk bodice, puffed sleeves and a skirt trimmed with a series of fine horizontal pleats at the hem. She wore it over a long-sleeved habit-shirt of white-embroidered muslin that was almost transparent, and revealed what she hoped Sir Dominic would find to be intriguing glimpses of her upper bosom and arms. She had no idea what secrets were to be disclosed this afternoon, nor if the news was good or bad; she had an absurd need to be dressed well to arm herself against any eventuality. It was odd, she mused, how waiting felt like the worst thing in the world until it was almost over, and then one craved ignorance again as a preferable state. Thus might Marianna feel in her hut, as she waited anxiously for news of Melusina…

Sir Dominic was accompanied by his groom, and it scarcely needed his warning frown to prevent her from bombarding him with a dozen urgent questions during the phaeton ride. Fishwick was a highly trusted servant who had known the secret of Maria's disappearance, but that didn't mean his employer had shared the rest of the matter with him – the blackmail, and all their suspicions. 'I had a brief note from your brother, asking if we could meet at my mother's house again, which I have arranged. I know little more than that,' he told her. He'd squeezed her hand reassuringly as he handed her up into her seat, but there could be no other form of communication between them for the moment.

When they arrived in Clarges Street, Fishwick took the ribbons and drove away; they might be a long while about their business, and Sir Dominic would not wish to keep his horses standing. 'Your sister should arrive soon, if she has not already,' he said in a low tone as they climbed the steps. 'Francis said in his note that he felt it important she be here, and he is right, of course. She will have come veiled, to conceal her identity as far as possible, and will announce herself to my mother's servants as you. But the time for such concealment is almost past, I hope.'

They were, in fact, the first to arrive, but Francis appeared a few minutes after them, with Maria and Lady Primrose on his heels. They were all shown into Lady De Lacy's larger drawing room, since they were too numerous for her private sitting room, and there was an awkward little silence as they all removed their hats and seated themselves. Cousin Sarah was not present, and Dominic's mother was looking particularly tragic in purple and grey, with a great many trailing scarves. Dominic and Maria smiled at each other rather ruefully, on this their first meeting since her flight, but there was no time for any sort of conversation between them.

Francis, very pink in the face, said, 'I'm very grateful to you, Lady De Lacy, for allowing us to meet here. Excessively kind of you, ma'am, I must say. And though it's not to the purpose and we should get on with our business, I'm happy as a grig to see both my sisters together, after so many years! I hope... But it's not the time.' They murmured agreement; Maria was seated in the middle of a large sofa, with Meg on one side and Lady Primrose on the other, and clasped a hand of each. Sir Dominic was at his mother's side, in case of spasms, and Francis had the place of honour, in a gold Louis XV armchair with a rather thronelike aspect that was oddly appropriate in the circumstances.

'I trust we're all up to snuff on the matter – no secrets here?' Francis said, and they all nodded. 'Well then, I have to tell you that my sister Margaret, Meg, was quite right. Dashed shocking thing, and I'm sorry to have to say it in front of all of you, but there's no dodging it: the old b... the old gentleman has been doing exactly what you feared – making free with Maria's fortune. The better part of it's gone, according to what Clarke was able to discover.'

Meg did not know if she made some sound, to hear all her suspicions confirmed, but she was aware that she was clutching Maria's hand convulsively, and that her sister was clinging to her just as fiercely in return. So it was true!

'That's why he was blackmailing me!' said Lady De Lacy sharply. 'He knew that when Dominic found out, as he must after the wedding, he could say nothing. What an utter scoundrel! Oh – I'm sorry, dear girls, but I cannot restrain myself from naming him so. I hope you will forgive me.' She didn't sound enormously sorry, in truth.

'You will hear no disagreement from us,' Maria responded instantly, spectacles glinting fiercely. 'He is all that and more. He has grievously wronged all of us. The question is, what are we going to do about it?'

'Well, the horrid old rascal hasn't done me any direct harm,' said Lady Primrose bluntly, 'and I'd sure he doesn't know of my existence, so it's not for me to say, but I think he should be horsewhipped – to begin with – for what he's done to you, Maria. Then shot, possibly. I'll have to think seriously about it.'

'Quite right!' agreed Lady De Lacy with bloodthirsty relish. If Lord Nightingale had entered the room at that moment, Meg would not have given a farthing for his safety.

'That's not all,' Francis said, 'and I'm in full agreement with all of you. Bound to be, because Clarke – excellent fellow – has discovered that he's been messing about with the entailed property as well. Selling pieces of land he has no right to sell, actually forging my signature on legal documents. All manner of shocking things!'

Meg said, frowning, 'Does my father know you know? I'm not blaming you for it, I'm sure it couldn't be helped, but I don't see how your lawyer could ask to look at all the papers without raising grave doubts in my father's lawyer's mind. Even if he didn't think anything was amiss, he must surely mention the matter to Lord Nightingale, or he'd not be doing his duty to his employer.'

'Ah, well, that would be correct, Meg, except that young Clarke is a deep one. He went to see the fellow in his office with no appointment, thought he'd surprise him – Sallow, his name is, little rat of a man. Clarke took his measure in an instant and pegged him for a blubbering coward, and so he took a high hand with him from the start. He told him he knew for certain that Lord Nightingale had been up to all manner of skulduggery – even though he actually knew nothing of the sort, only suspected it – and said that he'd make sure Master Sallow went down with him if he didn't help prove it. Who d'you think will get transported to Botany Bay, he said, or hung, for that matter – a peer of the realm, or a ten-shilling lawyer with no powerful friends to save him? Apparently the fellow knew exactly what was amiss, started bleating about how none of it was his fault, he'd only been obeying his master's orders, and after that he did all he could to help, in the hope of saving his own neck.'

Francis showed great animation as he continued. 'I've written proof that would satisfy any court in the land – there's documents supposedly signed by me on dates I wasn't even in the country, if you can credit it, but taking a toddle to Paris with a couple of other fellows, friends of mine. Can call a dozen witnesses to prove I was gambling in the Casino when I was supposed to be sitting in Lincoln's Inn dashed well signing away my sister's fortune, and my own. There's no doubt about any of it, I promise you. We've got him.'

Someone – perhaps everyone – breathed a deep sigh of relief.

'So now,' Sir Dominic said, smiling at Meg, 'we only need to confront him. Your father can have no notion that anything is afoot, and we may take him by surprise and sweep him entirely off his feet. When shall we do it – today?'

36

Lord Nightingale's butler raised his eyebrows at the curious little family deputation that arrived in Grosvenor Square a short while later, but he could hardly deny admission to his master's three children (one of whom was resident in the house), accompanied by Miss Maria's intended husband. Primrose had discreetly gone home, after squeezing Maria's hand and wishing them all luck, and Lady De Lacy too had decided not to come; she had no desire to see the odious blackmailer again, she had said, since she could not trust herself to address him with anything resembling common courtesy. She depended on her son to say and do all that was necessary, and was presumably now reclining on her fainting couch with her smelling salts, contemplating ingenious methods of revenge in the manner of Lady Macbeth or Clytemnestra.

They were ushered into the drawing room and awaited their unwitting host in tense silence. It seemed to take an inordinate amount of time before he made an appearance, and Meg had just been about to suggest that they go to confront him boldly in his library when the door opened, and her father stood blinking on the threshold, surveying them impassively.

Even with all she knew of his wickedness, and all she had suffered at his hands, it was hard to reconcile the harmless-looking scholar she saw before her with the ruthless and cruel actions she knew he had perpetrated. Lord Nightingale was tall, like his children, and had presumably once been fair – his brows and lashes were sandy, but he covered his hair, or his lack of hair, with an old-fashioned wig, which made him appear older than his sixty years. Endless hours of study had left him stooped and pallid, and like his older daughter he wore gold-rimmed spectacles perched on his nose. His dress verged on the shabby, his face was heavily lined and his expression unreadable. His silence made an extraordinary impression on his younger daughter. Would he not speak? He must be astonished to see the two children from whom he was estranged here, together, in his house. Surely he must fear discovery, and wonder how much they knew. And yet he said nothing.

The moment of silence stretched, and then he shuffled forward into the room and the waiting butler was able to close the door behind him and exit smartly. 'To what do I owe the honour of this most unexpected visit?' Lord Nightingale said drily at last. His voice, appropriately, was papery thin, little more than a rustle, as if from long disuse. 'It must be something vastly important, that you have all come to interrupt me so rudely when you know, or should know, that I am busy with my most important studies.' His tone did not alter a jot when he turned to Meg and Maria, who stood close together, and said levelly, 'I suppose your bitch of a mother sent you?'

Meg gasped and a gloved hand flew to her mouth. Before the Baron could turn on her and ask her what the devil she and her sister were about – the words could almost be seen hovering on his parched lips – his son stepped forward and said fiercely, 'If you weren't an old man and my father, to my sorrow, I'd dashed well knock you down for that foul remark! You must know perfectly well why we're here!'

'I know nothing of the kind,' Nightingale said waspishly. 'But I presume you're going to tell me. I have never had a high opinion of your intelligence, Francis – you must take after your fool of a dam rather than any member of my illustrious family – but I'd assume you can manage to explain yourself adequately in simple words.' An unpleasant little smile hovered around his lips and he snuffled disagreeably, as though he was congratulating himself inwardly upon a witty riposte. He appeared to be oblivious to the almost palpable waves of loathing coming at him from every person in the room.

'I am happy to do so,' said Francis stiffly, his face flushed. Maria, who stood by him, reached out and put her hand on his arm, and he achieved a grateful little smile in her direction before he continued. 'In simple words, then, so that you may understand them, we have discovered exactly how much you have cheated us, Father. My sister's portion, stolen from her, and the entailed estates, plundered. You have even forged my name on legal documents, and I can prove it.'

'Nonsense.' Lord Nightingale appeared tranquil and unaffected.

'It's not nonsense,' Meg said hotly. She had forgotten how easily her father filled her with rage; it was one thing to know all he'd done, and another to see him calmly denying it, as though he could distort the very nature of reality by his unshakeable belief in himself. 'Francis can prove that he was abroad on an occasion when he was supposed to have signed an important document. He has the forged paper, and he also has witnesses who will swear that he was in Paris with them on the date it was drawn up.'

'They dashed well will,' Francis growled. 'They'll be delighted to.'

'No one will believe a word your ramshackle friends say,' his father answered serenely. 'I am sure you must have bribed my idiot of a lawyer, or something of that disreputable nature. My word as a peer and an eminent scholar will naturally count for far more than theirs or yours. Imbecile boy! And in any case, I can't believe you really want to air our family secrets in public. The illustrious Beau De Lacy, who is to be your brother-in-law so very soon, I am sure has not the least desire to do so.' His eyes found Sir Dominic's; unbelievably, the old man was still smiling, his smug confidence apparently unshaken.

'You may be confusing me with my mother,' said Sir Dominic icily. 'I would never have given in to your unconscionable blackmail if she'd told me of it directly, and I won't do so now. Spread any tale you like about my family; I'm sure it will be drowned in the enormous scandal that will be created when the extent of your theft and fraud is exposed to everyone.'

'You're bluffing,' Lord Nightingale said, his smile slipping a fraction. 'You're all bluffing. You wouldn't dare expose me.'

'Do not continue to delude yourself, I beg you. It would give me a great deal of satisfaction to enlighten the whole world as to exactly what you are,' Sir Dominic told him. 'It would be nothing more than you deserve, and I don't think for a moment that anyone in this room would shed a single tear if you were imprisoned or transported. If we refrain from seeking legal remedies for your many crimes, it is not out of any compunction for you, or fear of scandal. It's only because between us we have had a better idea – a much more fitting punishment.'

'De Lacy's hit the nail on the head. The truth is, we have a mind to try a little blackmail of our own,' Francis said steadily. Meg could see that he shared – as they all did – in the exhilaration of facing her father down and doing so as a team. 'You should appreciate that, I'd have thought – just like one of your blasted dull Greek tragedies. Hubris, that's the ticket! You will pay for your dashed hubris by auctioning off your precious collection and paying us back what you've stolen from us.'

'I will do no such thing!' Lord Nightingale said. His face was ghastly pale now, and his eyes were wild. Clearly the threat to what he held most dear in the world had hit home, and he was taking his assembled family seriously at last.

'You will, or Francis will place all his proof in the hands of a magistrate and demand he acts on it,' Maria said. 'We shall all go there together, right this instant, and denounce you in the strongest possible terms. If you imagine for a second that I will allow you to get away with stealing my inheritance, and my brother's, you don't know me at all. You don't know any of us. Which frankly doesn't surprise me, since Meg has been living here and masquerading as me for days and days and you haven't even noticed. You may think you're very clever, Father, but in all the ways that count you are actually exceedingly stupid!'

'I will cast you off, you impudent hoyden!' he cried, staggering a little and clutching at the back of a chair to support himself. 'You are no longer any daughter of mine! I have no children! I disinherit the whole pack of you!'

'I may be an impudent hoyden, but at least I'm not a thief and a swindler! And you can't cast me off. That's a ridiculous thing to say, because Francis is my trustee too, and he will make sure I receive every penny of my inheritance, won't you, Francis?'

'Of course I will! And, while we're at it, I know you haven't been paying my stepmother and Meg all the monies you owe them for their upkeep, and I will take care of that, too! There are going to be a lot of changes in this family, and since you're plainly not fit to be head of it, I'm taking over! You will no longer have control of any of the revenue from the estate or the funds, and if you object, sir, I will gladly see you in court!'

'Bravo, Francis!' his sisters said in unison. Their brother seemed quite transformed by the events of the last few days, and was almost visibly growing in confidence with every moment that passed, while their father, in a strange sort of symmetry, appeared to shrink into himself. His lips were moving convulsively, and Meg thought he must be telling over a list of the precious things he was so soon to lose. She felt a pang of sympathy, but then remembered all his deliberate, wicked cruelty and hardened her heart.

'I will pay you a small allowance for your personal needs, and arrange appropriate accommodation for you, but there'll be no more bankrupting the family by buying fusty old manuscripts!' Francis went on inexorably. Lord Nightingale's face twitched with acute pain as these words made their impact on him, but he made no other sort of response.

Meg had been aware for a little while of some sort of unusual disturbance outside in the hall; it was hard to imagine what it might be, in so well regulated a household. She certainly could not conceive that the butler would be so foolish as to attempt to interrupt what he must be aware was no ordinary family encounter by admitting a visitor, however insistent they might be. But she soon found she was mistaken; the door opened somewhat abruptly, and a voice that was not quite level, as if the servant too had suffered a severe shock in recent moments, announced, 'Lady Nightingale!'

37

Dominic watched in fascination as a lady of perhaps forty summers strolled into the room, perfectly mistress of herself and of the highly unusual situation. Hermione Nightingale was tall, built along magnificent lines, and greatly resembled her daughters, though her hair was a little darker and her eyes more green than blue. She was dressed rather eccentrically for a woman of rank, in a shapeless round gown of no particular colour which appeared to have undergone ungentle treatment in recent hours. It was sadly creased and liberally stained – it was almost too good to be true – with what appeared to be ink. Lady Nightingale clasped a substantial leather bag that must surely, he thought, contain a manuscript, and which she had obviously not wished to entrust to the butler's care. Her unconventional appearance in no way diminishing her poise, she surveyed the room, smiling at her daughters, her stepson and Dominic himself, though he was a stranger to her. Then she said superbly, regarding her estranged husband with a critical gaze, 'Good God, Augustus, you look simply frightful! Do you never go outside or take any exercise? What in heaven's name have you been doing to yourself since I left?'

Lord Nightingale's mouth was hanging open in his grey face; he seemed to have no answer for her, and perhaps he had temporarily lost the power of speech altogether at this fresh shock. Meg crossed the room swiftly to her side and embraced her warmly. 'Mama!' she said, emerging from her arms a little dishevelled. 'I am excessively glad to see you, and your timing is superb, but how come you to be here, and today of all days?'

'Wrote to her myself, Meg,' Francis explained, rubbing his nose, a little embarrassed. 'Must have forgotten to mention it to you in all the excitement. Was pretty confident we were going to discover that the old... that my father had been up to something dashed havey-cavey, so I thought Her Ladyship should be here to see the upshot of it all. Sent my valet to Bath by the mail coach, got him to hire a post-chaise when he got there. Glad it's come off all right and tight – very good to see you after all this time, ma'am.'

'Thank you, Francis, it was most kind of you to think of me,' she said, bestowing a beaming smile upon him. 'It was very clever of you to arrange all the details, and the carriage journey – most comfortable, really, compared with the stage – has allowed me finally to finish my manuscript, which I will now be able to deliver in person. Matters have worked out excessively well, I think.'

'I am very happy to make your acquaintance, ma'am,' Dominic said, stepping forward and bowing low to her. 'I am Dominic De Lacy, and I look forward to the opportunity of becoming better acquainted with you.'

She surveyed him comprehensively from head to foot, smiling a little. 'I apprehend that you are the highly eligible young man my daughter was so desperate not to marry.'

'One of your daughters, ma'am, to whom I owe an apology. Not, I trust, the other.'

'Well, certainly as society is currently arranged you can only marry one of them. It would be as well to make sure you pick the right one,' she replied tranquilly.

'Oh,' he said, 'I promise you, I have.'

Maria said gleefully, 'I knew I was right! I knew you'd be perfect for each other almost as soon as I met you, Sir Dominic. I warn you, I shall always take the credit for this match and remind you of it often!' Dominic smiled briefly at her, but all his attention was focused on his beloved.

When he looked up from her at last, he saw that Lady Nightingale had crossed the room to her eldest daughter's side, and rather tentatively reached out to her. 'I'm so sorry, my dear Maria,' she told her now. Her apparently unshakeable confidence seemed to slip a little now, and she did not attempt to conceal her uncertainty. 'I should never have left you here with your father, and if you cannot forgive me for it, I do not blame you. I have been a terrible mother to you, and will be forever grateful if you allow me at least to try to make amends for it, though I do not know if I ever truly can.'

'I won't deny that I have been angry with you,' Maria said. Tears were streaming down both their faces unheeded, and Meg made a small sound of distress that caused Dominic to wish that he could put his arm about her, to give her what comfort he could. 'For five years I have blamed you for leaving me, and I have been jealous that you took Meg, so that I lost her too. But I know better now. I know that you were faced with an impossible choice, and made the best of the situation you found yourself in through no fault of your own. My father is hideously selfish, and took pleasure in driving a wedge between us – our estrangement was his intention all along, and if I persist in being at outs with you, Mama, I am only doing what he wants. I refuse to give him that satisfaction any longer. The responsibility for all the dreadful things that have happened in this family is his, not yours.'

Lord Nightingale had been standing, unheeded, apparently uncomprehending, still clutching the chair back, as all this emotion swirled around him. It was impossible to tell if Maria's words caused him any distress – Dominic would have wagered that the potential loss of his beloved collection was what had devastated him, rather than the openly expressed scorn of his family. His wife turned to him again and said, 'Augustus, you are a ridiculous little man, really, and now that I see you again after so long, I wonder that I was ever frightened of your scorn and your harsh words. I have every confidence that Francis has arranged matters so that you will do no more damage, to us or to anyone else you encounter. I hope your poor sister Susan too can be freed from your petty domestic tyranny, and make a better life for herself at last. I do not know how she has endured you as long as she has, and I am sure that you have kept her financially dependent on you on purpose; it is all of a piece with your other wickedly controlling behaviour.'

'I haven't forgotten her, ma'am,' Francis responded promptly. 'My idea is that this house should be let – my father hardly needs such a great barn of a place just for himself, and lord knows I have no wish ever to live here – and part at least of the profit from that should go to helping my aunt Greystone establish herself just as she wishes.'

'That's a very good idea,' said his stepmother warmly. 'Really, Francis, I must say, you have thought of everything in a most impressive and gratifying manner. My sister-in-law may come and live with me for a while, if she would like it, while she decides what to do, and she is welcome to remain forever if that is what she would prefer. I apprehend that I may soon have ample space in my home, if Meg is indeed shortly to be married.'

'I tell you what,' Francis said suddenly, 'I'm not a literary sort of cove, like some of you, and God knows I have no desire to be, not my line at all, but I must say, this does remind me of something. That play I was talking about the other day, I've been racking my brains for the name of the writer johnny, but I dare say it'll come to me eventually. Can't say I understood all of it, but it had an ending much like this. There was a villain in it, smoky sort of fellow, wanted to marry some lady well above his touch, but he was shown up, all the confusion sorted out, and in the end everyone else got married! Quite a striking thing, and dashed appropriate!'

'You're quite right,' Meg told him, her eyes glistening with unshed tears. 'It's *Twelfth Night*, isn't it? Shakespeare, you know, Francis. "Journeys end in lovers' meeting, Every wise man's son doth know"!'

'That's the ticket!'

38

The newly invigorated Mr Nightingale took charge of the situation now, and ushered his unresisting father out of the room, explaining that his lawyer Mr Clarke, and Lord Nightingale's man Sallow – who clearly had decided which side his bread was buttered and gone over wholly to the opposition – were waiting in another room to supervise the signature of papers that would place all of the Baron's financial affairs, and those of his family, in the hands of his son. 'Some of this concerns you, De Lacy, if you're to marry Meg,' he told Dominic as they left the room, 'and I may need a witness or two besides, so if you wouldn't mind accompanying me...? I'm not quite sure why you switched from Maria to Meg, though I can tell right enough that you're all dashed happy about it, but I daresay the writer fellow Whatshisname would have understood it better – sort of thing he specialised in, wasn't it?'

Dominic agreed, his voice quivering only slightly, that it was, and with a swift, intimate smile at his betrothed he followed. The women were left alone together, and a little silence fell after all the uproar, which Maria broke by saying

A Gentleman's Offer

with a touch of defiance mingled with anxiety, 'Mama, I must tell you that Lady Primrose Beacham is my love, and that we mean to set up house together!'

'I was beginning to suspect something of the kind,' said Lady Nightingale drily. 'I am very happy for you, my dear, and look forward to meeting her directly. I hope you will not insult me by implying that I should be expected to disapprove. I disapprove of nothing in life except meanness: an absence of love and liberty, such as your father exhibits. And Francis is quite right, you know – everything really has worked out with quite remarkable neatness; if I arranged it so at the end of one of my novels, I would surely be accused of the excessive use of coincidence.'

'Not coincidence, Mama – providence,' Meg said with a smile. 'Concordia: the universe operating in harmony for once. And if the solution to our comedy of errors should truly be excessively neat, we should expect now to see Francis happily settled along with the rest of us, perhaps with one of Lady Primrose's sisters – to avoid introducing entirely new characters who've never even been mentioned before at this late stage in proceedings, you know.'

'That's a thought,' Maria said, much struck, taking her jest quite seriously. 'She does have a great many sisters, mostly unmarried, and Francis seems estimable, perhaps even destined for great things, always supposing he has the right woman to take charge of him. I am sure such a thing could easily be arranged, without the least awkwardness, if between us we put our minds to it.'

'It might work, you know,' said Meg, torn between incredulity and amusement. 'I think he's rather lonely, and certainly nobody could be kinder and more generous. He'd make a lovely husband for a woman capable of appreciating all his many good qualities. I hope Primrose will choose quite the best of her sisters for him, and perhaps we can throw them together in a natural sort of a way, and see what comes of it. It may quite easily not answer, of course, if they should happen to dislike each other.'

'Nonsense, why should they? A great number of extremely pink children will come of it, if I am any judge,' said Lady Nightingale ruthlessly. 'But I think it's an excellent idea: well done, everyone. We should certainly dispose of the dear boy sensibly ourselves, if we can, rather than allowing him to blunder about choosing for himself and bringing goodness knows who into the family. How much more smoothly the world would run, to be sure, if women of good will had the organising of it instead of men.'

Meg sometimes found her mother a trifle alarming, and was suddenly and strongly reminded of Maria, when she had blithely informed her that it was a perfectly simple matter for Meg to assume her identity and marry Sir Dominic. Perhaps Maria would grow to be as formidable as Lady Nightingale over time. Perhaps she herself would, come to that. The thought made her smile. She thought that Dominic would be perfectly able to cope with it, and she had already decided that Primrose was equal to anything.

It was agreed among them that Lady Nightingale would not remain in Grosvenor Square, where she could not be comfortable, but would accompany Maria back to the Duke's house, once she had delivered her precious manuscript to her publisher in Leadenhall Street, putting it directly in Mr Newman's own hands. Another guest would make no matter in the Fernsby household, she was assured, and everyone was aware that mother and daughter had five long years to catch up on. Meg suppressed a desire to go with them; they must be allowed some time together without her presence, she thought, in order to mend their own relationship quite apart from her. And besides, it seemed most unlikely that Sir Dominic would finish his business with Francis and the legal gentleman and leave the house without seeking her out.

'I am conscious,' she mused, 'of a slight sense of anticlimax. Was my father always to be so easily defeated? He put up no fight at all, but gave in more or less instantly, greatly to my surprise. And yet, though I have spoken boldly of not being afraid of him in the past, in truth I have always been a little in awe of his sheer unreasonableness, and scared what he might do if I defied him over anything serious.'

'I too, I think,' agreed Maria readily. 'I've always found it so much easier to evade him than confront him: to smile and agree, while doing more or less exactly what I wanted behind his back. That can only take one so far, as I recently discovered. But it's this matter of my marriage that brought everything to a head. If he hadn't decided to try to conceal his fraud by arranging a match for me with a man he thought he could control, it might have been years before I'd have plucked up the courage to try to escape from him. Perhaps I might never have done so. My aunt never has.'

'Oh, I think you would,' Lady Nightingale assured her, smiling. 'You are after all my daughter, and besides you had a strong enough incentive, I should hope.'

'It was all caused by his fatal flaw, just like a tragic play. Francis would tell us that there's some dashed Greek word for it,' Meg said mischievously.

'Hamartia, dear,' her mother replied. 'You should know that, if he does not. And it's quite true – Augustus brought it all on himself, if can only be made to see as much. But I doubt it – it's far too late for him to change, in my opinion. What use is it to read the great writers all one's life, if one does not learn wisdom from them? But what caused him to crumble so completely, I believe, was the sight of us all united against him. Where could he turn? He's just a foolish blustering bully, when all is said and done, and I wish I had realised as much many years ago, and stood up to him then, and not allowed my children to be so cruelly separated. I remember that dreadful day when we left, and how you both cried so pitifully... But it does no good to speak of such painful matters, I am aware.'

'It's all water under the bridge now, Mama. It seems that Meg and I find ourselves exactly where we need to be now, with exactly the right people, and that's what matters. We may have been separated physically, but you have helped to make sure that we have stayed as close as we could be. And now nothing can keep us apart. Just let anyone try!'

Meg echoed her sister, and now it was her turn to weep joyful tears. 'Just let anyone try!'

39

When her mother and her sister left, after many more tears and fond embraces, Meg went to see her aunt, after informing the butler that she required speech with Sir Dominic before he too departed.

Mrs Greystone was alone in her dreary sitting room, wringing her hands and looking extremely anxious. 'I almost thought that I heard your mother's voice in the hall a while ago, but naturally I told myself that I must be imagining it, Meg dear,' she said faintly. 'I am so overset I scarcely know what I am seeing and hearing. And did we not have a great many visitors earlier? But we never have visitors, certainly not groups of visitors with ladies among their number, so I have no idea who it could have been. I fear your father will be very much displeased, if anyone came unexpectedly to disturb him, and you know that he will make us suffer for it, quite as though everything was our fault when of course it is not; how could it be? Well, I dare say you don't know, though Maria would, but you will find out soon enough how very uncomfortable he is able to make the whole house, if only he should be in a bad temper. Oh, I do hope he is not! It quite puts me in a state of nervous collapse. I shall have a spasm!'

'There is no need for you to fear his temper any more, Aunt,' Meg said soothingly. 'He has no more power to make you uncomfortable, nor anyone else for that matter.'

'He isn't... he isn't dead, is he, dear? Because if he is, I really do think you should have told me straight away, however disagreeable it might be. There's dinner to be thought of, you know.'

It was quite striking, how unconcerned Mrs Greystone seemed to be by the prospect of her older brother's demise. A cynic might even have imagined that she welcomed the possibility. 'No, he's not dead, ma'am, but he is shorn of all his power. I promise you he is. Francis has done it – Francis was one of the visitors you heard earlier, and you're quite right, my mother was here too, and asked me to tell you how sorry she was not to see you. But she'll be back tomorrow, and very much looks forward to spending time with you then and having a comfortable coze.'

'Hermione, under this roof, after so many years? I do not understand how it can be so!' said Mrs Greystone, trembling. 'Tell me everything, instantly, before I go off into strong hysterics!'

Meg sat down and explained almost everything that had happened – Lord Nightingale's fraud and theft and forgery included – and ended with Francis's plans for Mrs Greystone's support, and Lady Nightingale's offer of a home under her roof for as long as she should wish it. Her aunt stared at her in growing astonishment, and when she had done said slowly, 'Is it really true? Oh, not that my brother has done these dreadful things – I don't have any trouble at all believing that, I am sure he is capable of anything! But that I need no longer live with him, and can go into the country with your dear mother?'

'Quite true,' Meg assured her. 'Should you like to do so? Mama hoped you might, but she was not quite sure. She will be glad of your company, you know, for as long as you would be so good as to give it to her, since I believe I shall be leaving her to be married quite soon.'

'To Sir Dominic, dear child?'

Meg blushed. 'Yes. Maria… My sister could not like the idea, but I confess that I do.'

'I don't understand it at all, but I suppose it doesn't signify as long as you are happy. It's like a dream,' her aunt said wonderingly. 'A good dream, not one of those cheese ones. Is your mother's house quite small?'

'I'm afraid it is. It is a fine little Queen Anne house, built in Bath stone, just on the edge of a village, with an orchard full of old fruit trees. It's where she grew up, and it has just two bedrooms for guests. You will take mine, though, I hope – it looks out over the gardens at the back of the house, and then down the hill to a stream. It's very different from here,' she said a little dubiously. The house in Grosvenor Square might be neglected, but it was undeniably grand, and so very large.

'You don't understand, Margaret,' Mrs Greystone said fiercely and unexpectedly. 'I hate this house!' This extraordinary statement was almost hissed, so vehemently did she utter it. 'I hate this house, I hate London, and I hate having to manage everything for my brother when he is – and has always been, ever since he was an unpleasant little snuffling boy who bullied me and cut the head off my favourite doll – so excessively unreasonable about absolutely everything! To live in quite a small house, without great numbers of servants to instruct, and in a place in the country that is clean and free of this nasty London climate with its smoke and fogs in winter and stifling heat in summer – I can't imagine anything better. When shall we be able to leave, do you think, dear girl?'

'I am sure that matters may be arranged in a few days or so. If the household is to be broken up, there are the servants to be thought of,' Meg said, rather taken aback. 'They cannot simply be turned off, naturally; careful provision must be made for them. I wonder if Hannah will wish to go with Maria, or with my mother, or with me? Or alternate between us, perhaps.'

'I dare say you will be astonished how many of them will have their own plans,' Mrs Greystone said, surprising Meg once again. 'Many of them are quite advanced in years, and if a decent pension can be found for them – which I should hope it may be, for anyone who has put up with your father for any length of time deserves to be amply compensated for it – I should not wonder if most of them will wish to retire and never more be sworn at, nor have another boot or cup thrown at their heads again. And those who do not wish to stop working, or who are not yet old enough, must be helped to find good new situations, of course.'

This new energy and decisiveness in her aunt made Meg's head spin, and she could only agree. She left the older lady to her dreams of a life in the country, far from Lord Nightingale's unreasonable demands, and began to climb the stairs to her bedchamber, wondering how much longer the legal negotiations could possibly take.

She'd almost reached the upper landing when a door opened below, and masculine voices were heard in leave-taking. She stopped, hoping that nobody would think to look up and see her, and heard the door open and close again as some at least of the visitors took their leave. 'Meg?' said an amused, beloved voice from below. 'Did you tire of waiting for me at last?

I am sure I cannot wonder at it – we have been an unconscionable long time, and I am so sorry!'

40

Meg ran lightly down the stairs to Sir Dominic. 'Come back into the drawing room,' she said, heedless of the hovering servants, and led him with her into the chamber that had so recently been the site of the great family confrontation.

'Is all well?' she asked, drawing him down to sit by her, their hands clasped. 'I was just saying to my mama and to Maria, I find it almost incredible that my father gave way so easily. They both agreed that if they had known he would crumble so readily and completely, they might have stood up to him years ago – Mama in particular. It seems so odd that it should be so.'

'It's hard for me to judge, since I have had so little to do with him before. But yes, all is well; the papers are completed, and Lord Nightingale has resigned control of all financial affairs. Francis is in charge now. He intends to insert an advertisement in the newspapers to say that Lord Nightingale has renounced all financial control of his affairs and all power to enter into contracts, and that anyone who claims to be his creditor must apply to Mr Clarke within a stated time, as no debts will be settled after that point. Once that is done, Meg, your father will have little standing in the world, and if he does spread rumours about anyone – you, my family, your sister – nobody will believe him, thinking it mere senile spite.'

'Are we really free then, all of us? It hardly seems possible,' she said wonderingly.

'We are, my dearest love. And you are free to choose exactly what you wish to do. But I hope that what you wish to do is take me, though God knows I am yours already.'

He was holding his hand out to her in supplication, and she came swiftly to his side without a second's hesitation. 'What I wish to do is write, and travel, see the world, spend time with my mother and my sister, and live an interesting life at last.' His handsome face was shuttered, expressing only polite interest, but she was beginning to know him better now, and could sense the deep anxiety that lay beneath his impassive exterior as he waited to hear what she would decide. He must know, after all that had passed, that she could ask for nothing more than to spend her life with him – but he needed to hear her say it. 'And I wish to do it all with you. I do not say that there would be no joy or pleasure in a life without you in it – but I do not think there would be very much, my dearest. The world would be a dull pencil drawing, instead of full of bright and wonderful new colours. Will you marry me, Dominic, if all the confusion can be disentangled and it can be arranged? I hope you will. Remind me, though, exactly how long have I known you, sir?'

'Oh, my darling, I have no idea. A few days, perhaps a fortnight, or forever. Just long enough for me to know that I love you beyond anything I had believed possible, and that my life will be a hollow shell if I cannot persuade you to marry me. It has been a hollow shell for the longest time, till I met you. But I hope you have needed no persuasion. I hope you know that I desire nothing more than the opportunity to make you happy. If you do not know it yet, I will devote my life to proving it to you.'

She squeezed his hand with fierce intensity. 'Oh, Dominic, I do love you! Of course I do – how could I not? It is most mortifying to think that my sister was so entirely right and will never let me forget it! But am I to take her place, then, in my own name, and marry you next week? I don't know if that's even possible.'

'I don't know either, I must confess. It shall all be exactly as you wish – next week, or next month, or in six months' time.'

'Six months is a terribly long time to wait...' she said, smiling up at him.

'Well, I think so,' he replied. 'But I shall be guided by you and what you feel is right, my darling.'

She grinned up at him. 'Well then, Dominic, I wish it to be next week.'

'Then it shall be as you desire. Naturally it can be done – if I have you by my side, I feel I can move mountains. What is a mere clergyman or two, or even a bishop, to a man in love? I will overbear them and set all to rights, even if I must brave the Archbishop of Canterbury!'

'I am very happy to hear it. But what shall we tell the world? Not that I care for that,' she hastened to add. 'You must know by now that I do not. But we are obliged still to think of Maria's situation. It would be ridiculous to have come so far and done so much, and then to embroil her in a great scandal after all.'

'In fact, my love,' he said, his smile growing, as though a great spring of happiness were welling up inside him and could no longer be contained, 'your brother believes he has the perfect solution to avoid the least suspicion of scandal, and I have a great desire to see your dear face as I tell you it. It seems that yet another member of your family has a talent for fiction.'

'Go on!' she said, torn between amusement and anxiety. It was true that Francis seemed a new man, full of vigour and resolution and determined to do the best for his family, but it was hard to imagine a solution that between them she and Dominic had not yet thought of.

'Francis suggests, my angel, that we say nothing at all,' he told her, his voice wavering on the brink of laughter. 'Nothing at all, and let the information creep out – or not – on its own. This is where he is confident that your preposterous names would work to your advantage at last. I dearly regret that you were not there to hear him explain it to me. I have a great and growing affection for your brother, my love. He told me that if people should ever say in later years, "Dash it all, De Lacy, were you not meant to marry the lady's sister? I could have sworn you were!" I should merely look blank and reply, "Of course I was not; what an odd idea, old fellow. Their names are so very similar, by Jupiter, I fear you must be confused!"'

Meg gasped and spluttered, and then they both burst into whoops of mirth, laughing so hard and so long that before they were done they were obliged to cling to each other for support.

At last Sir Dominic said, 'The beauty of it is, he may well be right, marvel of nature that he is. It is almost impossible to underestimate how self-absorbed people are. If we act with great assurance, I am sure we can carry it off. Gossip generally comes when individuals behave as though they have something to hide, or something to lose. Or, of course, if you do dislike the beautiful idea, we can face everyone down boldly – take out an advertisement in the papers, and say, "Sir Dominic De Lacy and the Honourable Mr Francis Nightingale wish it to be known that the announcement previously made by Lord Nightingale of the marriage, etc., was inserted in error, and the lady in question is, in fact…" The implication would be that your father was not quite in his right mind when he made the arrangement. It is not perhaps in the best of taste, and will cause a great bustle at first, but if we are seen to be on good terms with your sister, nobody will think I have jilted her in your favour, or anything of that nature. There will inevitably be talk, but I am sure it will subside at length. It's riskier than the first option, I believe, but it must be for you and your sister to decide between you.'

'We must discuss it with her, and with my mama and with Francis, I suppose,' she mused, mopping her eyes, little bubbles of laughter still rising in her every now and then. 'Perhaps they may think of another solution. He is grown so excessively clever, he may have a dozen more startling ideas up his sleeve.'

'I should not wonder at it, so let us do so. But not now! Your family – always excepting your father – are excellent people, my love, but I have had enough of talking for a little while...' And then she was in his arms, held tight and close and secure, and they were laughing again and kissing each other all at once.

When their first excited flurry subsided, Meg found herself stretched languorously along the sofa, her body covered by Sir Dominic's tall frame, though he had somehow contrived it that his weight did not oppress her; instead, she found she liked it. He was engaged in unfastening with great care the tiny mother-of-pearl buttons that closed the placket of her habit-shirt. His objective seemed to be to set his lips upon the bare skin of her neck and upper bosom which the fine muslin shirt so imperfectly concealed. 'I must confess,' he murmured against her flesh, making her shiver deliciously, 'that there were moments in both of our recent serious and important family meetings when I was very gravely distracted by the sight of you in this garment, so nearly transparent as it is. The embroidery is exquisite, but your beautiful warm skin beneath it has been tantalising me almost beyond my power to endure it.' At last he had unbuttoned her as far as he was able, and he pulled the fabric wide and began kissing his way down her neck, towards the swell of her breasts and the deep cleft between them. His hands were about her ribcage, and she wriggled in pleasure at the sensation of being so firmly held and so thoroughly worshipped. He was aware of her tiny movement instantly, so responsive was he, and whispered, 'Am I holding you too tightly? God forbid that I should hurt you or make you uncomfortable.'

'No,' she almost moaned, bereft of the delicious pressure. 'Not tightly enough! And don't you dare stop!'

He chuckled and obeyed, and she fixed her hands deep in his glossy hair, giving herself up to sensation. She did not know how it had come about, but her shoes had come off, and Sir Dominic was lying snugly between her legs, her knees raised, her stockinged feet either side of his shiny hessian boots, rubbing against them, and against the back of his calves; this action conveniently caused her to spread her legs wider and raise her core so that her belly and her mound pressed up against his hard body, through the frustrating layers of fabric that covered them both.

He had discovered in his exploration that her bodice fastened at each side – the silk-covered buttons that ornamented it were not merely decorative, but functional too. Once he had undone them all, the silk folded down and revealed her chemise above her stays, made of the same fine Dhaka muslin as the shirt, and equally transparent. 'My God,' he said, very deep and low, and then his lips were on her nipple, which peaked obligingly to meet him, and he was sucking on her fiercely through the fabric. Her hands tightened in his hair and she whimpered in pleasure, wrapping her legs around him, her heels pressed against the backs of his thighs.

Her chemise closed with a ribbon, and once he had undone that by tugging determinedly on it with his teeth, he was able to push the thin, damp fabric aside and bring his lips and tongue directly to her naked, sensitised skin, making her moan with pleasure. She felt heat building inside her, begging for release and, scarcely aware what she was doing, she released his hair and took his right hand from her waist, raising it to her hot mouth, kissing and sucking on his fingers as she had done once before. He groaned in response, and moved his fingers in and out of her mouth, stroking the tender skin inside her lower lip, as he still tongued her hard, erect nipple and gripped her tightly with his other hand about the narrowest part of her body.

'Touch me,' she murmured against his wet fingers, nipping at them with her teeth. 'Touch me now, Dominic, my love.'

Slowly and tantalisingly, he drew his fingers from her mouth, and raised his body from her so that he could slip his right hand up under her gown and petticoat. He brushed the top of her stockings and stroked the delicate skin there, above her knee, but she moaned impatiently and, laughing in breathless understanding, he made his way up her thighs to the damp curls between her legs. 'Yes!' she said fiercely as he slipped two seeking fingers between her lower lips, finding her swollen pearl of Venus as she jolted at the sudden contact and pressed herself against him. She was wet for him, and he used the evidence of her arousal to ease his movement around her delicious sensitive nub, and back and forth to her entrance. His mouth was still at her breast, and with an exquisite instinct for what pleased her, he presented her with his other hand to suck on, which she did eagerly.

Soon she was gasping against his fingers, then sucking on them hard as they moved in and out of her mouth, an action which he mimicked, slipping inside her and away again, building a rhythm as she arched her back and welcomed him. His slick thumb rubbed her clitoris and she peaked and clenched on his clever fingers, seeing stars exploding behind her closed eyelids as the almost unbearably intense waves of pleasure crashed over her and carried her away. He didn't stop, mercilessly prolonging her spasms until at last she was obliged to moan an incoherent plea for release, or she would expire from pure sensation. He let her go, but claimed her mouth, kissing her long and deep and slow as she clung to him, the extremities of her body tingling as the waves ebbed.

'What about you, my dearest love?' she whispered at last against his lips, dizzy and satisfied, but conscious of the hard erection that had been pressing into her thigh all this long while, and showed no signs of diminishing.

'Never mind me,' he said between kisses. 'I shall not die of it. It's not so very long until we will be married, and there can be no question of debt between us, even a debt as delicious as this one. I will not take you here, however comfortable this sofa is. We have soft beds and short summer nights and long, long summer days in our future, my dearest love.'

'You paint a delightful picture,' she said, stretching like a cat and smiling up at him. 'But nonetheless, I have been brought up to believe in equality between the sexes, and therefore, sir, I think it is high time you locked the door!'

EPILOGUE
TEN WEEKS LATER

Dominic and his three companions crested the wooded ridge that overlooked his country house and looked down into the hidden valley below, catching their breath for a moment. It was late afternoon in a glorious September, and the old stone building was bathed in rich golden light, as if it had been dipped in honey. The central portion, which bore traces of the battlements and narrow arrow-slit windows that betrayed its ancient origin as a border castle, stood higher than the more modern, symmetrical wings on each side. On the central terrace, above the banks of white and purple flowers, he could see Meg, a tiny figure at this distance and yet one who held his heart entire and safe in her hands. She was tidying away her papers, he could see, weighting down the loose pages securely with a bright Venetian glass paperweight he'd given her and setting her writing table straight; she must have done working for the day. She was alone, but as he watched he saw Annie come out to join her for a rare moment of shared peace; he could hear his nephews scrambling about behind him, looking for the perfect tree to climb and pestering their father with endless questions that he answered with astonishing patience.

The Gilbert family had not been here before, and the boys seemed to be loving every moment of their stay, not least because De Lacy Court offered them opportunities for constant mischief, with its many panelled rooms, hidden staircases, extensive grounds, and the River Wye close by with its deep swimming pools. It was a wonderful place for children, Dominic thought, though he hadn't spent much time here in his own boyhood, because his mother disliked the remoteness of the place. But there was plenty of time for such matters in his own future; in a fortnight or so, he and his bride would be taking ship for France and all the adventures that the Continent had to offer them. Paris first, and then wherever their fancies took them.

His brother-in-law Tom came to stand by his side, a solid figure with a ready smile and an air of calm competence. 'The boys were wondering if we could go fishing tomorrow morning, Dom, though myself, I'd think that every fish with any sense for ten miles in either direction has been scared away and won't come back till these two monsters leave.'

'Do fish have sense?' Toby asked. 'They don't look as if they do. They look calm, mostly, but quite stupid.'

'Fishy sense enough to avoid you,' his father told him. 'Your mother would tell me it is wrong to bet, but I would wager a chocolate cake against either of you catching anything – or any of the rest of us, for that matter, with you splashing about and causing a great commotion. And I expect at least one of you will make sure to fall in.'

'It's not falling in if you mean to do it, Papa,' Nick told him seriously.

'Well, I don't mean to do it. Not with my favourite boots on. When you do fall in, your uncle can pull you out.'

'I may, or I may not,' Dominic said. 'It depends on how irritating you are being. Shall we head back now, urchins? It'll be time for you two to eat your supper soon. I expect you're hungry.'

'We're always hungry!' they chorused, and Nick added, 'We will ruin you utterly with… with our 'normous appetites, Mama says!'

'Let's go, then, while your legs are still strong enough to support you,' Tom Gilbert agreed. 'I'm sure your mother and Aunt Meg must have had more than enough peace and quiet by now. They'll probably be bored with it, and missing us, and finding the house altogether too quiet.'

The boys ran yelling down the slope, dodging agilely between the trees until they reached an expanse of sheep-cropped grass, at which point they lay down and began to roll with increasing speed down the hill. Their father and uncle followed them more sedately. 'I think I can see an episode of picking sheep shit out of two very dirty coats – which were no doubt clean this morning – in your immediate future, Tom,' Dominic said with the breezy unconcern of the currently childless.

'I don't doubt it. If I'm really lucky, they'll find where a fox has been, and roll in that, as dogs do.' Dominic shuddered fastidiously and agreed that this horror seemed all too likely.

The boys had been packed off into Hannah's care for a much-needed bath by the time the men reached the terrace, and indeed, two small, filthy jackets sat waiting, along with a stiff brush, for Tom's fatherly attentions. 'I refuse to allow those garments in the house in that condition,' Annie told her husband with mock severity as he grimaced comically and agreed that he would of course deal with the revolting objects to the best of his ability before handing them over to the servants for proper cleaning.

The ladies had been drinking something cold and pink from frosted glasses, and Meg rose to fill two more from a crystal jug. 'It will be nice to have a quiet evening, just the four of us, before the hordes descend tomorrow,' she told them, smiling. Mrs Greystone, Lady Nightingale, Maria, Lady Primrose and her sister Lady Violet were all expected some time the next afternoon, with, naturally, the indispensable masculine escort of Mr Francis Nightingale to ensure their safety. Dominic knew that Meg looked forward eagerly to seeing how the matchmaking plans were proceeding, and confessed to a little curiosity on the matter himself. Francis deserved to be as gloriously happy as the rest of the family, he thought. The sale of Nightingale manuscripts had been arranged for later in the autumn and was already causing a great stir in antiquarian circles; Francis was managing everything magnificently, and Mr Clarke had proved to be so indispensable that Lady Primrose was seriously contemplating him as a match for another of her sisters.

The new Lady De Lacy handed her husband his glass, and he pulled her down to sit on his lap for a moment, putting his free arm about her and inhaling the intoxicating scent of her hair as she rested contentedly against him. Lieutenant and Mrs Gilbert, some eight years married, smiled tolerantly at the lovers and strolled away arm in arm, making a tactful pretence of admiring the glories of the late summer garden, and the rich colours in the sky that presaged another spectacular sunset over the Welsh hills.

'How is your Melusina doing?' he murmured, brushing her

bright curls with a kiss as she settled more comfortably into his embrace.

'Oh, terribly, poor thing,' she told him, blue eyes sparkling with laughter. 'It's a curious circumstance, but she can barely go a day without falling into some dreadful danger through the machinations of the evil Count Malabarba and his henchmen.'

'I particularly enjoyed it when she was tied to the bed in the lonely turret, her clothes in utter rags,' he said, tightening his arm about her and setting down his glass the better to hold her as she wriggled deliciously against him in full awareness of what she was doing to his self-control. Dinner might well be a little late tonight, he thought. 'You know I'm always happy to help with research. It's my husbandly duty, in fact, and as such I take it very seriously. What do you have in mind for her this time, poor suffering creature?'

Lady Nightingale's publisher had offered Meg a contract, on reasonable terms, if she could have her manuscript finished before she left for France. He planned to publish *The Italian Twins' Tribulations, or Melusina and Marianna*, anonymously, with its author described tantalisingly on an elaborate title page as A Noble Young Lady, Lately Married to a Gentleman of Fashion. It should do rather well, he had assured her.

'I'm almost finished,' she told him with a quick smile. 'This last scene of deadly peril is to be the final one, the climax of the whole story, you might say, and so must be something special.'

'Do you have any ideas for this, er, climax?' She almost always had ideas, he'd found. And he too was not uninventive. In that respect, as in so many others, they found themselves well matched.

'One or two...' she said, and leaned forward to whisper in his ear. There was not the least need – there was no one nearby to overhear, however shocking and unladylike her words might be – but as her sweet breath tickled his skin and her fingers slipped inside his jacket to toy purposefully with the fastening of his shirt, Dominic had no objection.

'Time to change for dinner,' he told her, standing easily with her in his arms and carrying her inside, through the quiet old hall and up the elaborately carved wooden staircase towards the large four-poster bed that awaited them in their chamber.

'It's hours till dinner, sir,' she teased. 'Am I to be ravished repeatedly, like poor Melusina?'

'I like the sound of "repeatedly",' he said as he carried her. Her arms were about his neck and his hand caressed the swell of her thigh just where it met her bottom. There were fabrics between them currently – muslin and lawn and cotton, buckskin leather and wool and linen, but soon they would be naked, or naked enough, and able to give and receive pleasure, and learn each time a little more about each other, in a joyful journey of discovery that they had barely begun.

'Though Melusina is never completely ravished, as I understand it, but is always rescued at the last possible moment,' he told her as they reached the top of the stair and set out along the minstrels' gallery. 'It must be exceedingly tiresome for the poor girl, I should think. But I swear that you shall not escape my wicked plans, my lady!' He achieved an evil laugh, echoing around the great hall very much in the style of one of her villains, that made her giggle as she clung to him.

'Good!' she said. 'I don't in the least want to escape you. And I have wicked plans of my own! You must not take off your boots, Dominic!'

'I've begun to worry that you only really want me for my boots,' he murmured, manoeuvring her expertly through her bedchamber door and pushing it decisively shut behind him.

He laid his precious cargo on the bed and stood looking down at her in what he hoped was a suitably dashing and villainous manner. Judging from her expression, and the way she licked her lips, it was.

'I think I've proved that you are much more to me than boots,' she said, settling comfortably back against the pillows. She'd lost her satin slippers, unregarded, somewhere in their journey up the stairs, and she reached out one stockinged foot and ran it tantalisingly up the inside of his leather-clad thigh until it reached the fall of his breeches, where it stopped, as well it might. He took it in his hand and pressed it against him; she wriggled her toes, and he groaned pleasurably. 'So much more,' she said. 'And now, since I feel that you are more than ready to do it, I want you to make me a duchess.' Slowly, slowly she pulled her foot from his grasp.

'What do you know of such shockingly unladylike cant terms, madam?' he asked her teasingly, even as he stripped off his coat and waistcoat, and pulled his shirt hastily over his head.

'I couldn't even tell you where I heard it,' she said, biting her lip as she looked at him, bare chest and boots, and cockstand straining against his tight breeches, the open desire in her eyes inflaming him even further. She saw that too – they were so closely attuned to each other – and she very deliberately pulled up her skirt and petticoats so that her long, beautifully rounded legs were exposed up to her bright blue garters and beyond. 'But I remember hearing it and thinking, Mmm...'

'You imagined, wanton creature, that one day a man would carry you upstairs and throw you on a bed, pull up your skirts, just like the Duke of Marlborough supposedly did to his duchess when he returned home from the wars, and take you without even stopping to pull off his boots?' He was unbuttoning his breeches as he spoke and springing free.

'I don't think the stairs were a feature,' she said seriously, never taking her eyes off him, her hand creeping up her thigh to toy with the dark blonde curls that covered her seat of Venus. He stood, erect, and watched her hungrily. 'Nor the bed. I would have been perfectly satisfied to be ravished on a sofa. Or a sofa table, come to that. But we have guests, of course. Probably the Duke of Marlborough was too grand to worry about such matters. Or the house was bigger.'

She was an endless delight to him. 'Blenheim Palace is undeniably a trifle bigger than this house – that's probably why they made it so very large, don't you think? But despite all that, I'm going to make you a duchess,' he told her. 'I'm going to put your legs about my ears and plunge right into your glorious wetness, and I am confident that soon you will be... perfectly satisfied. But let me watch you a moment first. I love you always, but most of all when you are wicked and shameless and surprising.'

'Like this?' She slipped her fingers deeper into her curls, between her lips, and stroked herself and stretched out languorously on the big bed, as he watched and jolted at the wonderful sight. 'Like this?' she said again, unbuttoning her bodice with her left hand and pulling down her chemise so that she could cup one magnificent breast and begin playing with the taut nipple.

'Just like that,' he said, and then he could wait no longer and pulled her close with ruthless intent. She left off touching herself and reached eagerly for him, and he slipped into her in a glorious rush of heady sensation that set them both gasping.

'Oh God,' she moaned against his neck, moving with him, digging her fingers into his buttocks, wrapping her legs around him, 'sometimes slow and tender is good, my love, but sometimes fast and hard is better!'

'I'm sure the Duchess would have agreed!' And then both of them moved far beyond the power of speech, though they cried out as they came together in a great outpouring of ecstasy.

'Dominic, do you think,' she said much later, cradling his head between her breasts and smoothing back his disordered honey-brown locks with a loving hand, 'that people will truly discredit the evidence of their own senses and actually believe that you had always intended to marry Miss Margaret Nightingale, rather than Miss Maria Nightingale, all along? Even though the engagement was announced in the newspapers in black and white, and we held that dreadful party to celebrate, and everyone congratulated me thinking I was my sister?'

He was drugged with pleasure, and said lazily, 'I don't see why not. My mother tells me that nobody has questioned the matter in her hearing, or even looked at her oddly. She is in Brighton, you know, and must have heard if rumours were circulating. People don't give a damn, my love, if one behaves with enough style and conviction. Has Francis not said that it shall be so? And is Francis not a phenomenon, now that he has been unleashed upon the world, and likely to be Prime Minister one day, or something equally startling?'

'Admiral of the Fleet. Or Archbishop of Canterbury, perhaps.' He kissed one perfect breast in appreciation of the idea, and then again, in appreciation of the breast. 'I dare you,' she said, almost purring, 'to mention the idea to my mother, and to Maria. You might say it in jest, but they will take it entirely seriously. They both disapprove of the established Church, for excellent reasons, but that would not by any means stop them from...'

'Arranging his ordination by the end of the month,' he

finished for her. 'He would be a bishop, I imagine, in a sennight or two, with them at his back. Canterbury could only be a step or two away. Do you mean to be as terrifying and unstoppable as your mother, when you are older, my darling? And never to take no for an answer?'

'More so!' she said. 'And in that vein, I believe you promised to ravish me repeatedly, did you not?' Sir Dominic admitted readily that he had, and furthermore that he was a man who always kept his promises.

Dinner was *very* late that evening.

***

MORE FROM EMMA ORCHARD

Another book from Emma Orchard, *For the Viscount's Eyes Only*, is available to order now here:
www.mybook.to/ViscountEyeBackAd

ACKNOWLEDGEMENTS

I wrote my first novel in my kitchen in lockdown. I'd never have developed the confidence to do it without the encouragement of all the complete strangers who commented so positively on my Heyer fanfic on AO3. But the real inspiration came from my good friends in the Georgette Heyer Readalong on Twitter. I'm particularly grateful to Bea Dutton, who spent many hours of her precious time setting up and running the readalongs. I can't possibly name everyone – there are too many of us – but thank you all, amazing Dowagers, for your continuing support with this novel and far beyond it. Your friendship is very important to me. We've supported each other through some tough times, and had a lot of fun too. Many of us will never look at Paddington Bear in the same way again.

Thank you to all of the reading community on Twitter/X, and now on Instagram.

I've been obsessed with Georgette Heyer's novels since I first read them when I was eleven. They have their faults, but they've provided solace and escape for millions of people in tough times, and still do, so thank you, Georgette, even though you would have absolutely hated a lot of what I write. This might be my most Heyerish book yet in many ways, and if you know her work you'll see the inspiration – particularly *False Colours* and *The Corinthian* (sigh). I'm always (I mean always) available for Heyer chat on social media…

Thanks also to my family – Luigi, Jamie and Anna – for

putting up with me while I wrote one novel and then another in quick succession. And then another five. Thanks for understanding when I just have to write another 127 words before lunch so I can stop on a nice round number.

My lovely work colleagues Amanda Preston, Louise Lamont and Hannah Schofield, have also been extremely supportive: thanks, Team LBA!

I am very lucky to have a superb agent in Diana Beaumont of DHH. She has believed in my writing from the first time she read it, and will always be my champion. Her editorial suggestions are brilliant, and she's just an all-round star. Thanks too to everyone else on the teams at Marjacq and DHH. I know better than most people how important the whole team at an agency is.

Many thanks to everyone at Boldwood, including Cecily Blench for the fantastic copyediting, and to Team Boldwood as a whole for your amazing professionalism and unflagging enthusiasm – all of you, in every department, all the time. And of course most of all grateful thanks to my wonderful editor Rachel Faulkner-Willcocks, whose superb edits have made this a much better book. I know as I'm typing this that the amazing, talented Rachel Lawston is just getting started on the cover art, and I can't wait to see it. And thanks as ever to Gary Jukes for making 'doing proofs' a highly enjoyable experience. One of the many special things about Boldwood is the wonderful spirit of mutual support that the authors share, so I'd like to thank you all, particularly the fabulous Jane Dunn and Sarah Bennett, for your generosity and friendship. Jane, the *Rivals* chat has been priceless.

Finally, if you're reading this because you've bought the book, or a previous one: THANK YOU!

ABOUT THE AUTHOR

Emma Orchard was born in Salford and studied English Literature at the universities of Edinburgh and York. She was a copy editor at Mills & Boon, where she met her husband in a classic enemies-to-lovers romance. Emma has worked in television and as a Literary Agent, and started writing in 2020.

Sign up to Emma Orchard's mailing list for news, competitions and updates on future books.

Follow Emma on social media here:

- x.com/EmmaOrchardB
- instagram.com/emmaorchardbooks
- pinterest.com/EmmaOrchardRegency

ALSO BY EMMA ORCHARD

A Duke of One's Own

What the Lady Wants

For the Viscount's Eyes Only

A Gentleman's Offer

You're cordially invited to

The Scandal Sheet

The home of swoon-worthy historical romance from the Regency to the Victorian era!

Warning: may contain spice 🌶

Sign up to the newsletter
https://bit.ly/thescandalsheet

Boldwood

Boldwood Books is an award-winning fiction publishing company seeking out the best stories from around the world.

Find out more at www.boldwoodbooks.com

Join our reader community for brilliant books, competitions and offers!

Follow us
@BoldwoodBooks
@TheBoldBookClub

Sign up to our weekly deals newsletter

https://bit.ly/BoldwoodBNewsletter

Printed in Great Britain
by Amazon